INFESTATION

ALSO BY JAMIE THORNTON

FEAST OF WEEDS
Germination: Book 1 (Novella)
Contamination: Book 2
Eradication: Book 4

OTHER NOVELS
Rhinoceros Summer

OTHER STORIES
Wishflowers
Trip

Feast of Weeds Book 3

INFESTATION

Jamie Thornton

IGNEOUS
BOOKS

IGNEOUS BOOKS
PO Box 159
Roseville, CA 95678

ISBN–10: 0692495908
ISBN–13: 978-0692495902

BECAUSE SOMETIMES STAYING ALIVE ISN'T ENOUGH

CONTENTS

December

CHAPTER 1

Since before I can remember, my goal in life has been simple: stay alive, don't get hurt, don't get caught.

If you're one of those people who count three goals in that sentence and love to point out those kinds of things you can just go to hell right now. You're probably one of those people who make fun of those other people who post internet comments with spelling and punctuation errors too.

Just so you know, it doesn't make you smarter or righter than them.

What it does make you is a dick.

It's the kind of thing Corrina would do—I'd bet you $20 on it, if I had that kind of money, but I don't because I'm a runaway teenager who used to be a runaway kid.

I'll wait while you catalog your snobby thoughts and acerbic zingers.

Here's your chance.

Probably something about how there's no way in hell some-one like me could mess up grammar but use a word like acerbic correctly, right?

Well then this story isn't for you so put it down right now. Preferably in the library so someone actually worth something might find it and read it for free and get something out of it and not tell me how to count or where to put my commas or what words I'm allowed to use and how I'm allowed to use them.

Now that we all understand each other and only the right people are still reading, I can get started.

It's winter time and with that comes fog. I like the fog. It's moody and hides things easier. It's causing Maibe and me some trouble though. We've lost the rest of our group and something bad went down. How could it not with Vs running loose and soldiers fingering their triggers like a woman's—well, Maibe might read this and she's only thirteen and even though when I was thirteen I knew all about that sort of thing I don't think she does. I like thinking I could help keep it that way for her. At least for a little longer.

As I was saying, Maibe and me stayed behind to guard their backs, but now it looks like we'll need to save their asses and no matter what I think, I know Maibe won't let us leave without finding Corrina so—

"GABBI, DO YOU THINK THEY'RE OKAY?"

I stopped writing in the journal and looked up from where I sat on the van's bench. A dim flashlight, domed with an old, cloudy Tupperware container sat in the middle of the floor between us. Maibe was on the opposite bench, a wool blanket around her shoulders, scratching an insect bite on her neck. Curtains that Mary had made, before we'd lost her to the V virus, were attached with magnets to the back windows. The vent on top of the van let in the only fresh, freezing air. Yeah, it was cold, but the air needed to circulate. Spencer had learned that the hard way and I had learned from him.

We hadn't slept much in days and not at all since Leaf and Ano and the rest had been captured. We should have been sleeping.

I put down my pen. "No, I don't."

Her eyes widened and the circles around them darkened.

She hadn't expected honesty, I guess.

"But we're going back for them," I said, forcing myself to sound more sure than I felt. "We'll get them back and then they'll be okay."

She smiled, then her smile disappeared as if it had never existed. I knew how that sort of thing happened. I expected more of it to come both our ways before it got better, if it ever got better. But that's why I made myself simple life goals: stay alive, don't get hurt, don't get caught.

"How come we can't stay in a house?" Maibe asked. "It would be so much warmer and we could've locked the doors and maybe found some extra food and slept in real beds."

She pulled her dingy pink sweatshirt lower on her forehead. It had been days and she had yet to take that thing off. This bothered me a great deal because surviving on the street meant a kid needed to blend in—that meant look clean and put together—if she didn't want the police or social workers to pick her up. But then I remembered that sort of thing didn't matter anymore. Those people probably looked as homeless as us now, if they were still alive. Maybe they even looked worse since they wouldn't know all the tricks to keep yourself clean and warm without luxuries like running water.

"Gabbi?"

I realized I hadn't answered her yet, but I didn't see why I should. I got up and checked the curtained back windows for the millionth time. Our bicycles were on the ground a few feet away. A V was across the parking lot, punching the back of a bus bench and throwing trash around. I dropped the curtain back into place. Vs locked onto you like a wolf going after a rabbit. It hadn't noticed us yet and I wanted to keep it that way.

The crumbling red of the fitness center's sign took up most of the view through the front windshield. The van hadn't moved from where we'd abandoned it months before. Months ago, when things were just the normal amount of messed up for a kid living on the street, Mary had gone crazy for a second in the fitness center's showers and I had been so scared because she'd been about to hit me and Mary wasn't like that. But the worst of it was when Mary had infected us with the V virus and turned us over to the scientists and the soldiers to get the cure. Sergeant Bennings said Mary had killed herself. But I didn't believe it. No way she would just give up like that. No way.

I glanced at Maibe. She was still waiting for an answer. I sighed. "When you're hiding, you want to do it in plain sight, in a place that locks and that won't get noticed. Think about how big a house is, how many windows it's got, how easy it is to break into."

"But what if we wake up and…and we try to leave, but Vs surround us?"

"A running vehicle is safer than a house. Way safer."

"But you said the van won't start."

I bit back a retort. She was right, but it didn't matter to me even though it should. When Spencer, Leaf, and the others had stormed the fairgrounds yesterday with a V mob at their backs, they had gotten themselves captured. All I could think of was getting us to the van. To our old home base.

I looked up at the crumbling, yellowed fabric of the van's ceiling and tried to think about what would prove it to Maibe. "Picture yourself in your house when all this started. Did the Vs get in? Even though you locked the doors and windows and—"

A strangled sound came from Maibe's side. Her eyes glazed over, her jaw became slack.

I jumped from the bench. My papers hit the floor with a smack and the pen bounced and rolled somewhere out of the light. I yanked off her blanket, grabbed her by the shoulders, and then I slapped her—hoping to surprise her out of the memory-rush.

But then she screamed.

My muscles froze and my brain locked up. Too loud.

I slapped her again because I like to learn things the hard way, I guess. She screamed again and I swore something groaned low and close to the van.

"Get on your feet, Maibe," I said, fierce desperation in my voice. I didn't dare touch her. "Stand up, walk around. Push it back and shut up." My breath came in short gasps, the cold air in the van turning it into mist.

Slowly, slowly, she closed her mouth. Her eyelids blinked once, twice, and then focused on me. "I'm okay."

"No. Get up and walk around."

Her shoes struck the floor like the sharp closing of a book.

"Quietly," I said.

She paused, shoe in midair, then put her foot down toe first. The space around the flashlight allowed for only a few steps.

I peeked through the window. The V had stopped punching the bench and was back to throwing around trash. I let out the breath I'd been holding.

"You freaked," I whispered. "You just totally freaked when I slapped you."

Maibe waved her arms around and kept walking. Exercise was the only thing we knew that sort of worked to beat back the side effects of the cure. "I was having a memory-rush and… it's my zombie trigger, I guess—getting slapped."

"No kidding," I said. "But for the record, zombies eat brains, they don't scream like that."

"My aunt used to—"

I held up my hand and forced it not to shake. Three red dots marked where a flea or a spider or who knew what had bitten me. No surprise that bugs tried to eat us up, we didn't hang out in the cleanest places. Corrina had showed us how to make something out of oatmeal so the itching would stop, but I hadn't been paying attention. "I don't really want to know, kid. It's enough to know that it's one of your triggers. FYI, one of mine is heights. Do you know any of your others? A slap to the face and…"

Maibe shook her head. "I didn't even know about that one." The flashlight cast spooky shadows onto her face and high-lighted the lined, wrinkled, aged look of her skin—the cure did that. It was weird on a thirteen-year-old like her, as if a prop artist had done a bad makeup job, but no amount of scrubbing would take it off.

I touched my cheek and felt the same webbed texture. "We're only here for the night," I said as much for me as for her because a little voice in my head said that going back to the van had been the act of a scared sixteen-year-old girl running from the friends who needed her help. My stomach twisted into knots. I should have gone in to rescue them right away. That's what Ano and Leaf would have done.

"Tomorrow, we'll take the bikes and go in like stealth ninjas to save them all from their stupid selves." I pictured the looks on their faces when I came to save the day. Leaf, Ano, and Jimmy would be grateful, Ricker would act like it was no big deal, but Spencer would act annoyed and like he was just about to save himself and the others and why did I interfere? But he'd feel grateful deep down and that's what mattered.

Maibe settled back into her blanket with a sigh. "I don't know how to be a stealth ninja. In the movies, people always died when they left the shelter, or when they tried to save someone, or when they went outside, or—"

"This isn't the movies," I said. "And just so you know, a shelter is the most dangerous place out there. It gives the illusion of safety, but that's where people really get hurt." She couldn't know that I meant homeless shelters, group homes, and the like, she didn't know that much about me. But what applied there applied elsewhere. Get any amount of people together in a place that was supposed to be safe—like a family in a house—and horrible things happened behind closed doors and under darkness.

"But in the movies—"

"This isn't the movies!"

"But—"

"I can't sit here and not know what happened to them—not help them out!"

"I wasn't saying that, Gabbi, I wasn't—"

I jumped up angry and unsettled because deep down—in a dark place I didn't want to admit existed—for a split second, for a half second, for almost no time at all, I'd thought about running and leaving them behind because they'd gotten caught but I was still free. My foot accidentally hit the flashlight and knocked it over. The rays danced around the cabin sides. A shadow passed across the back door's curtained window. I stumbled back, shocked at the movement. My arms swung around to keep me from falling. Before I realized it I grabbed the curtains and tore them away and the magnets pinged to the ground like a handful of pebbles.

It was a girl, not much older than us. The trash-throwing, bench-punching V from across the parking lot. Her blonde hair looked like a bird's nest. Her face was dirty and streaked with crusted blood. Her blue eyes were crystal clear and totally insane. They were the opposite of empty. They were full of emotion, full of some interior knowledge, full of hate—and they were locked on my face.

The girl tracked me. Blue, angry dots that could see me but didn't really see me. Mary had looked like that at the end. The V virus was the scariest thing. It's like it took everything bad that happened to you and made you relive it over and over again like a song on replay.

Did I dare go outside? And then what? I wished Mary were there. She would know what to do.

I picked up the magnets and forced myself to begin fixing the curtain back into place. My fingers didn't want to work and the magnets kept dropping and pinging against the metal floor. I had fought off plenty of Vs by now—that wasn't the problem. But she was just a girl and I didn't want to deal with any of it.

"She's not going away," Maibe said. "You know she won't."

The V slapped her hand against the glass and smeared it, leaving behind a bloody streak. Her knuckles were cracked open, probably from all the punching she'd been doing. Everything drifted away and I was back on the hot sidewalk and there was Officer Hanley and the air conditioning blasting cold air out his open window. Mary had wanted us to run and I was so angry. I was mouthing off to Officer Hanley and the guy had slammed into the police car. We'd lost all those seconds to run away, because of me.

"Hey." Maibe grabbed my shoulder. I flinched.

The girl's hand—the Vs hand—mirrored mine. I told myself there wasn't a real girl in there anymore. This V would rip me apart if I let her. I swore I could feel her hot breath on my face—

Maibe finished attaching the curtain for me with shaking fingers. The girl was blocked out by an inch worth of glass and a little bit of cloth with a pattern of pink ice cream cones against a yellow background. Mary's idea of a joke. I blinked, shuddered, dropped my hands to my side.

"What memory-flash did you have just then?" Maibe whispered. "You just froze up and your face turned angry and scared all at once."

"I don't want to talk about it. We shouldn't be talking at all."

Silence. Except for the V breathing.

"She already knows we're here," Maibe said finally.

A sick feeling entered my stomach. I didn't know what I was doing. I didn't want this job. I didn't want any of this. "She'll go away if we're quiet."

"They never go away," Maibe said.

There was the sound of shuffling steps. The V girl had come around to the front windshield. Another V joined her.

This one was an older man. Hunched at the shoulders and looking as if he would have needed a cane to walk in any other situation. My heartbeat throbbed in my ears. The Vs would surround us, smother us, block all the light and hope for escape. Why had we hidden in the van?

I grabbed for the flashlight and switched it off, plunging the van into darkness. I stared at a ceiling I couldn't see anymore except for the faintest rim of light around the vent, and I prayed and prayed for the Vs to go away.

The only sounds were the two of us trying not to breathe, and the Vs bumping up against the van, and the shuffling that meant more were coming to join them.

CHAPTER 2

I CHANGED INTO MORE LAYERS, pulled a knit beanie tight over my ears, put on knit gloves with the fingertips cut off, and set to making coffee. The little camp stove had fed me and Spencer and everyone else many a cold night. A warm can of beans made all the difference in luxury eating compared to eating it cold.

I positioned the stove under the vent. Spencer always told the story about this guy he had known who'd killed himself because he'd slept all night with the windows closed and then had lit up his stove in his enclosed car. Stupid. I didn't understand how the guy hadn't felt it coming and just cracked open a stupid window and I wondered if Spencer had made the story up, which he'd been known to do, but then again, I never forgot to open a window, no matter how cold it got outside.

I handed Maibe a cup of coffee and offered cream and sugar packets hoarded long ago from some breakfast splurge at Denny's. She held the cup, sniffed it, took a tentative sip, and curled her lip.

"You never had coffee before?"

"No." Her dark hair haloed her face. I'm sure she would have looked young if not for the double infection turning her skin into an old leather sofa beat to hell. Someone else had infected her with both the V virus and the bacteria cure weeks before we'd met. It was one of the few things she didn't like to talk about.

I kept myself from rolling my eyes, but it was a close call.

She must have seen me hold it back though because she said, "My aunt wouldn't allow it."

I handed her a bowl of steaming oatmeal next. I'd done the same morning after morning for everyone. Spencer made the coffee, I did the oatmeal, Mary made bacon or eggs or potatoes, and we'd all eaten out of bowls in our laps, knee-to-knee on the benches.

Yeah, we might have been a bunch of kids living in a van, but in the homeless street world, the van meant we had been rich and we tried to make life better for each other whenever we could.

I shook my head. I couldn't let my mind wander, otherwise I'd become ripe for a memory-rush and Spencer and the rest didn't have that kind of time.

Something shifted.

The bowl in Maibe's hands shivered.

I noticed the wood walls, the metal door, the field that led to the trees that led to the river.

A part of me screamed at myself to snap out of the memory-rush. We were in the van and it was me and Maibe and we had to get to the others.

SUNLIGHT PULLED ME OUT of the memory-rush. The rays glared in my eyes because the ceiling vent was wide open.

I sat up and looked around. The van was back, the windows were curtained, the front windshield—

The Vs were gone.

Maibe was gone too.

Panic made me dizzy and the van's walls and windows and cabinets blurred as if I were taking a turn on a carousel. I scrambled through the vent and pulled myself onto the roof. My weight created depressions in the metal that popped back up when I stepped away. I scanned the parking lot, the gym's entrance, the street full of houses built just long enough ago for the paint to fade.

There. Movement on the street.

It was happening so fast, I didn't understand what I was seeing at first.

Five Vs. Maibe out in front. The V girl was closest to Maibe, the old man last of the bunch.

Maibe was sprinting down the block, drawing the Vs away. She ran just like Mary had run when that V in the plaid shirt had chased us. Mary had made us split up. The V had followed her and bitten into her and I cursed and jumped off the van's roof before the memory-rush could go any further. I needed to move or I was going to lose it and Maibe would die for nothing.

As soon as I went weightless in the air I knew I was going to land wrong. I tucked like I'd learned to do while jumping off moving trains. The shock of the ground was jarring and I thought about how fast I would die if I managed to sprain my ankle right then.

A yell from Maibe snapped me to attention. I slammed open

the van door and grabbed for my crossbow—a stolen piece of property thanks to the local hunting supply store. I ran after them but they disappeared around a house. I ran anyway, thinking I'd catch up just in time to watch them tear Maibe to pieces and it would be my fault because I hadn't found a way. The V girl had freaked me out and I'd hid and pretended everything would be okay if I ignored it for long enough.

My breath came out in gasps, but my legs were used to running. Halfway down the block a figure darted out from a side street.

I skidded to a stop, dropped to one knee, and raised my crossbow.

Maibe looked at me like I was crazy as she ran by. "Come on, Gabbi!"

I sprinted after her, fear mixed with admiration. She'd outrun them by herself. She'd actually done it.

When we made it to the van I bent over and took in huge, gulping breaths while pressing my head against the cold metal. If she had died, I would have been alone. "What were you thinking!?!"

"I knew I was faster than them," Maibe said. Her hair was in disarray and she didn't even carry any weapons. "But we don't have much time." She showed me her arm.

One of the Vs had bitten her. She'd be lost to the fevers soon.

Suddenly I was moving through the air as if I'd been hit by a car. The street and sky switched places. My crossbow flew away from my hands as if tied to a string someone had yanked. Air rushed into my ears and I landed on my gloved hands and bare knees and cheek. The shock of the asphalt sent tremors through my skull. My eyes couldn't focus and the world spun.

I raised stinging fingers to my cheek and felt wetness.

There was a growl, low and deep, behind me. I flipped over and stared into the eyes of what had once been a man but was now a V. He must have been drawn by the commotion we'd made.

He leaned over me, too close. Burst capillaries formed red rivers through the whites of his eyes. His breath stunk of spoiled milk. Half of his face seemed paralyzed. The other half showed a rigid snarl. I waited for him to rip me apart. He cocked his head like a dog might, opened his mouth so I could see his straight pearly-whites and the thousands of dollars he must have spent to make them so before the virus took him. He growled again and clicked his teeth shut with enough force to take off a finger.

The Vs eyes widened in fury, like he was reliving every angry moment of his life all at once. I dared not move.

A metal bat swung into view and slammed into the back of the V's head. He dropped like a brick.

I scrambled to the side, crab walking to my crossbow.

Maibe stood over the unconscious V, hesitating now that he was down but not dead. Would Maibe have the guts to deliver a second blow and finish him off?

I readied my crossbow but waited to see.

She held up the bat and then dropped it to her side.

I aimed and shot into his head. His body hiccuped and stilled.

"Coward," I said even though she had outrun a pack of Vs all by herself.

She looked ashamed. "Did you really have to—"

"Them being sick doesn't give them a free pass to hurt us." I went to the van. "We've got to keep going before you lose it."

She turned and puked.

It was like we were on speed as I made us gather our stuff: some food and water, the bat I bungee-corded to my back, a knife I insisted Maibe carry. We grabbed up the bikes. Our breath came out in long twirls of mist that made me ache for a smoke. The fog had a light brown tint to it because of the sunrise and the fires. The air smelled like a gross mixture of damp campfire and overcooked meat. The fires would only get worse with no one to put them out.

Maibe pedaled for a couple of blocks before the memory-fevers took over. I tried tying a shopping cart to my bike and dragging her along but the noise was terrifying.

I pushed her into the nearest dumpster and kept my crossbow lifted and ready to shoot anyone who dared show their face.

She stayed in the fever for hours. She tumbled back and forth on old food wrappers and lumpy plastic bags. Her face was flushed and when she moaned I tensed, waiting for Vs to hear it. I used the bungee cords to tie her hands and feet together—that was the rule Spencer had made. It kept someone in the fevers from hurting themselves or anyone else. But there was nothing else to do except watch and pretend I couldn't hear the terrible memories she was reliving—and stand guard until my arms couldn't lift the crossbow anymore.

I think I shot off my crossbow once. I don't know if it had been at something real. Sometimes the memories are like that—ghosts that fly into reality and become part of the scene around you.

MY ARMS HAD TURNED TO JELLO by the time she came out of the fevers. I could barely pull myself back over the edge of the dumpster. We picked up the bikes I'd abandoned on the side-walk when Maibe went under. Before the infection had taken down the city I'd done my bike up with silver streamers and a skull and crossbones sticker.

As we pedaled, life returned to my arms. We didn't speak to each other. She couldn't talk and there was nothing I could say. Though there were plenty of signs that life had been around at some point, there was nothing alive now: abandoned cars, broken glass, a hydrant that gushed water and flooded one street, bodies laying still on the ground.

I'd bet my best sleeping bag that Faints filled every house in sight. They were like the opposite of Vs. They went comatose and sometimes did their own version of sleepwalking, but they were mostly neutral. When me and the rest of us had almost come out of the fevers, Dr. Ferrad was there too, recovering from her own fevers. She'd told us that Faints were people who only caught the bacteria—though she didn't know how that was possible. The bacteria wasn't supposed to be contagious like the V virus.

What mattered about Faints though was they didn't come after you like the Vs did, but they could still cause trouble, plus they were super creepy all sleepwalking around with smiles plastered on their faces half the time.

Yeah, I'd told Maibe houses weren't safe. And they weren't. But I also couldn't bear to step inside one and run into a Faint.

We rode by a car with its windows busted and a body humped over the steering wheel. He could have been drunk and passed out like my dad used to get, except blood spatter marked up the pieces of windshield glass on the hood and road, and his head seemed sort of caved in.

"I think I'm going to be sick," Maibe said.

I felt perfectly fine and wondered what that said about me. "Just don't look."

We passed through a four-way stop with a stalled car in the middle. Mary sat on the hood of the car, her jet black hair falling around her shoulders. She waved and smiled at me as if nothing were wrong. My bike wobbled and I lost feeling in my fingers. I knew it was a ghost-memory, but I couldn't see anything except her until I slammed into the stalled car and tumbled over the handlebars and through the spot where she'd been sitting. She disappeared then as I lay splayed out on the hood.

I closed my eyes for a moment because I was so tired of it all.

The squeak of a wheel made me open my eyes again. Maibe had picked my bike off the ground and flipped it over. The skull and crossbones sticker was all scratched to pieces now and half the streamers had ripped off. She was trying to spin the front wheel and unbend what couldn't be unbent.

"I need another bike," I said, but my voice trembled. We'd already lost so much time. Either I walked the rest of the way, or I searched a nearby house for another bike. "We'll have to search the houses."

"We can't go in," Maibe said. "We can't! You said houses were dangerous, the most dangerous, the—"

"I need a bike," I said simply. I limped over to a garage with a dark strip at the bottom. Maybe it wasn't locked and I wouldn't need to enter a house at all. There was no hum of electricity, only the smell of grease and oil and metal. I stood up, put both hands underneath the lip of the garage door, and the door went up with a screech. Geometric shapes edged the interior. Something red and metal and bike-like gleamed in the corner. Something else smelled like wet socks that hadn't been allowed to dry.

My muscles knew before my brain could process it. Two people stood against a workbench, backs to me. Faints.

Faint skin looked like ours. It was weird because V skin didn't—theirs was like normal.

We could walk to Cal Expo.

There was no good reason to step into this garage, to the bike waiting like a present in the back corner. I could lower the garage door and turn around. I almost did because the Faints creeped me out worse than the Vs, worse than others like me and Maibe—Feebs—with weird skin and even weirder memories. Faints were still people, still alive, but locked in somehow differently than Vs.

"Is there a bike?" Maibe said from behind me.

"Shh," I said and dropped my arms. Sometimes you could wake up a Faint and that was even worse. "Yeah, but it's not worth it." I said this in a whisper as I turned around and walked down the driveway. I wouldn't risk bringing the door back down, better just to leave.

"What?"

"There's Faints," I said, trying not to let the fear show in my voice.

Maibe cocked her head and drew her eyebrows together. "So?"

"So," I said. "We're moving on."

"That's it? But they're Faints, they're not going to bother you, they're not going to do anything except maybe run through some old memory about taking out the trash or changing the sheets or cooking dinner. Did I tell you Faints saved Corrina and me?" Maibe waved her arms around in pantomime. "The Vs had followed us and she had gotten bit and the virus was flaring up again and—" Her voice trailed off and she looked at something over my shoulder.

The two Faints had moved to the garage opening. A black and white spotted cat twined in and around their legs, meowing outrageously at their lack of attention. They held hands. A middle-aged couple underneath the afflicted skin. Something about the look of the man, the scruff of his growing beard, the disarray of his hair, the mean hook of his nose, the way that he gripped the woman's hand, like she was a possession he intended to hurt—it made my knees weak and wobbly.

I willed back the tendrils of memory that crept out—long nights spent curled in a pink comforter listening for the yelling and fighting and the crash of glass. The creak of my bedroom door opening, the sour stink of alcohol—he couldn't hurt me anymore and I wasn't letting anyone hurt me anymore and this was just a Faint and they might be sick and needed my pity but they couldn't hurt me and—

"Can I help you?" said the woman in the driveway. My head cleared as I focused on her face. Her eyes were still glassy and unfocused, but something had triggered her to run a memory out loud. "Can I help you?" She scratched her wrist and looked at the man without really looking at him. "George, go see what they want."

George dropped the woman's hand and took a step down the driveway. I stepped back, and back, and back, until the car and the crippled bike and the dead Vs were between me and him.

"Gabbi?" Maibe said, her tone containing equal parts question and concern.

"I…" I leaned against the metal car door and slid to the ground. My palms burned as if someone had placed my hands on a hot electric stove, not someone, not anyone, but him, him over there behind the car, walking down the driveway to continue his business, as he liked to call it, walking down the hallway to drag me out of my room and into the kitchen and before I could stop it the sky and the Vs and the fog disappeared and there was only darkness and burning and his laugh.

CHAPTER 3

MAIBE STOOD OVER ME with a red bike in her hands talking about Faints and smoke. I blinked, groaned, shook my head, told myself to get over myself. I'd had that same damn memory-rush before. It wasn't new and it wasn't real.

My tongue felt so dry. I coughed and stared at a patch of blood on the knee of my jeans. Was it mine or a V's? Either way it needed to come off. The best way to get caught and sent back would be to look like I didn't belong. To stand out with dirty clothes or a sunburn or that layer of homeless grunge that happened when you couldn't shower for four days in a row.

My head cleared.

I remembered it wasn't that kind of world anymore.

Part of my brain believed it, but the rest of me couldn't give up a strategy that had worked so many times before. My stomach cramped at the thought of leaving that blood in place like I held a blinking "homeless kid" sign above my head.

Acid burned my throat. A sip of water, I needed a sip of water. I forced out a word. "Backpack."

Maibe stopped talking and brought over the bag. I ripped into the main compartment, took out a plastic water bottle, and chugged it. Cold water relieved my throat. The memory-rushes were a pain in the ass, but the alternative—becoming a Faint or a V—was worse. I didn't like how the rushes made me feel: groggy, young, powerless, but I reminded myself that I had left. I had taken control of my future and they hadn't ever caught me, not after that first time.

"We should go before more Vs show up or before the couple comes back out," Maibe said. "I got the bike ready while you were out…they were nice, the people I mean, not that they knew it was me or what I was doing."

I rubbed my temples and then used the car to help myself stand. Everything seemed steady enough, though my hands still burned from my skid on the asphalt. I swung a leg over the red bike. The garage door still gaped open, and through it another door to the house was open.

In the rectangle of light two figures moved around. The air smelled sour as if food had been left to rot. I secured my backpack and crossbow and took off down the street. Behind me, Maibe's shoes slapped on the pavement as she scrambled to follow. I spent a half second of thought on apologizing to her for taking off without even a thank you, but I decided to screw it. The blood flowing through my veins as I pumped the pedals helped beat back the last bits of the memory-rush.

For a while, the only sounds were the birds, the whir of our tires, the squeak of a pedal. A few blocks down, three Vs appeared between houses and ran out to us, their arms flailing in the air. We pedaled faster and our bikes kept us ahead them.

We picked up two more Vs on the next street.

Five more on the street after.

We stayed out of their reach and for a while even thought we'd lost them.

Some of the streets billowed black smoke and we couldn't avoid it once. Flames licked up the side of a two-story before jumping to the next roof. The burning plastic and glass and wood, and who knows what other chemicals, forced tears down my cheeks. I wondered how many Faints were still in those buildings and then told myself not to think about it. I pulled my knit beanie low over my ears and brought up the collar of my jacket to form a poor man's filter. It helped, but Maibe's hoodie didn't have enough fabric and she started coughing up a lung behind me.

There ended up being no way around the fire, so we retreated several blocks before finding another outlet. That's when the Vs caught up to us again.

We flew down the trail, trying to get as much distance between us and the Vs as possible. A few miles later we made it to the fairgrounds' gate entrance—the chain-link fence, the gatekeeper box, the makeshift barricade of cars and junk and barbed wire that separated us from the parking lot, and beyond that, the curve of a wall where Cal Expo really started.

"So how do we get in?" Maibe asked, looking at me with a confidence I didn't feel. "What's the plan?"

I could have told her—I should have. I didn't have a plan. The Vs were a few blocks behind us but would catch up soon. The plan was to get to Cal Expo and find a way inside. Spencer could have done better. He'd always been the idea guy, the one with the solution to our hungry stomachs, shelter for a cold night, talking our way out of the halfway houses, keeping us out of trouble with the pigs and the pimps and the do-gooders.

"Trust me," I said. I waited for her to cuss at me, yell at me, do something to stand up to me. That's what Ricker would have done, and Mary and the rest too.

That's what Maibe should have done.

You never trust someone who suddenly wants to take responsibility for you. Never.

I didn't know what to do next, but I pretended that I did by walking along the fenceline. Even though it was cold, sweat broke out on my forehead. I didn't know what I was going to tell her. I did know we could not fight the dozen Vs headed our way. I gripped the chain-link with both hands until the metal turned my skin purple. I wasn't the one who got people out of messes. Mary had known that, Spencer knew it. We were going to die against this fence and—

And then I saw it, by the hedge, in the dirt.

Underneath the fence was a hole big enough for a teenager to fit through.

The dirt felt damp from the fog. It soothed my stinging hands and smelled like heaven compared to the smoke we'd been breathing. I pulled myself out the other side, scratching my back on the chain-link edges. Maibe crawled after me. I helped her up and brushed off the leaves that clung to her sweatshirt.

Dried smoke-tears had left dirt tracks down Maibe's cheeks. Red rimmed her eyes. I opened up the last of our water bottles and used it to scrub our faces and douse off the dumpster smell. I couldn't stand being dirty another second longer, even with the Vs behind us.

The hedge and hole were part of a narrow greenbelt strip that ran from the fence to the curved wall of the racetrack. It separated two parking lots and wasn't more than a dozen feet wide. Trash floated in crazy twirls across the empty space. The place looked unguarded, though a group of spindly oak trees lining the greenbelt blocked a clear view. Either the people inside the fairgrounds had turned stupid or they didn't have enough people to set up this wide of a perimeter. Lucky for us either way.

I took off along the greenbelt. Maibe followed.

A skittering sound made my heart pound in my throat. My shoes sunk into ground made soft and slippery from decomposing leaves. Smells of wood and grass hit my nose. I didn't let us stop until we passed through the trees and back onto the strip of asphalt that bordered the racing wall. When we did I fell onto my knees and rested my forehead against the wall. We'd made it inside, now all we had to do was find Leaf and Ano and the rest of the group and figure out how to save them. Easy—yeah, right.

There was a scratching sound…I looked back the way we'd come.

The barricade still stood untouched, but the bush on the fence was moving. It shook like a wild animal ran circles around its base, and then it went still.

I narrowed my eyes, trying to bring it all into better focus. There.

A figure pulled itself through our gap in the dirt.

The person stood up. It was a hundred, maybe two hundred, yards away and something was very wrong.

Sometimes it was hard to tell a V from a distance if it was

standing still. There were no telltale signs of their virus like with Feebs and Faints until you got close. Sometimes when Vs moved their limbs, they jerked around like the two parts of the brain were telling the body different things. That's what this one looked like. He stood up and sprinted across the lot in our direction. The bush shivered again and a second one came up. In the time it took this second one to stand, a third one followed.

"Let's go," I said.

I followed the curve of the wall. The noise of a rifle went— pop-pop-pop—above us. I turned back and the first V lay on the asphalt, unmoving.

So maybe there was a guard, but he hadn't been doing his job until now.

Another two pops and the second V went down, but the third one kept coming and it was smart enough or lucky enough to run into the greenbelt and the trees blocked the shots.

There were shouts above me. The third V weaved between the trees, disappearing, appearing, nearing. A fourth V scrambled through the fence and another waited, almost patiently, in line.

I grabbed Maibe's arm and took us onto a maintenance road and then behind the back of a building. Two buildings formed a sort of alleyway between them. On our side was emptiness. On the other side the alley opened up to a type of square where people were sorting supplies, preparing food, handing out clothing, packing up boxes and loading the boxes onto trucks. But where were the trucks going, wasn't everyone who needed the supplies already here?

A table of blankets sat in the alleyway. Inspiration hit and I walked up to the table as if I knew exactly what I was doing. I grabbed a stack and pushed half of them into Maibe's arms.

I didn't let myself think too hard on the lack of guards other than a passing thought that it sure looked as if someone was trying to get people killed. A part of me couldn't understand leaving the route we'd just run unprotected. Unless there weren't enough guards anymore.

It didn't matter. The uninfected would lock me up in seconds if they saw who I really was. They believed they were the last real humans on earth. They wanted their old houses and cars and jobs and they wanted to tell people like me what I could and couldn't do. They judged me for living on the street and would kill me for getting sick with the virus and bacteria that THEY had gotten me sick with.

Maibe touched my arm, bringing me back. I flinched. She drew her hand away.

"We've been asked to take this to the sleeping quarters." I pulled my hood low over my forehead, repositioned the backpack and crossbow on my shoulders, and carried the blankets high enough to obscure the bottom half of my face. Maibe's wide, unblinking eyes flitted between me and the people ahead.

"We're just going to walk in there? That's the plan?"

"If we act like we belong, no one will question it. If we act like we're supposed to get caught, we'll get caught." It was the very first thing you learned on the street. Don't stand out. Blend in.

"Okay, but everyone knows you can't just walk into…into… it's not this easy, it's never this easy in the movies."

The kid and her damn movies. I closed my eyes in frustration. She wasn't wrong, but she wasn't right either. And mostly, this was the only plan I had. "It's not going to be easy. Use your eyes, look around, but don't look like you're looking around. Figure it out—are people talking to each other? Then look like you're talking. Are they working alone, in pairs, in silence? Do that. Are you clean enough to blend in? Being too dirty is a surefire way to stand out. If everyone around you can smell you, then they know you're not like one of them, that there's something wrong about you and they'll call the cops in." I realized my mistake too late.

"Cops?"

"Soldiers, guards—whatever. Come on." I began to walk away.

"Gabbi? Wait, okay. Just hold on."

I stopped and gritted my teeth. I didn't have any better ideas. This was it.

Maibe held the blankets under one arm, the fabric so big and bulky it spilled to the ground in haphazard waves. "You said we need to blend in, right? That's what you said, you said we can't be too dirty or talk too much or—"

"That's what I said."

"We're too clean now and you have to leave behind your crossbow and backpack."

I cocked my head, my frustration fading. I really looked at the people we were about to step among. There was plenty of noise. Different stations where some people cleaned gear, washed dishes, moved boxes of supplies. There was even a hint of yeast as if someone was baking fresh bread. She was right. Nobody wore a backpack like mine, and definitely not a weapon.

I went to the closest trash can, lifted off the top, and removed the plastic bag that contained a few candy bar wrappers and soda cups. I bundled our weapons and supplies in one of the blankets and set them at the bottom of the can. I replaced the plastic bag and covered the top.

"Where'd you learn to do that?"

"Storage space is expensive," I said and shrugged my shoulders.

"So what about being dirty?"

I cringed at the next steps. It didn't matter, but I couldn't shake the secret feeling that it did. Using up our water bottles had been such a waste.

"Run your hands along the ground and wipe it on your face."

Maibe also pulled out hair from her braid. I undid my ponytail and plunged my hands into the strands to tangle them. I hated being dirty because this was the way to get caught.

But it wasn't, it wasn't anymore.

"Done," Maibe said.

I picked up the remaining stack of blankets and we walked through the alley. "You did good to notice that, Maibe. You probably saved us."

"I know," she said.

I glanced over and saw the kid was actually smiling. A small smile crept on my lips. "Don't get cocky. You may have outrun those Vs at the van and helped us from getting caught just now, but you're still just an oogle."

"A what?" she said around the smile.

"New to street life," I said. "But you're catching on fast. Faster than I did. You might survive this after all."

Her smile grew and I decided to make sure that she did survive this.

We entered the grim bustle of people who'd never expected to be here. Still, they were idiots for not taking the Feeb vaccine. They were the uninfected, those still considered human according to whoever was in charge. If they became infected by a Faint or a V—that's what they would turn into. They'd be gone forever. Being a Feeb meant the bacteria kept the virus in check.

Yes, there were side effects—the skin, the memory-rushes and fevers and ghosts, but the point was it still was YOU. Mostly.

I made us walk straight through the middle. There were people of all ages. Men, women, some kids. All bundled against the cold in grungy layers of clothing. If they looked too closely at our faces and hands we'd be discovered but no one did because they couldn't believe a Feeb would just waltz through like it was nothing—and a V couldn't hide itself for long.

Close to a hundred people moved around and not one stopped us until we reached the other side of the square. A man in fatigues held a rifle lazily against his shoulder and stood to the side of a metal door that went into the building.

A guard meant there was something worth guarding. Maybe prisoners. Maybe Spencer and the others.

I lifted the blankets higher and kept walking. He motioned for me to stop and I did, but not until I was in the shadow of the building. I felt Maibe's weight press into the back of me, using my body to hide herself. I hugged the blankets to my chest. We were maybe a half dozen yards away. Close enough that he knew we meant to go his way, but hopefully not close enough for him to notice details about our skin. He hadn't raised his rifle yet, so I took it as a sign that he couldn't see our Feebness yet.

I opened my mouth to speak, not knowing what to say but hoping something would come to me. "He said to bring some extra blankets."

"Who told you that?"

I rolled my eyes like it was the dumbest question in the world. "You know who."

"Sergeant Major Bennings made this a restricted area."

Ahh, Sergeant Bennings. He'd been the white suit who'd

shot us up with the bacteria vaccine.

"Well, he's the one who wants the blankets, so—" I shrugged my shoulders. "We can give them to you and you can take them, I guess. We're supposed to help with food prep right now anyway and they're going to get mad if we take too long." I shifted my weight from one leg to the other.

"Is it chili?" He raised his eyebrows in a hopeful expression.

I knew what that felt like, the anticipation of eating your choice of comfort food instead of whatever weird leftovers people felt compelled to share. Not that I held it against them, food was food and I hadn't been a picky eater in a long time, but still, being able to choose what to eat, when to eat it, and how much of it to eat—that would always feel like a luxury.

"Yeah, chili. They found a whole case of cans, and she's in a good mood tonight, so there's even going to be real beef I think. At least, that's what she was talking about. Oh, my god, it smelled so good when I left to bring the blankets. And, okay, this is a secret, though it won't be for long because everyone's going to smell it, no way to keep the smell down—"

"What?"

"They're making fresh bread. They've already tested a batch of it just to make sure the yeast was still alive and it works and oh, my god they let me have a slice and it was...warm." I pointed my chin in the direction of the building. "I don't really like going in there. If you take the blankets, I can try to come back with a slice."

The blankets in Maibe's hands tumbled to the ground.

I froze and stared at the guard to see what he would do. Maibe quickly bent over and picked the blankets back up. I recognized the look on his face. Spencer had played me many times just like this. The guard was too busy figuring out what the most responsible thing would be to do while still getting that slice of bread.

"I can't leave my post." He narrowed his eyes. "But get in and out fast and bring me a slice of that bread while it's still warm." He straightened and lifted the rifle to his side. "Move it."

I lifted the blankets even higher and kept my head turned as we scurried through. "We'll be right back."

Once we made it to the end of the alleyway, it dumped us into another open square, but this one was empty of people except for a trio of soldiers that held a prisoner by a long pole and noose.

I walked us along the back wall until a planter, pole, and shadows hid us from the clump of people.

"Gabbi?"

"What," I hissed. Should we go for the building they'd just left or for the building they were dragging the person to?

"Do you think they really have fresh bread here?"

I looked sideways at her and shook my head. "Maybe, but we're not getting any of it."

"Oh." Her face fell even though she did her best to hide her disappointment. A thirteen-year-old wasn't supposed to care so much except that this was about food, and food could make or break a thirteen-year-old.

"I'll make you a fresh loaf when this is all done, okay? It's not that hard."

Her eyes brightened and her mouth turned back into a smile.

A commotion across the square drew my attention back to the problem in front of us. A boy who looked near Maibe's age came running up to the group. Uninfected.

"Dad! Dad!"

A soldier from the group stepped away and said in a voice loud enough for us to hear, "Alden, don't come over here." Sergeant Bennings' voice. "I told you not to come over this way."

"There's trouble at one of the gates," Alden said. "Some Vs got inside."

"Why didn't someone else come?" Sergeant Bennings said.

Maibe looked at me. "Do you think those are the Vs that came in after us?"

"Probably," I said.

"I think I know him. The boy. We went to school together."

"That's great, come on." I moved us closer, skirting the edge of the square. "Don't skulk," I said. "We're not trying to hide. If it looks like we're hiding—"

"—then it looks like we don't belong," Maibe finished.

"Good," I said without looking back.

All of the soldiers' focus was on the father and son and the prisoner. The Vs chasing us through the gap in the fence had created the diversion we needed. We could probably sneak in unnoticed. Except who knew what waited on the other side of those glass doors? It could be empty or full of soldiers.

Maibe drew in a sharp breath. "That's Corrina."

"What?" The noose was tight around the prisoner's neck, her clothes were well worn and could have been what she'd been wearing last, but I hadn't paid much attention. It was jeans and a t-shirt and sneakers. The outfit of choice for millions. Her back was to us as well, but the hair did look familiar. But really, it was a miracle she'd survived as long as she had so I doubted it was her, but then she was enough of a do-gooder dumbass to get caught, so it could be her.

"It's her, I know it's her. Just look!" Maibe's voice rose slightly at each word.

"Keep it down, stupid."

"It's her," Maibe whispered.

The prisoner turned her profile to us for just a moment, but it was enough to confirm Maibe's suspicion. Corrina's hair and prominent nose and sharp chin were unmistakable, even at this distance.

"We've got to help her." Maibe moved forward a step.

I dropped the blankets and caught her arm. The wool tumbled to the ground in a messy heap signaling something wrong to anyone who looked. "Not like this with a bunch of soldiers around. Are you crazy?"

She pulled against my arm. I badly wanted to pick up those blankets and bring back the semblance of safety they gave me, but Maibe looked likely to run and blow the whole thing. "Stop and think. They're taking her exactly where we're going to go. Maybe they're taking her to Spencer and the others. We have to wait. We have to follow and wait for darkness or some sort of cover."

Maibe finally relaxed. "Okay."

I dropped her arm and fixed my stack of blankets. The stuffy, dog-like smell of the wool comforted me.

Sergeant Bennings returned to the group, said a few words, and then left with the boy.

The soldiers disappeared with Corrina through the glass doors of the building. Before the doors closed, they revealed a large warehouse with lots of spaces to hide.

CHAPTER 4

WE SLIPPED THROUGH THE UNGUARDED DOORS. Shadows inside
the warehouse tricked my eyes at first into believing people hid
within the aisles of machinery, furniture, sign boards, exhibit
frames. Cement formed symmetrical columns that rose to
impossibly high ceilings. Paint peeled off the columns in thick
chips, and dusted the junk beneath. Dirt, rat droppings, grease,
rust, who knew what else, covered the cement floor.

Maibe and I hid in one of the aisles. Above our heads ran a
network of catwalks attached to a spiral staircase of metal. Even
looking at them upset my stomach and turned my brain fuzzy
and made the memories crowd close. Soldiers, and strangely,
people in doctor uniforms, came and went through the door
at the far end of the warehouse. Someone had put up an entire
section of rooms with framing, plywood, maybe caging of some
type, it was hard to tell.

My heart skipped a beat when I examined the catwalk again.

The grating skirted just a few feet above the makeshift rooms like a metal skeleton. My feet lost feeling as I pictured climbing across. The grating was low enough for me to jump onto the ceilings of the rooms below it and high enough to freak me out. But no matter—I had found my way in and I would climb those stairs and that catwalk, memory-rush or not.

"I need you to stand guard while I go up high."

"But it's one of your triggers." Maibe rose from the floor. "The memory-rush will take over and I won't be able to get you down and—"

"I'll be fine," I said even though I didn't really know that. My stomach grumbled and I thought about the supplies left behind in the garbage can. Things had been moving so fast, I hadn't made us eat anything since yesterday. The sky outside had darkened considerably in the last hour which only increased the spookiness of the place—but my catwalk would be hidden as soon as I crossed the lip of the first room's wall. I didn't want to waste another minute, the itch of finally going into action begged to be scratched. Plus the sooner I climbed up, the sooner I could get back down.

Maibe set up at the base of the spiral stairs, behind a damp and molding cardboard box of marketing materials for a water-less cookware set. I grabbed a nearby screwdriver, thinking it would make an excellent weapon and maybe a way to dig the others out through the drywall.

I prided myself on climbing the stairs like a ninja cat, whatever that was, using yoga skills learned at the gym that had served me well on the streets when it came to dodging unde-sirable people, animals, vehicles. It felt as if I were climbing two stories even though it was probably not much more than one story. Sweat made the screwdriver slippery in my hand. I wiped my palms on my clothes and smelled that distinctive metallic odor that always happened when skin touched cheap metal. I jammed the screwdriver into my waistband and cursed and told myself to get it together. My head felt woozy and full of space, as if there wasn't enough oxygen this high up.

Maibe's waiting form disappeared over the lower horizon of the ceiling panels as I crawled. Now, other than the pale light that filtered in, everything was dark and I was safer than ever, like I was pressed between a sandwich made of ceiling and roof. I crouched to rest for a moment, to still my heart rate, to concentrate on my breathing, to feel something solid even if it was just the grate under my fingers. But it was a mistake to stop moving. The memories crowded in and my mind went dark and then lit up blue, everything was pale blue and I watched it all transform into a house and I knew the house.

The pale blue house stood alone and lightning lit it up in flashes because there were no street lights that worked on the bad side. The rain soaked through my layers of clothing and newspaper and the wind drove the rain into all of me and everything smelled like the rot in take-out boxes left in the dumpster too long.

Father carried the last bit of food—a box of crackers. He was drunk. That kind of red-faced drunk that made him walk around like a sailor on board a ship in a storm. The rain and the wind and the darkness soaked the streets and turned them into streams that would soon roar into rivers if we didn't take shelter soon and I waited for Father to notice the blue house because if I said it first he would never let us go inside. I was eleven and I wanted to go inside but I was afraid of Father's red-rimmed sloshy eyes that meant he would hit me soon and maybe my mother too.

My mother held my hand even though water slipped between our palms and she pinched hard to keep hold. She stumbled behind Father and the lightning showed how tired she felt and how she wouldn't stand up for me tonight if I made Father angry.

Father's feet stopped moving but his body swayed back and forth. "There," he said, swallowing the word like a gulping goldfish, but he said it.

People-shapes moved behind the windows and I clamped down on my mother's hand until she said, "Gabriela!" and yanked her hand away and I fell into the street river, the water splashing onto my face, cold, gritty, smelling of oil and those outside bathroom places we used sometimes. But my knees burned because I wore shorts but the water would wash away the blood and it would be okay once we got inside. Except there were people inside, or maybe demons inside, and then we would have to keep looking but then the river would drown us.

Father stumbled up the path and my mother followed and I ran after them. The water dragged my feet down like weights and the cold made my legs move slowly. He pushed on the front door and fell over inside because it hadn't been latched. It was open as if waiting for us to find it and use it but demons always liked to invite you inside, like you were meant to be there, before they revealed their true nature. Alli had taught me that at the last shelter Mother and Father had taken us. She said those were the places you had to watch for the most. The unlocked places.

But Father and Mother did not know about Alli's stories. They kept going and I followed because they would not care if

I stayed all night outside and that would be worse.

There were people inside, but it was so dark and only the lightning sometimes showed them. There might have been demons walking around, hiding in the shadows, and there was lightning and one of the shadows stayed a shadow. I ran to my mother and grabbed her hand even though she might slap me for surprising her. But she didn't notice.

"Just give me the box, Dennis. I'll keep it for us."

Father laughed and I was not sorry for the dark because then I didn't have to see the look on his face and then there was a ripping sound, the kind cardboard and plastic make, the kind food wrappers make.

Mother snatched her hand away from me and went to Father, arms outstretched, one warding her face and the other held out, the lightning freezing her pose like someone had taken a photo. "Don't do that."

"Don't even think you can tell me what to do."

Lightning flashed and he threw the cardboard box at her and swung his arm around and then darkness made him disappear, but the sound of flesh hitting flesh rose above the rain and howling wind and someone laughed and I screamed, "I'm not hungry!" but she didn't listen because the next flash showed her barreling into his stomach, but he did not move, not an inch, and then it went dark again but the wap of his hit sounded again and someone else laughed and then something hit me in the head and my thoughts spun in the dark until I didn't know which direction I faced. I ran into another room, away from the shadows and found stairs and climbed them and hoped and hoped there would be no shadows up there because the holes in the roof let water in and people and demons did not like to get wet.

The stairs creaked and a few gave way under my feet, but if I could find a place, just a little place where shadows could not fit. My head hurt, my stomach hurt, I couldn't see where to go and the wind howled and filled the whole house with howls like a pack of demons would snatch me out of the house and drop me and I was too high because I had walked up four floors and when they dropped me my body would split and seep blood and all of me would get washed away by the river so no one could find me. A window shattered and threw glass on my left side like little bullets and wetness came with it and more cold because the demons had broken in!

I ran and ran and smacked into a knob that punched into my chest and I clawed at the door until it unlocked and ran into the room and cried. "Please don't punish me no more!" My stomach hurt and my head hurt and I fell onto the floor. I shivered and waited for the demons to grab me.

"You ain't being punished."

I looked up and in the next flash of lightning I saw an older boy curled on a towel next to me like Aunt June's cat liked to do except this boy didn't hiss at me and looked like he didn't mind I was next to him.

"It's rain for the flowers and trees. It washes away the battles bad people wanted to have on the streets. It means the angels are trying to win," he said.

Light flickered and held and was a golden color from a lighter. There was another boy and a girl, and the boy looked older than everyone but the girl looked older than me but not too much. They sat cross-legged around a candle and did not stay shadows. My pounding heart slowed down and I sat up.

"I'm Leaf," the curled-up boy said. "That's Mary, and that's Spencer."

"Tell us your name now," Mary said.

"Gabriela," I said, a sob catching my name in my throat.

"No. Your real name," Mary said.

I felt confused and didn't know what she wanted me to tell them. Then I said, "Gabbi with an 'i'."

"Gabbi with an 'i,' are you here alone?" Leaf asked.

I almost gave a different answer. It was on my lips but then it changed at the last second. "Yeah," I said because it was both truth and a lie but mostly truth.

Leaf shared a look with Spencer but the dancing lightning from outside covered it up except Leaf said, "We're jumping the train to California. You can come if you want."

"It's better in California," Mary said. "It don't take so much storms to get rid of all the bad stuff out there."

"There are more angels there. My cousin told me," Leaf said.

The storm held its breath. I stopped crying. I wiped my cheeks and hardened myself to the shadows downstairs. I could hear the truth in what Leaf said because I really wanted it to be true. "Okay," I said. "I want to go with you."

THE MEMORY-RUSH FADED and my senses came back to me.

I moaned and pressed my face into the grate like I had pressed my face into that wood floor. My mouth felt thick with dust, but I was grateful the memory-rush hadn't been one of the bad ones.

I pushed on as soon as the memory let me. Weak people let the memories take over and made them feel sorry for themselves.

I wasn't weak like that. Even if I couldn't always fight off the
memories, I always tried.

I crawled along the catwalk and noticed there were lots of
dividers—at least twenty-four rooms to search. From above
them I realized they formed a sort of double-row semi-circle. I
guessed there must be a hallway in between. On the other side
of the rooms, opposite the warehouse from where I climbed up,
was a large room that opened like a hole beneath the grating.
In the middle of it was a dentist's chair with its back to me.
Spotlights shone down on it and a tray on wheels was next to
it. Equipment rimmed the edge. I knew how light refraction
worked and how bright lights inside that room made it almost
impossible for people to see me in the shadows. It took the rods
in the retina of the eye many minutes to adjust from light to
dark, that's why pirates wore a patch over one eye. Not because
they lost it in a fight, but because it kept an eye always at the
ready for seeing what needed to be seen in dark places like the
hold of an enemy ship or the coastline at night during a raid.

I moved across the grating until I reached the room's lip and
saw the profile of the chair. A person was strapped to it. My
breath shortened, my heartbeat increased, my fingers began to
tingle as I thought about jumping. If it were Spencer or Leaf
or one of the boys I was going to jump from this catwalk and
rescue them. I'd land on all fours, and we'd barrel through
the door, whatever door was closest, and I'd scream for Maibe
and we'd take our chances on the run, because you always ran
from a fight—

A person wearing a doctor's coat walked into the room and
the light made it obvious that this doctor was also a Feeb. I
moved silently across the grating until I faced the dentist chair

head-on. I primed myself to launch off the edge and onto the woman's back.

But then I saw it was Corrina strapped to the chair and I stopped.

I don't mean to say I wasn't happy to see her—well, I wasn't happy to see her—but I wasn't unhappy to see her, but she didn't need my immediate rescuing either.

She wasn't one of us.

The adrenaline rush faded and now that I knew where Corrina was, I crawled back to the cells and lowered myself to the ceiling. I dug at the drywall with my screwdriver. My hole took too long, this sort of thing always took too long, but I finally made an opening big enough to see through. This was when I discovered that all the drywall did was cover up a metal cage underneath.

The pinhole let light through, which made it easy to see who was in the cell when I put my eye to it.

A Feeb like me, but not one of my crew.

I did not speak a word or otherwise let the whimpering person curled in a fetal position on the cot know about my presence. I continued onto the next cell and repeated my steps with the screwdriver.

Once I punched through I saw this one also held a Feeb, his marks clear on his balding head. It was Officer Hanley. He paced his cell with his head buried in his hands and acted like he hadn't heard me. He was probably so deep in the fevers he couldn't hear anything. I moved on, feeling like I was in a sort of X-rated peep show. He'd gotten his payback but I felt sick to my stomach.

The next ceiling hole revealed Leaf and I almost teared up

from the joy of seeing his stupid, curly, unkempt hair while he carved into the wall with his fingernails. "Leaf," I said while pressing my mouth against the hole. I quickly took my mouth away to replace with my eye.

Leaf stilled for a moment, then resumed his carving.

"Leaf! It's Gabbi."

Leaf looked up with his Feeb skin marring an otherwise pixie-like face. He had stripped off all his winter clothes and wore his favorite yellow t-shirt because yellow was a bright, happy color and he liked to pretend the world was the same way. If anyone could be said to be the mother of the group, it was Leaf. I'd never understood how he had survived this far on the street, except that Spencer must have found him early on and took him in before the drugs and the survival sex that most of the rest of us had faced had done permanent damage. I'd made a pass at Leaf once, on a lonely night long before the Vs came on the scene, long before I'd known the true state of relationships in the group. He hadn't humiliated me when he turned me down. Even though I'd gotten hot with embarrassment he'd said something to make me laugh and it was like it had never happened.

If anyone was too good for the street, it was Leaf.

He smiled, but only one side of his face turned up. "Hi, Gabbi. That's the real you, right? Not some ghost-memory playing tricks on me? Though I guess if this were a ghost-memory I'd be seeing you instead of just hearing you, huh?"

"Leaf," I said in a strangled voice. I had to take my eye away to put my mouth over the hole and I hated to lose sight of him even for a second. "What happened? What have they done?" I switched back to my eye. Half of his face was strangely frozen.

I pressed my eye harder onto the hole so that its edges gouged my skin but I didn't care. It wasn't just his face, but one entire half of his body seemed limp. My nose breathed in drywall dust and my throat constricted.

"This is not a good place, Gabbi. Not a good place at all." And then he burst into tears but they only came out of one eye and he bowed his head so I could not see it and I wanted to scream.

"Leaf. Leaf! I'm going to get you out. I promise. I'm going to fix this, I'm—"

"Spencer's next door," Leaf said.

I switched back to my eye, cursing the hole's smallness. He'd turned up his face again. Wetness made one cheek shine. His good hand brushed it away. "Hurry up, Gabbi, if that's really you up there and not some side effect I had avoided the pleasure of experiencing until now, oh, the doctor will love this little development, won't she…" He turned his head to the side as if forgetting he talked to an actual person, to the person who was going to rescue him.

His head jerked and he gazed up. "Oh, there you are. In the hole. Nicely done, very sneaky, very Gabbi-chic."

I tapped out a message in Morse code because I couldn't speak around the lump in my throat: S-T-A-Y A-L-I-V-E.

Ano had made us learn the code from a stolen library book. We'd been traveling by train last year under big night skies, bright stars, and a feeling that everything was working out for us. We'd made a game out of learning it. We'd been headed back to California and dreaming about the future.

Leaf smiled. "I'll sure do my best, captain." He fake saluted with his good arm.

I scrambled up and over to the next room. I dug into the

ceiling, using all my strength, caring little now for noise and everything now for speed. This time I made the hole more like a diagonal ditch. Dust flew into the air and coated my face, my eyelashes, my hands, my nose. I sneezed and snot came flying out, but I didn't stop to wipe it, just kept digging until I punched through and widened it enough for both my eye and mouth.

Spencer stood tall beneath me, staring at exactly where I worked. Dust coated his dark eyebrows and hair, turning it into an old man gray color that better matched his Feeb skin. His arms were crossed, both eyes blinked, both arms moved.

"And does this rat have two legs or four?" he said quietly.

"Spencer." I whispered his name like a talisman of protection because that's what he was to me and the others.

"Ah, it comes on two legs, and is rather a sight, or should I say, sound, for sore ears." He cocked his head to the side. "Gabbi, what the hell took you so long?"

"I got here as fast as I could. I swear."

He held up a hand and my heart beat wildly. Could I have made it here faster, could I have done something different? Was this my fault? A sick feeling grew in my stomach that brought me back to long nights and dark moments and a hand gripping my bicep in such a way that I knew I'd never escape, no matter how much I screamed or kicked or cried.

"You better stop whatever thoughts are in your head right now. You are not a victim. You can't be. Victims don't survive the streets, and here you are, alive." He paused, stuck out his chin in that defiant, prideful way he had. "We're not victims either. So cut that crap out. We're alive and we're going to stay that way—most likely, anyway. Do you have a plan?"

"I…" I'd found them, that had been the plan. I'd found them

and figured the rest would come and I'd just see a way out. But all I could see was the hours it would take me to dig out a hole big enough for even one of them to fit through if I could get something that would cut through the cage wire and they were all in separate rooms and I surely would not get them all out in time and who would we have to leave behind?

"You never run without a plan, Gabbi. I thought you knew that."

"I do know that, I do…" It's how I'd avoided capture by the police and the shelters and the pimps. It's how come I knew how to make a fresh batch of bread and take a bath out of a bucket and sleep with the windows cracked in the midst of an apocalypse.

But I didn't have a plan for this.

Spencer sighed. "Just kidding, twit. I've got a plan and it's better than whatever dumbass thing you could have thought up."

Relief flooded me. You could count on Spencer. He would know what to do and I would be able to do it and stop trying to figure all this out on my own.

"They've been checking on Leaf in the early morning," Spencer said, "Take out the nurse and guard, and you'll have the keys to every prison cell in this section. Think you're up for that?"

"Killing an uninfected…a real person?" I'd only killed Vs up until that point and no matter how much I wanted to claim it didn't bother me because they were trying to kill me first—it did bother me.

"It may come to that. Whatever they did to Leaf—" Spencer's voice cracked. "He was screaming, Gabbi. I could here him through the walls and I couldn't do anything. I couldn't stop it." The tough, laugh-at-the-world facade peeled off for a moment, revealing a seventeen-year-old who was angry and sad.

I held my tongue for a long moment, examining myself to see if I was really capable of such a thing. And then like a ghost-memory, Leaf's broken face rose before my eyes. "Yeah. No problem."

"Okay find some place safe to hole up for the night. I'll figure out how to get a message to the others. Try to sleep or something." He turned and lay down flat on his cot, threaded his hands together, and put them behind his head.

"How are you going to get them a message?"

"I'll figure out something. I'll claw open the walls with my bare hands if I have to."

I realized I didn't know one thing and I wondered if it meant something really bad had happened, even worse than whatever had happened to Leaf, something so bad that Spencer couldn't even bear to bring it up. "Spencer?"

"Yeah?"

"Are Ano and Jimmy and Ricker…are they okay?"

"I don't know."

CHAPTER 5

I HAD FIGURED OUT A PLAN that was going to work. At the first
chance, I would go back to the trash can and get my crossbow. I
would round up more Vs somehow and bring them back and it
would give me enough time to get everyone out. It had worked
once before. It would work again.

In the meantime, I made us trap ourselves on the catwalk.
Maibe went into this whole babbling argument about not going
up there again. It was both the safest and stupidest spot to
be. In the aisles there were places to hide, but it could also be
patrolled. On the catwalk, I battled my fear of heights and a
tumble to the ground was our only escape.

Softly, Maibe said, "How are you doing this? How can you
be up there?"

I scratched at the bites around my ankles until it felt like it
was turning into one huge, itching mess. I'd break skin soon
if I wasn't careful but I didn't care. It kept me in the present

and away from the memory-flashes and away from thinking
about having to kill a guard.

"Maybe it's not one of your triggers?"

"No," I whispered. "It's one of my triggers." Instead of the
grating I imagined the hard floor of that upper story of the
house and Leaf curled up next to me on a towel.

The guard had come back while I'd been digging through
the ceiling—the guard I'd promised to get bread for. He looked
torn up, as if he'd been battling Vs. I wondered if he would
remember my promise and if that was going to get us caught.
I wanted to go back for my crossbow, but I couldn't, not as long
as the guard was back.

We waited for hours, watching and listening. My muscles
cramped and my throat felt dry, like if I even tried to speak all
that would come out would be a croak. The guard didn't leave.

The guard had to leave.

In the middle of the night, there was finally a commotion. I
sat up and tried to see through the shadows. If the guard had
left I would run down the stairs and for the door.

Two soldiers burst inside the warehouse. A light was turned
on, just enough to see they were running for the door where
Spencer and the others were.

People yelled and boots slapped on the cement and then
they were dragging out the doctor on a stretcher, and there was
Corrina too, and both of them were being taken away. They left
through the outside glass doors. Maibe sprang up and raced
for the staircase.

I was about to go after her, but then a familiar face caught
my eye. Spencer. A guard was dragging out Spencer.

I lost precious seconds thinking about what to do. They'd

be gone to the outside before I made it halfway down the stairs. There wasn't time for any of my plans now. I ran without thinking and launched myself into the air. Wind rushed passed my ears and my throat choked up. The darkness made the leap feel like it lasted forever. I landed on the soldier holding onto Spencer and my impact sounded like the wap my father's fist always made in my mother's stomach.

SPENCER GRABBED MY SHOULDERS and shook them. "Snap out of it, Gabbi. We need you now!"

Maibe stood behind him, backlit by light. The guard moaned in unconsciousness next to me. I was on my back, dizzy and shocked that I hadn't killed myself.

Maibe's hands shook and the keys she must have taken from the guard jingled together.

"Get out of here," I said. "Hide." My words sounded slurred.

"We have maybe a minute before they notice the guard didn't make it out with me," Spencer said.

I snatched the keys from Maibe's hand and hurried into the hallway. First I unlocked Leaf's cage, shouted for him to get out, get out now, then I went methodically through opening up others. Spencer grabbed Leaf around the shoulders of his yellow t-shirt, hugged him, kissed his forehead. Ano and Ricker and Jimmy's rooms were all in a row two doors down from Leaf's. They fell into the hallway like a circus car run backwards.

"Get the rest," Spencer said to me. He supported Leaf down the hallway because half of Leaf's body seemed sort of frozen. "Ano, Ricker, Jimmy—help Gabbi."

I went for the next door, the three boys crowding on my heels.

Maibe screamed. "They're coming! They're coming!"

Spencer poked his head back into the hallway, his face serious and commanding. His voice boomed. "Leave them and run."

Ricker, and Jimmy dashed away. I stuck the key in the next door. There were almost twenty cages left to open and release people who would have as soon spit on me, ignore me, or arrest me for being a runaway before all this had happened. But we were all Feebs now. They were outcasts like me, homeless, forced to create their own set of rules.

"Gabbi!" Ano yelled.

I left the key unturned in the lock.

I sprinted back out into the warehouse and a cacophony of shouts and gunfire bounced around. Figures flitted in the darkness. A beam from a flashlight fell on me, blinding my eyes.

I dived to the right, landing in a heap of boxes. The cardboard edges gouged my ribs and legs and neck. Lights flashed above me, but moved on. I forced myself up, scattering the boxes in multiple directions, and took off down one of the aisles. I didn't know what else to do. The others could have been anywhere. The tunnel effect dampened the shouts and the gunfire. I was dead if they managed to get ahead of me.

My shoes thumped into a thick layer of dust, as if I ran on a weird sort of carpet. A rectangle of light appeared ahead of me, then a shadow cut it into a polygon shape. I stumbled, afraid of what I was running to.

The outlines morphed into recognizable figures. Maibe supported Jimmy. Leaf limped unsupported but with Spencer hovering close by. Ano and Ricker held the door open and motioned us through.

"Go, go, go," Ano said as he pushed me outside.

CHAPTER 6

"HOW BAD IS IT?" Spencer said.

Jimmy's normally easy-going face was streaked with tears and dirt and blood. Maibe supported him with her shoulder under his and her hands wrapped around his chest. Jimmy's face went white as he lifted his hand away from the bullet wound on his arm—a gash three inches long and deep enough to still be seeping blood.

"It's a flesh wound," Ano said, pressing the skin on either side. "It needs to be cleaned and bandaged."

We had stopped at the fence edge that separated the water park from the rest of the fairgrounds. The rundown buildings, empty pools, and brightly painted three-story slides were a creepy background for our reunion. It looked abandoned, but on the far end, there was activity near the train tracks. Too far away to worry about at the moment.

"We have to go back for Corrina," Maibe said. She looked

earnestly at each one of us. "We have to."

"I don't think so. We've got to get gone," I said. "They're going to be looking for us and we've got to get gone and away from this crazy place. The bike trail is on the other side of the levee," I pointed to it. "We find a way onto it and take it out of town."

"But—"

"Look, I'm sorry, I really am," I interrupted Maibe. "But we can't do it, Maibe. We've got to run—"

"No, we're going back for the rest," Spencer said. "It's my fault she got caught." He tugged on the makeshift tourniquet around Jimmy's arm one last time before standing up. "Leaf, go with Jimmy and Maibe to the edge of the grounds. Find a way onto the bike trail, set a fire, then get gone. Gabbi, Ano, Ricker, you're coming back with me."

"I'm going too," Maibe said.

"I'm not staying behind either," Leaf said. The yellow of his shirt almost matched the yellowish gleam of his face.

Spencer looked at him for a long time.

"Dr. Ferrad hit a nerve," Leaf said. "When they were running some tests on me. It was an accident. They really are looking for a cure."

Spencer shook his head.

"Dr. Ferrad is here?" I said.

"She's the one who's been experimenting on us," Ricker said, loathing thick in his voice.

"She's trying to find a cure," Leaf said, his words coming out with a lisp.

"How can you defend them?" Ricker said. "They're monsters."

"I'm not defending them," Leaf said.

I had to look away because he only said it with half his face and it made me want to burst into tears.

"Gabbi, it's going to be okay," Leaf said.

I gritted my teeth and turned to Spencer. "This is crazy. You said we should always run from a fight."

"Not always," Spencer said.

CHAPTER 7

THE COLD AIR SUNK INTO MY CHEST and made my breath hiccup. We had spent two days hiding. Two days worth of avoiding the extra guards, the extra patrols, and looking for Corrina. I'd gone back for my crossbow, but that was the only weapon we'd yet managed to find. We knew where we were going next though. Ricker had overheard that morning while stealing food from their soup lines that they were planning to hang Corrina as a way to celebrate the New Year.

We skirted the fenceline. The evening light threw shadows everywhere. I trailed behind the group. I told myself I was watching our backs instead of dragging my feet. Spencer hadn't sent anyone away—even half-paralyzed Leaf, injured Jimmy, and Maibe in her silly pink sweatshirt. The three of them were too young, too injured, too weak. Mary would never have let them come.

Groans drifted out from the darkness, on the river's side of the fence, and grew louder as we approached a gate.

Spencer held up his hand.

A person lurched into view through a gap in the fence. A gap, it dawned on me, that shouldn't be there.

Dark shapes littered the ground. Unmoving lumps of clothing that had once been guards. Their uniforms gave away which side they'd belonged to. I tried to breath around the sudden tightness in my chest. How could we get Corrina and the others and fight off the uninfected and the Vs too? We were runaways, not soldiers, we stayed in the shadows, we blended in, we avoided stuff exactly like this.

"Check them out." Spencer said.

I pushed all thought away and went through the closest guard's pockets, then stopped, realizing I didn't need his money or his plastic. He was facedown on the ground and his neck was twisted. Broken.

"What happened?" Maibe said. She held a bloody knife in her hand. Part of me was glad she had the guts to take what she needed and another part of me was sad. I pushed it all away and focused on getting us all out of this alive.

Leaf limped over to the fence and brushed his fingers along the opening. "The Vs must have overwhelmed it." He kicked at the parts of a broken radio. The plastic bits scattered. "They might not even know about it."

The shuffle of feet on the fairground side of the fence drew our attention to a group of Vs yards away. Some ran, some walked, others limped.

They were moving away from us.

They were moving toward the noise and smells and activity of the camp.

"We have to warn them," Leaf said.

"They don't deserve a warning," Ricker said. "We don't have to warn them. The opening is right here. We just leave now."

I opened my mouth to agree with Ricker.

"We're not leaving without the rest of the Feebs," Spencer said.

"We don't owe them," Ricker said.

"I won't go," Maibe said.

Ricker looked at her, begging her to change her mind. "Maibe…"

I waited for Ano to speak up. His dark eyes surveyed the landscape. He'd picked up a rifle and a knife and looked too much the part of a soldier—hard, uncaring, set on doing damage. But I knew that wasn't him, was it?

Ano didn't say a word. He just let them argue it out in fierce whispers while the cold sunk deep into our bones and the mucky smell of the river mixed with the smell of blood.

Spencer started walking without a word. Maibe was the next one, and Jimmy after her. Ano and I looked at each other. We didn't need to say anything to know the other's thoughts.

Spencer had decided and we would follow.

Stay alive, I told myself. Don't get caught. I repeated this like it would automatically come true if I said it a million times.

Ricker caught up to us when Spencer slowed down at the base of a set of stairs.

"Jimmy. Maibe. Get up those stairs and keep lookout." Spencer pointed at where he wanted the two of them. Up high, out of the way, in direct view of the center of camp. The electronic sound of a man speaking suddenly filtered through the air.

Maibe dashed up and Jimmy followed. The voice droned on. There was a sick slap as a figure slammed into Ricker and took him to the ground. We'd caught up too close to the Vs and one of them had noticed us.

I panicked and jumped onto the V and bashed in his skull with the crossbow. Ano helped me drag the V off Ricker. Blood poured down Ricker's face. The V had bitten him on the head, not so deep, but enough for a scalp wound, enough to send him into the fevers at the worst possible moment.

"You'll be okay," Ano said.

I echoed Ano's words even as Ricker's eyes began to glaze. Ricker wiped his hand across his face, smearing the blood. He wasn't going to be much help now. I looked around for Spencer and Leaf, but they were gone.

"We can't leave him," I said.

Ano thought for a moment and then nodded. We propped Ricker between us, his arms slung around our shoulders. The crossbow hung at my side. We limped him up the stairs and every step felt slow, like walking in quicksand.

The entire camp seemed spread before us. A mix of tents, tables, and people on one side of the moat of water, and a stage lit up as if it were Christmas on the other side. Two people stood on boxes.

"Who's that with Corrina?" I asked.

"It's Dylan," Maibe said. "She found him. She didn't think she would find him. She was afraid he had died."

"He won't be alive much longer." Spotlights were trained on the two figures, highlighting the ropes around their necks.

"We have to stop them," Maibe said.

"There's way more of them than us," I said. "They're already on the ropes. They're dead and we'll be dead with them soon if we don't get out of here."

"They're not dead yet," Maibe said fiercely. "Take that back, Gabbi. Take that back."

Sergeant Bennings began speaking through his stupid microphone, like an emcee announcing the next act. "Any last words before the New Year?"

Dylan said something about love and Sergeant Bennings spoke again about finding a cure and making necessary sacrifices so that people like his son and his wife and everyone's sons and daughters and wives had a chance. He gave the microphone over to Corrina for her last words but she shook her head.

That's when Maibe stood up at the very edge of the perch. Even though it was night the security lights shined just high enough that her pink sweatshirt stood out like a star when she waved her hands around.

"Wait," Corrina said, her voice faint through the speaker system. "I have something to say." She began telling some weird story into the microphone.

I dragged Maibe out of the light. "What are you thinking?"

"She needed to know we were here," Maibe said. "She was giving up."

"There's nothing we can do—"

The camp erupted into shouts. The Vs had made it to the tables. People were running and fighting and dying. I spotted Spencer in the crowd and Leaf was on the other side of the moat, hobbling to the stage. My stomach dropped. Ano dashed down the stairs.

"Stay here!" I yelled at Maibe. "Keep Ricker and Jimmy safe!"

Maibe opened her mouth to protest.

"Please, Maibe. Please protect them." I couldn't keep the anguish from my voice.

She nodded.

I lost all sense of direction except that I had to follow Ano. It was impossible to tell V from uninfected in the dark like this with everyone looking equally insane and angry. A V slammed into my side and I went down under her hot breath, her scratching hands, her rabid eyes. Hands grabbed her shoulders and threw her off. Ano towered over me and held out a hand.

I grabbed up my crossbow and ran after him through the crowd, pushing my way through the stinking, hot bodies that had suddenly turned the night into a sauna. I broke through the crowd and fell off the edge. I was flying, falling. I hit the water hard. The shock stabbed a million needles of ice into me. The crossbow dragged me down and I imagined the dark bottom as an abyss that would swallow me up and never let me go. A boom shook the water, shook me to my core. My eyes were open but saw nothing, nothing but darkness, nothing but deep cold and wet night. I tried to get my feet under me. My shoes slipped on the thick muck of the bottom.

There was a bottom.

Energy surged through me. Water streamed from my head, my face, my arms, as I stood up. I lifted the crossbow and took in what I was seeing in the golden light of the stage. Corrina hunched over Dylan, spreading herself over him as if that would stop the bullet from the uniformed soldier standing over her.

I aimed the crossbow and shot it and closed my eyes just before the arrow buried itself into the soldier's chest.

When I opened my eyes Corrina stared at me in shock. I screamed at her to get out of there. She looked at something behind me. I turned and saw Sergeant Bennings had climbed a light pole and was acting like a sniper, picking people off. He turned his gun to the stage but then a V jumped onto his boot and he tumbled into the water. I sloshed through the moat, set my crossbow on the stage, and hauled myself into the light.

Dylan and Corrina were gone. There were two bodies. I ran by them, thinking to catch up to Corrina. We'd find somewhere safe and then get back to the others and then—

A yellow shirt. One of the bodies wore a yellow shirt.

I froze, the knowledge sinking into my muscles before it registered in my brain. No. It was the light. The lights only made the shirt look yellow. It wasn't really yellow. It wasn't—

Spencer scrambled across the stage, his face a mask of grief, his jeans torn and bloody. He tumbled to one knee next to the shirt that couldn't be yellow.

Leaf.

That was Leaf with the bright red spot like a target spreading from the center of his chest. That couldn't be Leaf. Not the kindest one of us. Not the one who deserved more than any of us to get something better out of this life than what he'd gotten.

A keening sound filled the air and I realized it came from my own throat.

Spencer gathered Leaf into his chest and rocked him. The boom I had heard underwater. That had been Leaf dying. That had been my friend getting killed for helping someone he shouldn't have cared about. But that wasn't Leaf. Leaf always cared. It didn't matter whether Corrina deserved it or not.

"We should never have stayed. We should have let her hang." The water that streamed off me puddled next to him, thinning the blood into something pink. Her life in exchange for Leaf's wasn't right. This thought wormed deep into my heart like poison.

\\ | /

January

/ | \\

CHAPTER 8

They killed Leaf.

We left him behind. Dead on a stage. Blood spreading away from the hole in his chest.

He saved Corrina and Dylan but not himself.

Spencer should have never let him come with us. Spencer should have known better.

I PUT DOWN THE PEN AND PAPER because it was too painful to keep writing. I don't even know why I did it, except that Mary had always done this with her blog posts. We'd hidden ourselves away in a warehouse later converted into a bar. All the alcohol was either missing or smashed. Thick dust layered the bar counter. A grungy claw-foot bathtub had been dumped at some point in a corner.

I helped Ano drag the tub into the middle of the two-story

space and we put Ricker inside of it. Ano found a bunch of rope and I helped him tie Ricker's hands and legs. We took turns staying with him through the fevers. We'd promised each other to never let one of us go through it alone. It helped to wake up to a face you knew wasn't going to hurt you no matter what the fever made you relive.

The camp battle sounds had finally faded into silence. We'd made a pile out of broken chair legs and set it on fire. The flames made shadows dance across faces covered in smoke, blood, mud, afflicted skin.

Maibe was here. Her body hunched, her knees pulled into her chest, her face cast toward the ground as she sat against Ricker's bathtub. She scratched a bug bite on her wrist as an afterthought. Jimmy had his injured arm propped on her shoulder. He stared with vacant eyes into the flames.

Corrina and Dylan were missing. We had not saved any of the other Feebs but we had gotten a lot of people killed.

Spencer was somewhere nearby.

No one dared search for him. I had never seen that mixture of grief and hate and self-disgust on him before, not even when we'd lost Mary. Not even when he'd discovered some particularly gruesome act a pimp had demanded of a kid or when we'd stumbled across a dead body swollen beyond recognition in the creek.

Jimmy's squinting eyes shifted to me every few seconds, waiting for me to do something. With Leaf dead and Spencer absent, they expected me to take up the mantle, to be responsible for them, to tell them what would keep them safe and alive and relatively warm for another night. Except I had no idea what to do.

"Gabbi, is there any food?" Jimmy whispered across the firelight.

I grabbed a granola bar out of my pack and threw it across the fire into his lap.

"Thanks."

"There's water too," I said. Whoever had taken the alcohol hadn't cared about the shelf of bottled water or the pen and papers next to it. I stood up and passed out the bottles. "We should move on soon. Get as far away as possible from this whole mess."

"We should go back to the boxcar," Jimmy said. "Go back to what we know."

Ano cocked his head, not quite disagreeing but not agreeing either. The boxcar had been our home after we'd been 'cured' and escaped Sergeant Bennings—before the rest of the city had fallen apart.

"We should run," I said. "You always run, Jimmy." I looked to Ano for agreement.

"But what about Mary? I thought you said she was coming back?" Jimmy said.

Ano winced.

I closed my eyes. All of me wanted to run, but I couldn't just leave the message I'd scratched into the wall—*Mary, we'll back*. She would wait for us and it would be my fault that we never came back for her.

Ricker shouted out something about his brother.

"We can't do anything until Ricker is out of the fevers," Ano said finally.

A door squeaked open and feet shuffled along the ground. I tensed and looked at Ano across the fire. He held himself like a statue. At first whoever it was blended into the darkness, but then slowly took shape as it approached the fire. Spencer had returned. He went over to the water bottles. Ano relaxed.

"It'll be light in another couple of hours," I said. "That's when I think we should go back to the boxcar to leave a message for Mary."

"There's no point," Spencer said, his voice cracking.

"What if Mary's come back?" I said.

"Mary isn't coming back," Spencer said, not looking at me.

"You don't know that."

"I do."

Something about how he said it felt off. "You know something," I stood up. "What do you know?"

"I saw her. During one of the experiments. She's in their V cages."

"What did you say?" Ano shot up to stand next to me.

"If it was her." Spencer brushed a hand across his face. "I couldn't get close enough to be sure, but if it was her, she's all V now."

Fury rose up in me then, a small wave of it that grew bigger and threatened to crash into the sand and drag me under. "We should never have gone back for Corrina, what were you thinking, Spencer?"

Jimmy scooted back. Maibe stayed frozen in her cross-legged position against the tub.

Spencer took another drink of water, his presence looming over us. His seventeen years and experience on the street made him so much older than the rest of us. He was supposed to know what was best and tell us what to do and we'd just listen like we'd always done. Like we'd done with Mary, and going into the fairgrounds in the first place, and then going back for the other Feebs. All of that had turned out wrong.

A sick feeling swelled in my chest. Spencer couldn't be trusted anymore. I backed away from the warmth of the fire. Cold immediately slid down my spine. "Mary's gone because you told us not to run."

Spencer flinched, but I kept going.

"You all got captured, because you told us not to run."

Spencer didn't move this time.

I clenched my fists. "Leaf is dead. Because you told us. Not. To. Run."

Spencer's mouth turned into a snarl, but not a sound came out.

Jimmy was wide-eyed. Even Ano looked surprised. Maibe stared into the fire as if she couldn't hear anything.

"It's time to run, Spencer. We aren't heroes here. We're nobodies. We're the stray dogs people throw out onto the street when they no longer want to bother with them. We're the weeds people spread poison over. But we don't die, we stay alive. We stay alive because we run away. We. Run. Away." I lifted my hands in supplication and then forced them down to my sides. I didn't beg. I would never beg. To hell with him.

He turned and his nose stood out in profile, his hair like a clown wig, casting cross-hatched shadows on the wall behind him.

Ano coughed. "We should run."

"We should run," Jimmy said.

Ricker moaned in the fevers, but I knew he would have agreed with us.

I looked at Maibe and her pink sweatshirt drying at her feet.

Her hair stood out in all directions like Spencer's. She opened her mouth and I waited to hear her vote.

"All right," Spencer said, almost in a whisper.

Maibe closed her mouth and put her forehead to her knees, hiding her face.

"All right, what?" I said.

"We'll run."

CHAPTER 9

BUT WE COULDN'T RUN.

The fever was a bad one. Ricker never talked about what happened before finding us, but I could guess. Sex for money, beatings, going hungry and being afraid to sleep because someone might jump you, and that was after whatever had been done to him to make him run away.

When Ricker came out of the fevers, Maibe was still at watch by his side. He had screamed and strained against the ropes. She soothed him by crooning a lullaby.

When the fever broke her face was all he saw, but then we all came around and cut the ropes and lifted him out and gave him water and food and space to put himself back together.

But by the time Ricker had come out of the fevers, there was a lookout near the warehouse we were hiding inside.

We limited our movements to using the bucket bathroom Ano and I had set up. The water ran out the third day of waiting.

We weren't built to stay in the same place like this. Jimmy kept picking at his wound, Spencer would stay in the back room alone for hours and come out with a tear-streaked face. Ano and I forced Maibe and Ricker to do silent exercises with us to keep back the memories. But the itch to run was getting to all of us—guards or not.

On the fourth night, our breathing sounded like the beats of a familiar song run backwards. The cement was hard and cold underneath me. I licked my dry lips and drifted into the memory-rush that waited on the other side of sleep.

"Staying at my place means my rules," she said.

She was my grandmother but I had never met her before and when the lady with the kind eyes dropped me off I grabbed her hand and pleaded and said, "Let me please stay with you. I will be good, I promise," because grandmother's eyes widened when she saw me and when they did that her eyelids disappeared into the folds of her eyebrows. The pale blue eye shadow seemed to encircle her lizard-like green eyes as if she were already dead.

"We will pray in the morning and in the afternoon. No matter how long it takes God to hear you, he will cure you of your sins. In this I do believe with all my heart." Her hand fluttered to her blouse, a collared, checkered thing she'd overlaid with a beige sweater. In her other hand was a big wooden spoon. Smells of spaghetti came from further in the house, but she held the spoon like a weapon and the nice lady had already left. My father had never spoken of his mother, not once that I could remember and I remember thinking that he must have just been born out of nothing, all adult and red-faced and angry.

A screech interrupted grandmother's drone.

I opened my eyes to the twilight of early morning in the

warehouse. My tongue felt thick and dry. A pinprick of light shined through the upper-story window. The lookout used a flashlight sometimes.

I sat up and itched the angry red dots on my ankles to keep from thinking about how Grandmother liked to punish me for my sins. When I'd run away from her, CPS had caught me and decided to give it another try with my parents—but then there had been the storm and the blue house and Leaf curled on the floor next to me.

The itch to run increased. The warehouse was too small. We were in a prison and we would die here if we didn't get out soon.

The screech sounded again. Soft yet piercing. Like a rat's squeak. When I tried to find where the sound came from, I saw Maibe at the door, struggling to open it.

"What are you doing?" I hissed. My voice echoed through the cavern. "Are you crazy?"

"I can't stand it inside anymore," Maibe said. "I need to go back for Corrina. I can't just leave her."

"She's probably dead. I bet she is by now."

"Don't say that," Maibe said, raising her voice. "You don't know."

A voice inside me told me I was too mean, there was no reason to hate Corrina so much that I would purposefully hurt Maibe. But then I remembered Leaf and anger washed away any hint of apology. "Quiet down," I said. "You'll wake them up."

"Already accomplished," Spencer said.

Jimmy was still asleep, but both Ricker and Ano sat up. Spencer was laying down as if he couldn't be bothered.

Ricker rubbed his face. "What's going on?"

"Maibe wants to go after Corrina," I said.

"Maybe we should," Ano said quietly. His words somehow becoming solemn.

A flame of anger lit up inside me. How could he be so stupid? "Close the door," I said.

"Corrina survived for as long as any of us," Maibe said. "She saved my life a million times. She was alive last time we saw her—"

"Hanging from the rope of a noose," I interrupted.

"She got out of that. She…Leaf got her down," Maibe said.

"You go outside and you'll get us all caught," Ricker said.

"I won't," she said.

Long minutes passed. I waited for Spencer to say something.

She would leave no matter what we decided. She would go after Corrina on her own and Spencer wouldn't do anything to stop it. If I went with her to find Corrina would it be betraying Leaf's memory? Or did it even matter?

A deep sadness took over. It felt worse than the anger. We were all going to die and Spencer wasn't going to stop any of it anymore.

Maibe pushed at the door again.

"Wait." I strapped the bat to my back and slung the crossbow over my shoulder. I went over to Maibe. A breeze passed through the crack of the door that made goosebumps rise on my skin. "I'll go with you. Just let me help you with the door."

"But you just—"

"You'll get yourself killed without me."

I waited for someone to stop us. I rested my hand on the cold metal and peered into the twilight before sunrise. No one said anything. It was cold and empty and lonely out there. Almost as lonely as it was inside here.

I shut my eyes, but saw Ano and Ricker and Jimmy and Spencer for what they were—empty shadows, bodiless breaths, ghost-memories waiting to happen.

When I opened them, light flared out of the corner of my eye. The brief click on and off of a flashlight. I turned to Maibe. Her eyes were wide. She'd seen it too.

And now I heard it. The shuffling of steps, the almost silent creak of gear, the hint of breathing.

"Ano! Ano! Get them out. Get out of here!" I screamed this and threw open the door and dragged Maibe behind me.

There was a ping and a thud into the wall. Another ping into the door. We ducked and ran away. I wanted them to go after us and give Ano time to get everyone else out. I crouched once and shot an arrow in the flashlight direction. The gravel at my feet kicked pebbles into the skin of my legs. I looked down. A dart had missed me by inches. They weren't shooting bullets.

Maibe yelled for me to come on. She was already yards away. I raced to catch up. I wanted to hear Ano and the rest escape. I wanted to know, but I couldn't hear.

Me and Maibe dodged a broken fountain. Light flared behind us. They weren't trying to hide anymore. There were shouts, stomping feet, it sounded like an army. I looked over my shoulder to see how many there were, but the light blinded me and then the building blocked it all out.

CHAPTER 10

"CORRINA?" MAIBE'S VOICE FLOATED through the air like mist.

We had found Corrina like it was no big deal. Like she was just out on a walk, back from a shopping trip.

Vs wandered the compound, most likely drawn by the noises. I was sick with worry. Sick with being separated again.

Maibe hurried forward and Corrina cried out in joy or fear or shock or maybe all three.

There.

Swift and low like a wolf, a man in mud-streaked khaki pants ran toward Maibe and Corrina. I wondered if he was running from his own violent attacker, or if he was actually reliving running someone else down.

Corrina and Maibe had not seen the V coming. I raised my crossbow, took aim, fired.

The V went down, my arrow buried in his back. I sent another arrow flying, just to be sure. It nicked his shoulder and then skidded into the asphalt at Corrina's feet. She jumped. The stack of cans in her hands crashed to the ground.

Maibe spun around.

"Get your idiot asses inside," I said, knowing I might be calling other Vs to our spot but not able to stop myself. We had Sergeant Bennings people after us, Vs around us, and Spencer and Ano and Ricker and Jimmy gone again. I remembered when the list of names had been longer.

I did not help Corrina and Maibe as they gathered up the cans. Someone needed to stand guard for us. Might as well be me. Since when she'd first showed up with Maibe at the boxcar, something about Corrina set me on edge. She was too earnest, too flighty, too judgmental. People like her thought they could tell me what to do because they believed they knew better than me. She wanted to save me from myself and she had no right to do that. She had helped get Leaf killed.

Corrina led us to a barn-like building on the edge of the fairgrounds. I couldn't believe she was still alive. The barn was dark and musty and smelled of spoiled hay. We entered the building, Corrina first, then Maibe, then me. My eyes adjusted to the darkness quickly—light streamed in from cracks in the walls and ceilings.

Something rustled in one of the stalls and I raised my crossbow.

"It's Dylan," Corrina said, pushing my crossbow to point at the ground. "He's in the fevers."

DYLAN WAS LAID OUT ON HAY in one of the stalls. His low moans raised goosebumps on my arms. His right arm was thrown across his face. His legs disappeared into the hay. Sweat gleamed on skin that was beginning to show the wrinkles and tone of a Feeb. His facial hair was growing out in that rugged way I'd always preferred. Even unconscious and sick and changing, he looked muscled, healthy, attractive.

I snorted to myself. Yeah.

He'd infected himself with Feeb blood because of Corrina. He'd gotten himself strung up on a noose because of Corrina. Maibe and I were trapped in this barn now because of Corrina.

I stalked back to Maibe and Corrina deep in conversation about this or that. Who the hell knows. Something about more and more Feebs and Vs waking up.

"We can't stay here," Maibe said. "I think things are going to get much worse very soon."

I snorted. "Did you tell her how bad it already is?" I said.

Maibe nodded.

"But I can't move him. Not when he's in the fevers." Corrina stacked the supplies in a corner along with a few other odds and ends: a bucket, a sliver of soap, some canned food, a water bottle half empty. "He's lucid sometimes, but otherwise we'll have to carry him. He can't stay on his feet yet."

"How did you get him here?" I asked.

"That wheelbarrow," she said, pointing with wet hands to a dark geometrical shape in one of the corners.

"So that's what we use to take him out of here," I said. "We have to find the others."

"He's still too sick," she responded.

"But they're waking up," Maibe said. "The Vs get out of the fevers first."

I remembered when Mary turned. "It's only hours for them,

once they're infected."

"But Feebs take longer," Maibe said. "Days or even weeks."

"What about the Faints?" Corrina asked.

Maibe looked confused. "I don't know. Do you, Gabbi?"

I thought about it and shook my head. "I've never seen someone turn into a Faint. I've only stumbled upon them afterwards. I don't know what happens or even how they get sick with it in the first place."

"It's the bacteria," Corrina said quietly. "That's what Dr. Ferrad told me.'

"When?" I demanded. "When did she tell you?"

"There was this room they took me into," Corrina said. "A chair in the middle of this big room with lights and equipment."

My stomach felt sick. I knew exactly what she was talking about. The room with the dentist chair. The doctor in the white coat and with a clipboard had been Dr. Ferrad. I didn't want to admit I'd seen her there in the chair. I didn't want to admit I'd almost jumped and then stopped when I saw it was only her.

"She said a person turns Faint when they only get infected with the Lyme disease they genetically engineered to fight the virus," Corrina said. "A Faint happens when there's no Lyssa virus to keep the bacteria in check."

"But how?" Maibe asked.

Corrina shook her head. "Dr. Ferrad didn't know. She said none of them know. That's why they're running a bunch of tests."

"They're hurting people!" I said, stalking across the room because I couldn't stand to be still one second longer. "They hurt Leaf!" My throat hiccuped on his name. Dark feelings rose up and I crunched them into a little ball inside me.

"How many people will all this have killed by the time it's

burned out?" Corrina shook her head and closed her eyes. "It's sickening to imagine how many people are in the fevers and there's no one to help them through it, no one to give them sips of water or something to eat."

"Who do you think started this whole mess?" I shot back. I rested my crossbow on my shoulder and locked my face into a grimace. "Whose fault do you think this is?"

Corrina looked at me with her dark brown eyes full of sorrow, sadness, pity. But pity had only ever spurred on my anger.

"People like you, in your clean houses and white picket fences and white collar jobs making the rules for the rest of us who never wanted to play your game. Never wanted anything but to be left alone to make our own way, but you couldn't stand it, couldn't believe it, had to fix it—"

"What are you talking about?" Corrina said.

Maibe looked at me and then back to Corrina and then back to me.

The fury dribbled out of me and left only a dull ache. "Maibe's right, our ghost city is waking up. Almost a million people surround us right now and even if only ten percent survive, that's a lot more people than we can handle. And Sergeant Bennings knows we're here."

"You saw him?" a male voice said behind me. I whirled around and saw Dylan rising onto unsteady feet, wobbling like a drunk. Hay stalks clung to his clothes and his beard and hair. His eyes were the brightest blue I'd ever seen. But he did not even look at me even though he'd asked me a question. His eyes were only for Corrina.

"No. But it was his people at least," I said.

"We should get out of the city. Go into the foothills." Dylan coughed and began to crumple. I dropped my crossbow and wrapped my arms around his chest. His shirt was soft under my fingertips, his smell a cross between sweat and earth and musk. He leaned on me, almost draping my side, his body heat a shock. His beard scratched the skin on my neck.

Corrina rushed over and grabbed his other side, throwing his arm around her shoulders, lifting him off me. The pressure release left an ache I could not name, did not like, forced myself to ignore. She led him back to his stall while he mumbled about a place he called Dutch Flat. His head rolled and revealed glazed eyes. He regained consciousness for a moment and stumbled a few steps and turned and gripped Corrina's face with both hands and kissed her deeply before slumping to the ground.

I stood there knowing I should help and knowing I better not.

Maibe pushed past me and helped Corrina settle Dylan back into the hay. Corrina offered Dylan a few sips of water and brushed his hair from his forehead.

I turned away and picked up my crossbow.

He'd gotten himself captured, almost killed, infected—for her—and I was a runaway with a temper and a chip on my shoulder. I pushed open the door without waiting or listening or looking. A man, in ripped jeans and a green-collared shirt, sporting long gashes of dried blood, stood a few yards from the door. He had already turned toward me. His eyes were bloodshot, vacant, furious. His mouth opened in a grimace. He held up his arms before him, as if choking someone that would have only come to his shoulders. I raised my crossbow and he grabbed for it, choking it like it was the neck of some ghost-person he was trying to kill again and again.

I released the arrow and it buried deep in his forehead even as one of his hands clamped the fiberglass and twisted. The string broke, whipping a burning line of fire along my cheek.

He fell into a heap on the ground. I wished I could fall into a heap on the ground.

There was a scuffle of steps. The creak of gear. The glare of the flashlight. Behind the fallen V, a group of Sergeant Bennings' soldiers came into view.

CHAPTER 11

PART OF ME KNEW THE SOLDIERS WERE A GHOST-MEMORY even as I threw myself back inside the barn. "We have to leave!"

Maibe's forkful of beans froze halfway to her mouth.

Maybe the look on my face did it, but neither of them protested. Corrina and Maibe got Dylan into the wheelbarrow. His arms and legs hung out in what looked like uncomfortable angles and his head lolled to one side, but it couldn't be helped. Corrina packed in some of the canned food around his body.

I opened the door, slowly, peering through it for signs of Vs or Feebs or patrols. Nothing so far.

I opened the door wider, letting in more light. The space was clear and I motioned them out. Suddenly the strangest train whistle floated across the landscape.

"What is that?" Corrina asked.

I had no idea, but the sick feeling in my stomach said it meant nothing good for us.

THE BIKE SHOP WAS A MILE AWAY. We hurried as best we could with Dylan in the wheelbarrow and Sergeant Bennings' ghosts at my heels. I put down two Vs with my bat and wished the crossbow had stayed in one piece. But it was gone now and we would be gone too if we didn't hurry.

We broke into the bike shop through the back. I hooked a trailer up to one of the bikes and we fit Dylan into it as best we could. Corrina strapped his legs and arms to the rails of the trailer so they wouldn't drag on the ground. Vs began to pile up along the front store window. Bikes hung down like odd skeletons from the ceiling. We left the food behind. There wasn't room.

When the glass began to crack, white veins streaking it, we left through the back, pedaling past a group of Vs. A fast one in the front snatched at my shirt. I kicked out, almost tumbling off when my leg connected with her knee. There was a crunch and she fell. Corrina was behind me with Dylan, Maibe was in the back. I went first, taking us back to the boxcar because maybe Spencer and the boys would be waiting for us there, even though part of me screamed to get far away from the fairgrounds. I led us onto the bike trail and worried about the train whistle and Sergeant Bennings' men and the Vs that waited in the bushes along either side.

The boxcar was two miles away but it was back the way we had come. The fairgrounds was death. The city was death. Why couldn't we leave this place behind?

We could—if I was willing to leave Spencer, Ano, Ricker, and Jimmy. I immediately banished that thought.

The only sound was that of our pedaling, the wap-wap of rubber on the asphalt, the whir of wheels. I led the way down the trail, across an open field with half a dozen dots of people that shifted in our direction as we zoomed by.

The smells of swampy, brackish water deepened as the trail bent closer to the river. My breath puffed spurts of mist into the air as if I smoked a cigarette, which I badly wanted. I focused on bringing my legs up and down and keeping the handlebars straight and straining my senses to find a V or a Faint about to wreck our escape.

The bike trail drifted away from the river. Oak trees full of moss that hung like curtains from the branches separated us from the water. On the right was an open meadow, green from the winter wetness. Grass so vividly green against the white sky it hurt my eyes. Electricity towers five stories tall rose up from the mist like sentinels. We were close. My heart rate sped up. More dark figures dotted the landscape. A strip of gray formed in front of us, above our heads. The freeway. Underneath it, the trail disappeared into a black hole.

I slowed and stopped a half dozen yards before that cave.

We had to pass underneath to get to the boxcar, but anything could be in there.

I was still first. Corrina and Maibe behind me. Dylan moaned inside the memory-fevers. Further behind us, a group of Vs followed down the trail. There was no going back through that crowd.

A car hung down from the ledge of the freeway above. Twisted and mangled, windshield broken and glass scattered across the trail beneath. A body hung halfway out the driver's window. Injured, bloody, but the fog obscured the details and it was hard to know if the injuries were from the car accident or something else.

Better not to know.

I steered my bike to miss the worst of the glass and held my breath when my tire crunched over some of it anyway. There was no way I was going to stop and fix a flat.

Sounds changed once the underpass enveloped us. Now every creak and squeak and cough seemed to slap back at us from all directions. Our lights revealed dirt and trash and some homeless guy's sleeping bag, but no homeless guy. The dirt sloped up on either side. My light caught a swallow's mud nest attached under one of the T-beams.

There was a moan, low and long behind me.

I lost my balance and struggled to keep the bike upright. It weaved a snake-like path that almost tipped me onto some river rock. Corrina and Maibe zoomed by.

A shape limped out from the sloped dirt. I pedaled faster. My wheel ran into the back of Maibe's wheel.

"Are you okay?" she said.

"Go!" I said fiercely.

She'd set a foot down but now took off, popping out of sight into the bright fog on the other side.

I was about to pedal when the moan turned into a groan. "Please. I need help. My leg. I think it's broken." He came within a dozen feet. Definitely injured. There was a long gash in his thigh. He'd tied it with a belt and held both hands around it.

I fled into the fog after Maibe and Corrina.

"Please," he said, his voice already distant and echoing.

I told myself we couldn't stop for him. I told myself we would all die if we helped him.

A dark and terrible thought entered my mind. He would distract the Vs that followed us.

CHAPTER 12

OLD BULLY WAS PROPPED AGAINST the side of the boxcar. I'd never been so glad to see its tricycle wheels and snowplow-like attachment, even if it was spattered with V blood. They must have escaped and gone back for the bikes they'd abandoned when they had first rushed the fence. When Maibe and I had run for the van. When Leaf had still been alive and unhurt.

It was a reunion, but things had changed. The relief I'd felt, digging through the ceiling to discover them, that was there, in the background, but mostly I felt nothing other than a claustrophobic fear that made my throat choke up. We needed to leave. Every minute we stayed was more time for them to gather and cut off any escape. My message, scratched into the boxcar for Mary, stared at me as if somehow Mary would know what I had just done, that I had left behind someone who needed help. But I told myself she would have understood.

Ano rested a hand on my shoulder. He looked at the message

and then back at me. "We have to keep going," he said.

"I know," I shrugged him off. It's what we had tried to do with Mary, what we had done so many times before—when the situation got too weird, we left. We jumped a train, took a bus, hitchhiked out. This was both the same and different. We didn't know which way to go or where.

"We should take the freeway out of here," Ricker said.

"We could go deeper into the valley," Ano said.

Spencer said nothing and I almost didn't notice anymore.

I stood up and walked a few steps away. This was a stupid place. The river was a bunch of dirty ice water. The field was dotted with trouble coming our way. It was too close to Sergeant Bennings. This was where Mary and Leaf had died and it was time to get the hell out of dodge.

"We should go to Dutch Flat," I said. Was there something rustling in that bush? My hand automatically went to unsling the crossbow but it wasn't there anymore. I touched the bat instead and hoped it would be enough.

It was only a rabbit, its cottontail a white flash as it jumped away. I didn't relax.

"Where's that?" Jimmy said.

Dylan moaned from where we'd laid him out on the ground.

"Ask him," I said. He'd been in the fevers for hours now. He'd come out of it soon, for a little while, if his infection followed the same pattern ours had followed.

"Gabbi," Ano said and stopped. I just looked at him. I realized I had been avoiding talking to him. It was too hard with what had happened to Mary. He was the one who understood the best and he was the one I least wanted to talk to.

"Dutch Flat is in the foothills," Corrina said. She rested a hand on Dylan's.

Dylan sat up as if splashed by cold water. "In this little hollow below a ridge." His eyes were wide open but he didn't see us. "Less than two hundred people live there. I played there growing up, down by the river bed, before my grandparents died. The gardens always overflowed with fruit and flowers and vegetables and all of it is surrounded by tall pine trees…" He kept talking. Ano's eyes went thoughtful, Jimmy's went dreamy, and even Ricker had stopped chewing on his cheek long enough to listen.

"The bike path," I said when Dylan slumped back down like a windup toy that had run out of tension. "There's too many fires, too many Vs in the city and along the freeway. Better to take our chances on the bike trail along the river."

"Except," Maibe said. "That same bike trail drew a mob of Vs onto us the last time."

"But that had been the plan," I said.

"What about the train whistle?" Maibe said. "Maybe the trains are working now."

"If they are working, it won't be for Feebs like us," I said it more confidently than I felt. What if the trains were working? What if Sergeant Bennings was wrong and the whole world wasn't infected and there was a way out?

"We heard it too," Ano said quietly. His dark eyes stared at the ground before flicking up. He didn't really need to say much more. The grim look in his eyes said enough.

"We saw it on the tracks as it passed near the boxcar," Ricker said when Maibe looked confused. "A whole mob of Vs followed after it. We had to stay dead silent in the boxcar until they passed."

"I felt like I didn't even breathe for the whole time," Jimmy said.

"Wherever the trains are going, it is not for us," Ano said. "It was Sergeant Bennings and his people inside."

We all went quiet for a moment as if mourning the loss of something I couldn't quite put a name to. The trains were off limits now. The trains had always been the way we could count on to move from one place to the next. I wondered if that had been why parts of the camp were left unguarded—maybe they'd been evacuating.

"If we take the bike trail," I said finally, "then we've got plenty of water from the river. And if there's too many Vs, we can cut into one of the neighborhoods."

"We're going to Dutch Flat, right?" Jimmy said, looking around. "That's what we're talking about, right?" The eagerness in his voice was not subtle.

Ano elbowed him in the ribs and hissed into his ear, "Yes."

"Taking the freeway would get us out of here faster." Spencer spoke for the first time. He was cross-legged next to Old Bully, fiddling with the chain. "Isn't that what you wanted?" Spencer looked at me.

I repositioned the bat on my back. "I want to get out of here alive. That's what I want. Isn't that what you want?"

The group looked back and forth between me and Spencer. It was a contest I hadn't realized I had entered. I hated it. I didn't want to fight with him, but everything in me screamed that the freeway was the wrong way to go even with the Vs that might still be waiting for us at the overpass.

Spencer returned to the chain without saying a word.

That pretty much decided it—I had pretty much decided it. We would take the bike trail and deal with whatever problems that route brought our way.

I scanned our group of runaways. Jimmy was still nursing his wounded shoulder and had a shell-shocked look to him. Ano had turned inward, his face like a stone. Ricker never could hide his emotions. He was worried and perceptive—he knew we didn't know what to do. Spencer might as well not exist and I couldn't bear to look at Corrina or Maibe.

I hoped I was right about the bike trail.

I jumped into the boxcar. There were dozens of maps in a pile, one for every place we'd visited in the last three years. Favorite cities, favorite rest stops, favorite parks, friendly places—all of it was marked on the maps. I took the only one we needed.

We loaded up the bikes and closed off the boxcar. Deep down, I knew we weren't ever coming back again. I used a rock to scratch out the message I'd left for Mary. I kept her name untouched, carved into the boxcar like it was carved into my arm.

Everyone waited for me to finish, as if they couldn't leave until I said so.

"Dutch Flat is over seventy miles away. We should get going," I said.

"Seventy miles!" Maibe said, but didn't follow up with anything else. We all knew there were a lot of neighborhoods in those miles.

I took off without looking back.

The fog lay over the field like a blanket, hiding us from any Vs. Hiding the Vs from us. It muffled the sounds we made and also somehow seemed to magnify them. I rode Old Bully this time because I didn't trust Spencer to do it without getting himself killed.

The river rushed by on our right because I was taking us on the same bike path we'd traveled what seemed like a million times now. I scanned for movement, for sound, for signs of danger. Every lizard scrambling away, every bird spooked into flight, shot up my adrenaline levels.

The group of Vs that had followed me, Maibe, and Corrina were at the overpass—bodies strewn about in the grass, riddled with bullets. Their blood turned a whole section of the field red. I didn't look to see if one of them was the Feeb I had abandoned. I decided to believe he had gotten away somehow. But the dead Vs were almost more disturbing than if they'd been alive. Who had killed them? Where were those people now?

Smoke rose in thick columns on our left. It would only be a matter of time before the whole city and its surrounding suburbs burned. We biked for over an hour before I stopped us again. It made me nervous, that much time without any problems. A mountain of trouble felt headed our way, but I just couldn't see it.

I held up a hand when the river widened up enough so that a small island with a few trees popped up in the middle. We were coming up on the high school soon. A school I could have attended if I hadn't run away and wasn't trying to stay out of CPS hands. Those had always been the oddest-feeling moments, when I passed by a school in session and saw so many kids my age doing something so foreign to me now, something like sitting in a classroom listening to what someone else thought I was supposed to learn and believe. I wasn't like Mary, she had wanted to go back someday. Even Leaf had talked about missing school sometimes. I'd take a public library over a school any day, but still, I avoided schools whenever possible. I didn't like what it did to my stomach.

There was an obstacle in the middle of the trail. I almost breathed a sigh of relief. I knew it had been too easy. Nothing in life was ever this easy. I held up a hand for everyone to stop.

The starthistle and grasses grew tall here, almost waist-high, providing cover for whoever might hide in its depths, but it was the path I worried about. Two people were sitting on the ground. One was laid out flat and the other one hovered over him.

"They're Feebs," Maibe said behind me. Too loud.

The one who was sitting looked up at Maibe's voice. I didn't know what I should do, what I should say. I wanted to ride on by. Their clothes were dirty and ripped. Their faces were streaked with dried blood. The younger one's upper arm was wrapped in layers of bandaging. The man laid out on the ground looked overweight and his balding head was pointed at us.

"We don't need more baggage," I said.

The balding man struggled to sit up. The two of them exchanged a look that made me nervous.

"Hello," the balding man said, nodding to us. "I'm Laurel Gillen. This is Kern. Do you know what has happened?"

"What are you doing in the middle of the trail?" Ano said. He stepped next to me, a chain hanging from his hand. They were Feebs like us, but that didn't mean they could be trusted.

Laurel's eyes shifted to the chain. "We were taking a break."

"In the middle of the trail?" Ano said.

"That way we could see someone coming," Kern said quietly. His eyes seemed to burn into mine.

"When did you wake up from the fevers?" I demanded.

Laurel's focus shifted to me. "May I ask your name?"

I did not respond, only waited and crossed my arms across

my chest.

Laurel sighed.

"I'm Corrina."

I closed my eyes and gritted my teeth. We had a system for dealing with strangers. What right did she have to speak up?

"Hello," Laurel said, nodding in her direction.

She strode forward and offered her hand to them.

I hissed between my teeth. "What the hell are you thinking?"

They shook. Corrina tossed her hair over her shoulder and looked at me with a guileless gaze I knew she must be faking. "We can't keep avoiding everyone. We can't act like everyone we meet is the enemy."

"Yes, we can," I said. "If we want to be smart and get out of this alive. That's exactly what we should do."

Laurel held up his hands as if that might fix the tension in the air, as if that somehow made him more trustworthy. "We woke up several days ago from…whatever this is. My son, Kern here, had come visiting. I thought it was a burglary, but…they killed my wife." He went silent and pressed his thumb and index fingers onto either side of his nose as if trying to hold back tears.

Kern placed a comforting hand on his father's shoulder. "It killed my sister too—"

"Your daughter," I said to Laurel.

He nodded. "My wife and my daughter."

"—and we both got really sick, in and out of this fever, these memories…and then we woke up." Kern released his hand from his father's shoulder and held it out and looked at it in wonder. "We saw what had happened to us, but we don't know why. We had guns but lost them a ways back fighting off the crazies—"

"We call them Vs," Jimmy said.

Kern cocked his head. "Sure, kid. Whatever you say. We heard there was a camp. Like for refugees. We tried the hospital first, but…"

"Who told you there was a camp?" Ano said.

Kern looked at Ano for a long second. "On the radio."

Ano and I glanced at each other. They woke up a few days ago—were radios even still working? Maybe. But maybe not. I tapped my fingers against my thigh: W-A-T-C-H. Ano didn't bother to reply. The scowl on his face said his message would have been something along the lines of: N-O D-U-H.

Laurel shook his head. "Don't go to the hospital."

"We're not stupid," Ricker said.

"Did you kill those Vs back there?" I said.

Kern glanced at Laurel. "We haven't been that way yet. That's where we were headed."

"We think the camp is that way." Laurel pointed back the way we'd come.

"It's more like a prison," Corrina said. "You don't want to go there."

"But the radio…" Kern turned to his father. Laurel's face had collapsed on itself.

"The trains are no good either," Maibe said.

This seemed to bring both Kern and Laurel to attention.

I glanced at Ano. He cocked his head. He'd seen it too. "What do you know about the trains?" I said.

"We don't know anything about the trains," Kern said. "We told you we only woke up a few days ago."

"Are you sure about the camp?" Laurel said.

"We're sure," Maibe said.

"What the hell is happening?" Laurel looked around as if the sky would answer him.

"We don't have time to help you understand," I said.

"We're not sure how it started," Corrina said and began explaining her story.

I wanted to slap her and looked at Spencer to demand him to step in and end this farce so we could keep going, but Spencer wasn't listening to the conversation. He was looking ahead, past the two men.

A dark clump of figures stumbled into view, still far away but coming toward us. Of course an hour without trouble had been too much to ask.

Maybe the bike trail had been a mistake after all.

"Time to go," Spencer said quietly.

Laurel looked over his shoulder. "We should go to the camp. That way is open."

"Are you crazy or stupid?" I said.

"We can't stay on the trail," Maibe said, hopping from foot to foot.

A pause. "The high school, then," Kern said. "We were just there. There's fencing and a gate we can close."

And just like that the group followed these two strange men we had known for all of thirty seconds. I was left on the trail staring after them and at the oncoming Vs.

Corrina acted as if she were in charge now because, what? She was the oldest? That didn't give her the right to tell the rest of us what to do, especially when all our lives were at stake.

Jimmy turned and when he saw me still on the trail, said, "Come on, Gabbi. We need you."

This broke me out of my frozen state. I followed as they cut through the brush with the bikes. We ended up at the back parking lot of the high school.

"This way." Laurel motioned us forward. Kern jogged ahead to a chain-link gate that opened to a quad area between two buildings. The similarity between these buildings and Sergeant Bennings' was creepy. Government-built places always had this institutional feel, no matter how many windows they tried to include. I was about to point this out, that maybe these two men were leading us into a trap, when the clump of Vs broke through the brush behind me. They were all men, all approximately the same age and wearing similar clothes, and I wondered if they'd once been friends and what exactly they were remembering now as they ran for us. What was it that the virus made them relive with their hands out and their teeth ready to tear us apart?

"Gabbi!" Maibe's shout broke through my thoughts.

I pedaled through the gate that Laurel held open. I would make Corrina pay if she'd helped lead us into a trap.

My bike zoomed into a courtyard teenagers had used in a former life for breaks, its cement benches and trashcans and a few spindly trees mostly untouched, ready for the next bell.

The gate slammed shut, clanking against the pole. Laurel grabbed an unlocked chain that had once secured a garbage can in place and wrapped the gate closed. Dylan took this moment to wake up and was shouting questions.

Ano grabbed a thick branch and stuck it between the chain-links. Maibe and Ricker helped me drag a cement bench over to block the front gate.

Glass tinkled. Kern had thrown a trashcan through the windows of one of the classrooms. He took off his shirt, revealing a chest crisscrossed with bruises over muscles that flexed with his effort. He set the shirt on the window's edge and lifted himself through the gap, then came back out the door.

I didn't like how fast all of this was moving. I wheeled my bike up to Kern and leaned it on the outside wall.

"Welcome," he said, ushering me through.

"Yeah," I said. "We'll see."

CHAPTER 13

IT HAD BEEN ALMOST EXACTLY four years since I'd stepped foot in a real classroom. In this one, the desks were arranged in groups of four, facing each other instead of the front. Inspirational posters about working hard and making good choices littered the walls. Huge English textbooks lined two shelves next to the corner desk where stacks of papers and a computer sat.

Everything looked ready for the next class, as if winter vacation would end any day now and the students would file into their seats with backpacks full of books and minds ready to learn.

I laughed to myself. Yeah, right. Most people were varying shades of prick and that included teenagers too.

Kern wandered the classroom perimeter until he came upon a cork board displaying A+ student work. He ripped the board off the wall. The projects pinned to it went fluttering through the air onto desk surfaces and the linoleum floor.

"So you're Gabbi." He carried the board over to the broken window. Glass crunched under his shoes.

"Yeah, so what?"

"So…hi," he said, glancing at me and then away. The others filtered in, Dylan and Corrina last, his arm around her shoulders.

Dylan kissed the side of her head and she hugged him around the chest. He whispered something in her ear, then suddenly his eyes glazed over and he lost control of his legs. She almost dropped him but then Laurel grabbed Dylan's other side and together they controlled his fall to the floor.

Another memory-fever. Great.

"When did he get infected?" Laurel asked.

"A few days ago," Corrina responded.

"Five days ago," I said. "Leaf died five days ago."

Corrina flinched.

Kern finished securing the board over the broken window and crouched next to Dylan. "Let me see. I was training to be a paramedic someday."

Ano leaned against the wall. Not resting really, more like saving his energy. Jimmy sat nearby with Ricker and Maibe. Spencer was there too. They'd settled as a group in the opposite corner of the classroom, furthest away from the door and windows, behind the teacher's desk, creating some privacy, a cave within a cave.

"What's next?" I asked Spencer.

He shrugged.

"If we wait long enough, the Vs might go away," Maibe said. "As long as they don't find a way in."

"So in the meantime we're just supposed to trust those two?" I said.

"There's more of us than there are of them," Spencer said. "As long as no one else joins them."

"So us now includes them," I said, pointing at Corrina and Dylan. "When did they earn our trust?"

"They deserve it," Jimmy said.

I scowled.

"Get over it, Gabbi," Spencer said.

"Get over what?" I said, a menacing note in my voice. "What exactly am I supposed to get over? What exactly am I supposed to be okay with? People we hardly know, people who would as soon have ignored us in any other situation, suddenly telling us what to do as if they care what happens to us at all?"

"They do care," Maibe said.

"And even if they do," I said, turning on her. "So what? That doesn't make them right! It doesn't mean they know better than us or have the right to act better than us or that we're just supposed to do what they say because they say so!" At each word my voice raised in volume and I knew without having to look that the others had paused and were watching me rant. This made me feel both embarrassed and angry and there was nowhere to go so I had to just sit and face it when what I wanted to do was run away until the horrible feelings melted away.

"What's your problem?" Corrina said.

"You are," I said.

A shadow fell across me and I knew without looking that Corrina stood over me now. I rose slowly onto my feet because I could not let her loom over me like that, as if I had already submitted to her will.

"What have I done?" Corrina demanded. "Exactly what have I done to make you distrust me?"

"What haven't you done?" I said, anger working me into jitters.
"When have you listened to what we had to say, when have you
done anything other than judge and question our every move? I
saved your goddamn life on that stage, when you were hanging
from that noose. If it hadn't been for us, you would have killed
Maibe by now, and probably yourself and your boyfriend too—"

"You have no idea—"

"YOU have no idea," I said, pointing at her. "Leaf died because
of you." I was so angry I was losing my words and I hated her
even more right then because I knew I must sound foolish, like
a petulant teenager, and I hated myself for letting myself down
like that. "You have no idea," I said again and turned my back
on her and sunk to the floor.

Ano stared at me, daring my temper. He did not make me
feel ashamed. He understood even if he didn't agree. Ricker
and Jimmy avoided my gaze. Maibe stared and when I stared
back she stood up and walked away. Spencer looked out into
the vacuum of air around us, absentmindedly scratching his
knee—I hated how disconnected he seemed, as if he didn't particularly care what happened to the rest of us now that Leaf was
gone. I had no idea how to bring him back. I did not want the
responsibility of making the decisions for all of us but I most
definitely did not want Corrina to take that responsibility either.

Outside there was a rattle and scratching. A crack as the
branch broke. Kern jumped to one of the unbroken windows
and looked out. "They're inside the courtyard."

Ano rose from the floor in one fluid motion.

I pictured them tumbling in and surrounding the classroom
door. We should never have come here. "This is your fault," I
said turning to Corrina again. "We should have gone back."

"You wanted us to take the bike trail," Corrina said.

Her words pierced me worse than any V bite could have.

"Hate me later," she said, "when we have the time for that sort of crap."

I sat stunned at the accusation in her words and the truth that rang in them. The Vs were about to attack and I was still hurling insults.

She ran over to Dylan and yelled back at me. "Do something useful with that bat."

Faces began appearing in the frosted windows. One of them banged on the door once, then again, then harder. A splayed hand hit one of the windows and smeared yellowish fluid down the glass.

Corrina and Laurel tumbled a few desks in front of the door and I screamed at them to stop because the Vs weren't going to come through that way, the door was sturdy and they were blocking our only exit to the outside with a maze of desks.

The first window broke. Maibe shouted. Kern ran to the V, grabbed a three-legged stool, and smashed it over the head of the woman clawing her way across broken glass. The wood splintered over her but did not stop her.

Her vacant eyes stared unseeing into the room and I thought—she wasn't running for us, but away from something else that had scared her.

Kern took up a desk and threw it at the woman. It crashed onto her, pushing her back out of the window, but also enlarging the gap.

Two more Vs filled the hole, climbing over each other to get in. I raised my bat, ran forward, and connected with the head of another V. Blood sprayed and I tasted iron. The V behind him kept coming.

Corrina ran up with a textbook and smashed it across the Vs head. I waited for the V to move, but Corrina smashed the textbook down again and there was a crunch sound and the V twitched and went limp.

More glass sprayed around me and suddenly five Vs fell in and the classroom became overrun as others followed. I lost my grip on the bat. I dropped to the ground and looked for it. It had rolled near the teacher's desk where Maibe fought off a V by herself. I scrambled up and ran for her. A yank on my ankle took me down hard. I hit my head on the corner of a desk. Sounds and light disappeared. All I could hear was the roar of wind in my ears. All I could see were black dots flashing on and off. A burning pain erupted on my leg. Everything swam away except for the shuffling feet between the metal legs of the desks and chairs that squeaked as people ran for their lives while mine was ending on the linoleum floor of a high school classroom.

CHAPTER 14

THE FEVERS SMOTHERED MY BRAIN even as their grip loosened. I coughed and then tried to stifle the cough because I didn't know who was still alive and whether it included any Vs. It was too dark to see if their bodies were around, but the stink of blood and shit and other slimy fluids told me that whatever had died here was still very much present.

I wiped a hand over my hair and felt the crunch of glass. My leg lanced with pain when I even thought about moving it. I forced it to move anyway and I cried out.

Even though it was dangerous, I couldn't help but call to see if anyone else was still alive. "Hello?"

Nothing.

"Ano? Ricker? Maibe?"

Still nothing.

Faint moonlight filtered through the broken windows of the classroom. It cast only enough light to outline figures hung over the sill and draped across the desks.

I grabbed the nearest desk leg and pulled myself up, careful not to put any weight on my injury.

My heart fluttered in my chest. Where was everyone?

I hobbled to the closest body facedown on the ground. I grabbed his shirt, turned it over, and moved within inches of the face. Its iron, acidic stink overwhelmed me and I dropped him.

Not anyone I recognized.

I moved to the next body.

Another V.

The next one and the one after were the same. I shuffled around like an old person, dragging my leg behind me and gritting through each step.

I checked each body in that classroom. Each time I waited for the shock of recognition, but it never came.

I was in a room full of dead Vs. I had been left behind.

I slumped to the ground, too shocked to remain standing. How could they have done this? Where could they have gone? Why had they left me alone during the fevers?

A tear slipped out, making my cheek itch. I wanted to curl into a ball and hide somewhere and be safe and never come out. I furiously scratched at the tear and forced myself back onto my feet. I needed to think about surviving and nothing else. I needed to clean my wound before an infection set in. I needed to find my bat. I needed to find food and a safer place to stay.

I limped into the courtyard and went to the closest water fountain. "Please work, please work, please work," I whispered under my breath. I did not think I would make it if I had to travel to the river.

The water fountain shuddered and water came out.

I drank it up, then washed my hands as best I could, then gave myself a makeshift bath and lifted my wounded leg up to the spigot.

The moonlight was just bright enough for me to see the gash was deep but not into the muscle. I peeled my pants up to the knee and scrubbed the bite as hard as I could for over a minute while I tried not to scream in pain.

I wanted to strip everything off and clean the rest of me, but I feared trying to get my pants over my wounded leg. I settled for taking off my shirt and cleaning every other part I could reach without soaking my clothes. Where were they? Why had they left me?

I hobbled over to one of the cement benches and collapsed on the tabletop. There were bodies out here too, clumped near the wrecked classroom. I knew I should check them, just in case, but I couldn't bear recognizing one of them and I couldn't bear the thought of not recognizing any of them. I started to cry.

"GABBI?"

A female voice. Was it real? Was it my imagination?

"Who's there?" I said in the darkness. The moon had traveled past the horizon of the courtyard roof. I could not tell if I was asleep or dreaming.

"It's…Corrina."

"Corrina?"

I must be dreaming. She would not have come back for me.

A cool hand touched my hot forehead and it felt so much like the hand of the foster mom I'd wanted to stay with before they sent me to my grandmother.

"One of the Vs bit me," I said. She was the last person I wanted to see, but in that moment, I suddenly didn't care. At least I wasn't alone.

"What happened to the others?"

"I…I don't know," I said.

"Are you injured besides the bite?"

"My shoulder hurts," I said. "My head hurts like I hit it."

"I got bit too," Corrina said. "On my arm and they scratched up my legs pretty good."

"Did they leave us?"

"I think so. They had to. They ran and drew the Vs with them I think."

My head pounded as I tried to sort through a jumble of thoughts and memories. My mind grasped at the hope that I hadn't been abandoned, that this was only a temporary situation, that they were coming back for me and this had all been part of a last-minute plan.

The hand left my forehead, making me ache. No one had ever put a hand to my forehead before, especially not my own mother.

"I'm just going to lay down," Corrina said.

"Don't go," I said. I reached my hand out and brushed her arm and then grabbed it and moved down until I reached her fingers. "Don't go."

She squeezed back. "I thought you couldn't stand me."

"I can't."

She laughed softly and then went silent for a long moment before saying, "I have only ever tried to help you when I could. What did I do?"

I tried to pull my hand away. She would not let go. I released a long breath I didn't realize I'd been holding. Along with it went some of the anger I always nursed inside me. "You did nothing," I said finally.

"You don't get off that easy," Corrina said.

A flame of anger flared, then died back down. She was right.

"People like you—"

"People like me?"

"People like you," I continued, "People who—"

"—whose parents died when she was a teenager? Who was left an orphan at sixteen? Who lived in foster homes and was bullied mercilessly for being from a different country, who has never quite belonged and who was about to lose her house and job and boyfriend—people like that?"

I felt a mix of shame and defensiveness at her words. I'd wanted her to be a certain way because it was easier that way. "I didn't know," I said finally. I realized she had been trying to take care of us like Mary used to do and I couldn't bear it—so I'd been a jerk. No surprise there.

"You never tried to find out." She squeezed my hand as if to soften the judgment in her words.

"I…" I almost wanted to apologize. It was there, burning a hole in my chest. My mouth wouldn't let me finish the sentence. Maybe it was the pain in my leg, maybe it was the virus and bacteria messing with my head, maybe it was being left behind by everyone except for Corrina—I started giggling. We were in the middle of an apocalypse. Our conversation was ridiculous, but I didn't want it to stop.

"What?"

"You know you did make an ass of yourself from the very beginning."

"Maybe," Corrina said. "But you never gave me a chance."

"I almost did but…"

"But what? You remembered that wasn't your style?"

"Haha," I said. "Probably."

She started laughing. "I can't believe this. I swear I'm having flashbacks to high school right now."

"I never went to high school," I said.

She paused. "You didn't miss much."

We lapsed into silence. A cricket chirped for a few seconds and then all was still again. I drifted into sleep realizing Corrina still held my hand.

I woke up all at once when warmth hit my face.

My eyes flew open but then I quickly closed them again. The fog was gone and even though it was a winter's sun it shone bright and hard above me. Directly in my eyes.

My back ached. My shoulder was numb. My leg burned as if it were on fire.

I sat up and saw Corrina still asleep on the bench a few inches below my tabletop. Her arm slung across her eyes. Her other arm dangling to the ground. Idiot should have slept on the ground instead of half off the bench seat.

The bite on her arm wept blood. The scratches on her legs had crusted over.

Under the sunlight my bite wound looked gruesome, all chewed up. I tore up the cleanest part of my shirt and wrapped the wound as best I could to hold the skin together. There was no puss for now. I hope it stayed that way.

Bodies still lay everywhere and the flies swarmed the pools of blood. I gagged at a severed arm just a few yards away.

"Wake up, Corrina," I said and shook her gently. Better not to spend another minute here, better to get clear of this and breathe clean air again.

She mumbled in her sleep but did not move.

I shook her harder and moved her arm from across her eyes. "Get up!"

She cracked an eye open, closed it, then opened both eyes. She pulled up a sleeve to check out a bite on her wrist. I wondered what she had relived but dared not ask in case she would ask me in return.

She hobbled over to the water fountain and began rinsing off her wrist and splashing water on her face. "Did I dream it, or are we getting along now?"

"It wasn't a dream," I said.

"I was awake for part of your fevers. What…was that your mother?" She kept her back to me.

My relief faded. Did I owe her a description of my memory-fever? No, I sure the hell did not. But something else compelled me to explain to her what I'd relived, to make up for how I'd judged her, for how I hadn't given her a chance. "No, it was my grandmother. After I ran away the first time, they tried putting me with her. That didn't work out."

"Oh."

"Running away was the best thing that had ever happened to me. I couldn't have survived one more day with them."

"With your family."

"Yeah, with my so-called family."

"Okay."

"Okay, what?"

"Just…okay. Okay, I believe you. Okay, you made the right choice because you're still surviving. Better than a person like me." She turned and smiled to reinforce she was making a joke.

I half-smiled in return and rolled my eyes. "This doesn't make us friends. Just because we had some sort of heart-to-heart doesn't suddenly make us best friends—"

"But we're not enemies either," Corrina said. "Right?"

I took a while to answer because I really needed to think about it. It was time to get my priorities straight. Who was the enemy here? Was I really going to blame Corrina for stuff that was outside her control? I had better things to do with my time than let her get to me. That's what Leaf would have said. "Yeah. We're not enemies or anything, just don't mess up bad enough to test it."

"No promises."

"Bitch."

"Right back at ya."

We stared at each other for a moment, testing these new waters. It was uncomfortable, but I guess I'd get used to it eventually.

"Let's go find the others," Corrina said.

She held out a hand to help me up. I let her help me, and I only judged her for it a little bit.

CHAPTER 15

Sometimes being a runaway sucks.

Most of the time actually.

But it sure beats the hell out of going back to what I ran away from. No one will ever convince me otherwise and you're a terrible person for even trying, so stop.

I've written down everything like how I remembered it. That may not have been what happened to everyone else, but it's what happened to me as I saw it.

Anyways, I wanted to get all that down because I don't know what will happen next and I wanted someone to know I wasn't just some dumb runaway too stuck up or damaged or stupid to figure out I should have gone back to my grandmother or my mom and dad. I made the right choice, my choice, to run away. I will always be proud of taking control of my own destiny. I want everyone to know that.

"THEY CAN'T LAST MUCH LONGER UP THERE without water,"
Corrina said.

I put down the pen I'd stolen from the classroom before
we'd left. "I know," I said in a subdued voice. We were on the
roof of a house far enough away from the high school not to
attract notice—yet.

Three days. It had been three days since Corrina and I had
woken up surrounded by flies and dead bodies. We'd walked
out of that courtyard but hadn't gone far.

The stink had given it away.

Corrina and I had followed the smell to the far end of the
high school campus. The river and the bike trail were at our
backs. The sun had burned off the fog, but not the chemical
filled smoke from all the fires. The sky was a dull brown, the
sun like a runny egg yolk.

"How many are there now?" I asked, looking back down at
the binder paper I'd also swiped from the classroom.

"A few hundred. And more trickling in every hour or so." She
was talking about the Vs and how they milled around, lost in
their dementia.

The rest of our group was surrounded on the roof of one
of the classroom buildings. They were all alive. I think both
Corrina and I counted every five minutes, just to make sure it
was true. They were all still alive. Even Kern and Laurel.

"Message them again. See if Maibe is still puking her guts
out," Corrina said.

I took out a little pocket mirror and flashed a Morse code
message to Ano. He flashed back an answer.

"She's better," I said. "Sort of. Throwing up every couple of
hours instead of multiple times an hour. Though he says the

bite looks like its getting infected."

"She probably can't throw up anymore, not without more water." Corrina walked the roof line until she stood at the edge closest to the high school. The tops of trees blocked a portion of the V crowd, but there were plenty in plain sight. "I just don't get what drew them all here. Why all of a sudden? Why now?"

"Maybe our battle made too much noise. All the windows we broke."

"But none of us had guns and we were inside a classroom inside a courtyard."

"But they're really sensitive to noise," I said, irritation pricking my neck. I didn't necessarily think my hypothesis was all that good either, but she didn't have to dismiss it so quickly.

"But not THAT sensitive."

"Okay. So what do you think happened?"

Corrina returned to my side and sat cross-legged on the shingles. I folded the papers and stuck them in my jacket.

"I don't know."

"Look," I said. "More of them are waking up. Me and Spencer and the others, we were some of the earliest people in the city to get infected. It happened weeks before you got bit and you were probably one of the first regular people it happened to. So now, everyone else is waking up from the fevers either as a V, a Faint, or a Feeb."

"Maybe," she said.

"Well," I said, feeling exasperated. "What the hell does it matter why, only that it is, and they're going to die if we don't fix this?"

Corrina pushed her thick hair off her face. It was like an unkempt mane of a lion that had been dragged through a puddle of mud and twigs. I knew I must look about the same although I always kept my hair short but shaggy around my ears to pass sometimes as a boy.

"You're right."

"Of course I'm right!" I exploded.

"Quiet."

I wanted to slap her but fumed in silence instead. Of course she was right too. Now was not the time to raise my voice.

"We should create a diversion," I said, thinking about the crazy stunt Maibe had pulled at the van. She could have died, but it had worked. "Make some noise. Attract them away so the others can climb down and go for the bike trail."

"But with what? And won't that just get us stuck somewhere and then they'll have to return the favor?"

"Not if we're smart," I said. "We figure out a distraction and an escape route. More than one escape route. An escape route for the escape route."

She chewed on her lower lip and looked across the gap again, at the roof that held Dylan, a guy still recovering from the memory-fevers and still way too hot to have ended up with someone like Corrina.

"I have an idea," she said.

CHAPTER 16

SO THE PLAN WAS THIS: find something battery-powered to make noise close to the Vs and draw their attention away from the building. I would bike across the high school campus with the noise into the multi-purpose room. The Vs would follow me into the building. I would exit through the side doors, barring them behind me. Corrina would wait until they were all inside and then lock the entrance doors behind them. The Vs would be trapped and then we could help everyone down from the building and make our way back to the bike trail and get the hell out of town.

It didn't sound like the greatest plan in the world, but we couldn't think of anything better.

"Ready?" Corrina said.

"As ready as I'll ever be," I said. I straddled my bike and checked the bungee cord that held a battery-operated music player in place. It had taken us scavenging through four houses to find a cordless device with actual speakers instead of an iPod or other earbud player. The chains we planned to lock the doors with had been easy to find in the first garage we'd hit. The locks were a little harder, but we were ready nonetheless.

Corrina took off around the corner of the building, chains and padlock in hand.

I pushed the ON button and cranked up the boombox volume. I'd tested it once already, in the house, to make sure this 90s tech still worked at all, but I held my breath all the same.

The CD spun up.

Suddenly Lady Gaga blared, the instruments starting low and then quickly rising in volume and fullness. I straddled the bike and pedaled toward the crowd of Vs milling around the building. I dared look up for a second and saw six faces peering down at me from the roof's edge.

A mild wind started blowing against my back, carrying the sound better to the crowd.

Finally one V stopped fidgeting, cocked his head, and then turned to face me.

A lump rose in my throat. My mind screamed to turn around now, but one V's attention was not enough.

I pedaled to within a football field's length of the crowd. A few more turned their heads, then went back to bumping into one another.

"Hey!" I squeaked. I gulped down a deep breath and forced the next yell from my belly. "Hey! Over here!"

Now a half dozen Vs turned. I kept pedaling to them. Now only fifty yards away. I needed more.

Suddenly one began sprinting. Sprinting with a limp, but eating up distance all the same. I wasted precious seconds to make sure others followed his lead, and then I fishtailed the bicycle around. The boombox shifted, slipping halfway out of the bungee cord tie, dangling over my back wheel.

I straightened the bike but did not reach for the player. The lead Vs were only yards away now. In spite of the music, they were so close I could hear their hard breathing, the slaps of their shoes, those that still wore shoes, the grunt of pain from one of them, the smell of ripe body odor and urine and worse. In spite of my injured leg, I put all my weight into the downstroke and stood up for more momentum. I rode in a straight line to the open multi door and hoped the player would stay attached long enough to make it into the building.

I almost flew over the handlebars as the bike slowed. I screamed, pumped the pedals again. The bike moved slowly but did not fall over. A V had latched onto the player, pulling the player off my bike, but the cord was still attached, acting like an anchor.

I tried reaching back and unhooking the cord, but this only made me wobble dangerously. Other Vs closed in on the box.

"Corrina!" I screamed.

One V stared at me with bloodshot eyes. He twisted his head at the player and then back at me. Then he took a step toward me, then looked back at the player. Then another step toward me.

Corrina came running, the knife in her hand glinting in the sun. She slashed at the bungee cord. It snapped back and stung me on the cheek. A group of Vs collapsed on top of the player, but others still advanced.

"This way!" Corrina yelled. She ran backwards, facing the Vs, waving her hands around, yelling and screaming. "This way, this way!"

Suddenly the player died and the music stopped. Vs pushed past those who had stopped for the player. I jumped back on my bike and rode after Corrina.

The thick crush of their bodies sent an overwhelming aroma of sewer that enveloped me like a cloud. Their grunts and groans sent hot air across my neck. I knew, I just knew any moment that something would grab my shirt and yank me off the bike and I would fall to the ground under a pile of bodies and they would suffocate me with their filth and make me bleed with their violence.

My front tire crossed the building's threshold and slipped sideways across the slick, polished floor. My balance shifted, tilted. I slammed a foot down and a sharp pain shot up my shin. Corrina waved to me at the opposite side—the door open, the light silhouetting her body.

"Go faster!" she screamed.

I wanted to yell back something about how I would take my damn time if I felt like it. What the hell did she think I was trying to do?

Halfway across the space decorated with flags and banners displaying softball tournament wins, I risked looking over my shoulder. The door had created a bottleneck, but a half dozen had tumbled through and were racing for me.

"Go, go, go!" Corrina screamed.

I didn't look back again.

I flew past the doors and the sunlight blinded me with its intensity. My tires hit the rough asphalt with a slap and I traveled another few yards before forcing on the brakes.

Sweat slicked my hands and made them slippery on the handlebars. My heart pounded so hard in my chest I couldn't hear very well. My legs felt like jelly. Corrina struggled with the chains and lock. Vs pushed the door out a few inches.

"Watch out!" I raced back to her side, jumped off the bike and slammed my own weight into the door. My shoulder took most of the shock but I ignored the pain. Corrina wrapped the chains twice through the handles and clicked the lock in place.

"The other side," she said, a crazy light shining in her brown irises. Her face was streaked with dirt from somewhere. Her mouth formed a rectangular grimace around the teeth she bared. "You go around one way, I'll go the other."

"We should stick together," I said.

"No." She shook her head and took off.

I wanted to shake her. I didn't want to go around the building, I didn't want to meet a V by myself. I didn't want to be alone but she was already gone.

One of the Vs slammed against the door, bucking it out, but the chain held.

I scrambled backward and ran around the side, leaving my bike but pulling out my bat. A V turned the far corner and sprinted for me.

I centered my weight on my feet, aimed, took an extra second to breathe, and swung. She dropped to the ground. I continued running and slammed my back against the wall just before turning the corner. I peeked. The space was mostly empty except for a group of Vs struggling against each other to get into the building. The player lay scattered in glinting black pieces on the asphalt. I held back, hoping they would all go inside as long as they didn't see me.

The last V, a teenager who had maybe once gone to school here, was the last one in. I raced to the doors, threw aside my bat and grabbed the chains coiled in a pile behind the cement trash can. I pressed the doors shut and then there was another set of filthy hands over mine.

I yelped and jumped back.

"Cool it," Corrina said. "Hurry up."

I laced the chains through the handles several times. Corrina snapped on the padlock. We both stepped back, waited.

Shuffling feet, more groans, and that sewer smell again. The breeze made one of the plastic pieces skitter across the ground. A bird chirped.

One of the Vs slammed against the door. I jumped.

"Corrina!"

I followed the sound. Dylan waved and ran to her. Corrina met him halfway and he lifted her and kissed her hard on the mouth.

I walked past their little reunion and admitted to myself that if not for Corrina and her knife I would be dead by now.

The rest of the group straggled across the campus. Ricker and Ano walked on either side of Maibe, helping her stand. Spencer came last, behind Jimmy, Kern, and Laurel.

THE GROUP SAT IN A CIRCLE IN the middle of the athletic fields. It would let us see anything coming our way even as the knee-high grass provided some camouflage. Though it also made Jimmy break into a rash and itch like crazy.

Dylan was still awake, sitting with his arm around Corrina. Fires still burned, but the grass smell that surrounded us helped mask it.

Maibe's memory-fever was gone, but she kept throwing up.

The wound on her arm was festering. It was bright red, swollen, hot to the touch, oozing a pus that kept coming back no matter that we'd cleaned it three times. She needed medicine.

Ricker helped Maibe down onto the grass and she fell into a troubled sleep. He brushed hair back from Maibe's forehead. Ricker had always been whip-thin, but it was worse now.

No one spoke about the Vs trapped in the multi other than to thank Corrina and me for saving them. We were leaving the Vs to die a slow death. I sort of did and didn't care. They had tried to kill me and my friends. Sick or not, human or not, I wasn't going to forgive that. There were no right answers. Better not to think of them at all. We couldn't help them, we could only worry about our own safety. But that was easier said than done.

Kern pointed at Ano's arm of scars. "What're those for?"

When Ano only answered with a steady stare, Jimmy said, "For people who have died."

Kern looked around at each of us, his eyes catching on the ridged, white lines that formed messy, childish-looking names. He didn't say anything more about it. Instead he searched the inside of his bag and began pulling out little packets. He did it without a word, but the crinkle of plastic wrappers drew our attention. The yellow caught my eye first—peanut butter and chocolate. Bright, fire engine red for a package of candy. A green bag of vinegar chips. Even a few soda cans. He emptied the backpack until there was a small mountain of junk food in front of him. I tried not to picture how the chips would taste: salty and sharp on my tongue.

"So, who wants what?" Kern said.

Jimmy reached over first, but stopped before touching any of it.

Kern looked around and raised his eyebrows. "This isn't a trick or something. I raided a gas station when we first woke up."

"And you took all the junk that would make you sick?" I said.

Kern squinted at me. The bag of chips seemed to stare at me too. "I'm trying to say thanks for letting us tag along."

"We'd like to come along, if you don't mind," Laurel said.

"I mind," I said. "I don't know you and I don't trust you."

"We could use all the help we can get," Corrina said.

Corrina and I had come to a truce of some sort, but that didn't mean I had to agree with her, but I also couldn't get up enough energy to fight her on this.

"We could all help each other out for awhile," Dylan said. "I'm not back up on my feet yet, not really. Right now I'm a burden, which means you're more likely to get killed hauling me around—"

"We're not leaving you behind," Corrina said.

"I know," Dylan said. "I'm not suggesting that. But that does mean we could use more help, more muscle than just a bunch of kids."

"Go to hell," Ano said.

I silently cheered at Ano's words.

"Who do you think saved your ass?" Ricker said.

"That's not what I meant," Dylan said. "I'm sorry. I know neither of us would be alive without your help."

I waited for Ano to rip Dylan again, but there was only silence.

Jimmy looked back and forth between me and Kern. His hand still hovered over the chocolate peanut butter bar.

"Take it, kid," Kern said, smiling. "I promise I didn't secretly poison it—like Gabbi over here seems to think."

Jimmy still didn't move. Now everyone seemed to be looking back and forth between Kern and me. Everyone except Spencer. He still looked out over the field. I scowled.

A hint of a smile appeared on Ano's face. "I claim the chips."

Kern smiled back and tossed over the bag. I burned holes into Ano's head. He popped open the bag and crunched down on the first chip, looked at me, looked back at the bag. Laughed. He tossed the bag into my lap. "I'm full. Do you want the rest?"

I took the first, delicious chip out of the bag before I even knew what I was doing. Jimmy dove for the chocolate bar, which made Laurel laugh. Corrina and Dylan split a soda and Ricker took a package of candy. Spencer took nothing.

Kern drained his soda and tossed the can into the grass.

My first impulse was to snatch it up for the recycling money. I saw it in Ano too, the way his muscles tensed even though he was sitting. He shook his head and half-smiled.

"So what's next?" Laurel asked.

"We get out of the city," Ano said. "We get medicine for Maibe." He didn't say anything about Dutch Flat.

At the sound of her name, Maibe moaned. It was good that Dylan was awake, for however long that lasted. Maibe would need the trailer.

Kern looked at me for confirmation on Ano's words. I shrugged.

"Good chips?" Kern said.

I turned onto my stomach without answering and licked the last of the salt and vinegar from my fingers.

Kern laid flat on the grass on his back. He was only several feet away now. His arm stretched up and over his eyes to block the sun. This pulled up his shirt enough to reveal dirt-streaked, well-defined muscle, and a strip of hair that disappeared into his jeans.

I pinched myself hard and twisted around to stare up at the sky. Now was not the time for a crush.

I turned and focused on the blades of damp grass in front of my nose. An ant crawled along the underside as if its whole world hadn't fallen to pieces. You never trusted somebody out of the goodness of your heart—whether they shared junk food with you or not. They always betrayed you. But fighting off the Vs would fall to Ano and me, and we weren't enough, and I didn't know what should come next.

I tore the blade of grass in half and threw it into the air. It spun and drifted to the ground a few feet away. Let's see the ant put the pieces back together now.

CHAPTER 17

BEFORE WE LEFT, I slipped away to pee behind one of the buildings. I passed by the multi and rested my hands on the lock for just a moment. Shuffling feet and soft groans as if from a dream drifted from the door. Was it murder if we left them all inside? I shook my head. Be smart, Gabbi.

But it was hard to take my hands away. It was hard to walk away and leave them inside, in the dark, alone with themselves. I did that. I had gotten them in there.

I left the chain in place and walked away and told myself going soft now would only get us killed.

Kern and Laurel found bikes in one of the empty houses near the high school. They said they would lead the way on the trail. They said it was the least they could do to thank us for helping them. I didn't know what to think about that, except to let them ride in front. They were easier to watch that way.

We made good time on the trail for a couple of hours. It was twenty miles to Folsom Lake. Kern said there was a pharmacy just off the trail after reaching the lake. We knew there had to be other, closer ones in the neighborhoods that lined the river, but no one volunteered to search them out. The V sightings became less frequent as we got further from the city. The suburbs were still built thick along the river, but a wider greenbelt created a better buffer. Plus, there had been no refugee camp to draw the Vs out here.

Soon we hit the dam and the lake opened before us. It was noticeably empty even on this winter day. The waves were calm and lapped gently on the shoreline a few yards from the bike trail. The gnarled trunks of the oak trees stood sentry like they had always done. A few shorebirds squawked over a trash can chained to a speed limit pole.

For a second, I could pretend nothing had changed. We were a bunch of street kids taking advantage of our freedom to enjoy the lake. Maybe someone was going to light a joint and we would veg out to some music while letting the sound of the water hypnotize us.

Then Maibe moaned. Ricker was taking his turn on the bike trailer. He locked eyes with me and shook his head. "She's getting worse."

I caught up with Kern and rode alongside him as he scanned the trail ahead.

"What?" he said.

I was going to ask him how far until the pharmacy. Instead, I said, "What do you mean what?"

"I mean," Kern said. "Is there something wrong with me?"

"Why would there be something wrong with you?" I said. "Is there something you're not telling us?"

He flinched. "Chill out, woman. You were staring."

Had I been staring? "Don't call me that."

"Gabbi, then."

"Don't call me that either. You don't know me."

"What's your problem?" Kern said. He scowled at me, drawing his dark eyebrows together over his almost black eyes. "I've done nothing but—"

"You've done nothing to make me—"

"Why didn't you leave them?" Kern said.

"What?"

"I saw you. I saw you go back and unlock the door."

"You were watching me?"

"That's not the point," Kern said.

"I think it is."

"Why didn't you just leave them?"

"I did leave them."

"You didn't unlock the door?"

"I didn't."

"But you thought about it?"

"That's none of your business."

"You've killed them before."

"In self-defense," I said.

"It's the end of the world."

"It's murder," I said. "Even if we have to do it."

"It's the END. OF. THE. WORLD."

"It's still murder if they aren't trying to kill me first!" I said.

"But they ARE trying to kill you. That's the whole point," Kern said. "That's why you call them Vs. V for violent, as in, they will violently kill you if you give them the chance."

"We got you out alive. Why are you complaining?" I said. I

didn't understand how this conversation had gotten so out of control. I hadn't unlocked the door. I might have thought about it. I might have done it if I'd been myself, but I hadn't.

"I'm only pointing out some important facts here," Kern said. "Facts that might get us killed if others don't accept them."

"I don't need your facts." I gritted my teeth. It didn't matter if what I had thought about doing made sense or not. He didn't get to judge me for it and think I would just take it.

"Yeah, whatever," he said, shaking his head, dismissing me. "You're crazy."

He increased his speed and pulled ahead. I coasted and dropped back next to Maibe and Ricker. I hadn't meant to start an argument. I hadn't been looking for one. I'd wanted to know how far away the pharmacy was. I'd hoped to make him smile.

We rode a few more miles in silence. Kern stopped at a large intersection. Four cars were piled up in the middle. One was charred and melted into the street, the others mangled bits of red and green and blue metal. Glass was everywhere in a thick, glinting carpet.

"This is where we go in a bit," Kern said. "The pharmacy is in that strip mall. Across the street is a grocery store. Laurel and I will grab us more food while you all get the medicine you need."

I wanted to argue for keeping the group together, but Kern's judgment still ran through my mind. Maybe I WAS crazy for not trusting them. They'd been through a lot too. They'd lost people and woken up from the fevers, infected just like us with memories that kept betraying them.

"All right," I said, looking at Ano for agreement. "Everyone meet back here."

"I'll stay with Maibe," Ricker said.

"Jimmy," I said. "You should stay too. Help Ricker."

"I want to help get groceries," Jimmy said. His dark curly hair had matted around his ears. Chocolate crumbs stained his chin.

"And get more chocolate bars," Ricker said.

Jimmy looked away. Ricker poked him in the side. "You better get one for me this time."

Jimmy turned back, smiling.

"This is serious," I said. "This isn't some game!"

"We know," Ricker said. His smile became a scowl. "It's all death out there all the time. Thanks for reminding us."

I felt embarrassed. Of course they knew. I didn't need to ruin every time someone tried to lighten the mood. At least Ricker was still trying, which was more than I could say for myself.

"I'll go with you," Dylan said to me and Ano. His blue eyes were shockingly light against his dark hair. Sweat trickled down his forehead in spite of the cold. He'd stayed awake for the whole ride this time. The fevers were almost done with him, but not completely.

"We can't risk this," Ano said. "If you go down and there's trouble…"

"Stay with Maibe and Corrina," I said. "We won't be long."

Corrina whispered in his ear and he sank to the ground in silent relief. He was going down again.

"We need to find a second trailer." I said it so only Ano could hear. He pressed his lips together and nodded.

We separated. Ano and me to the pharmacy, Kern, Laurel, and Jimmy to the grocery store. Everyone else remained behind. It didn't feel right leaving them.

The inside of the pharmacy was cold and our steps echoed on the tile. The aisles were these huge shadows that loomed over our heads. Parts of the store had been ransacked, other aisles were in ruins, as if someone had come along and run their arms across the boxes to purposefully crash them on the floor.

There were two dead bodies in the back, both were clerks. We didn't look close enough to see what had killed them. I kept my eyes open for a trailer, anything that a bike might be able to drag, but there was nothing. The pharmacy gate was bent, almost ripped off its track. The shelves behind it looked—empty.

"No," I whispered.

Ano ran and jumped the counter. "All of it is gone!"

I heard a low growl and reached for the bat strapped to my back. The clerks weren't dead.

They rose from the ground like monsters out of the horror movies Maibe talked about. I cleared the counter just as there was a crash. Ano appeared at the gate, wide-eyed, his black hair a shock of darkness across his face. He was scared.

Behind him the pharmacy was totally empty, except for the five Vs headed our way.

We scrambled back over the counter and into the waiting arms of the two clerks. One was a large, older woman with a gray-haired perm, the other was a younger man with a goatee. They snatched at our clothes and screeched. The Vs behind us screamed. I screamed back and swung my bat. The goatee guy caught the bat and ripped it out of my hands. It flew across the store, slid along the tile, bounced off an aisle, and disappeared. Ano smashed into the guy's chest and sent him tumbling to the ground. The woman with the perm dug her fingers into my arms. The Vs behind us stumbled over the counter and one of them grabbed my hair. They were pulling me back and forth between them as I tried to fight them off, but they were too strong, too angry, too determined.

Lights blazed inside the store and made everything disappear into a sea of white. The woman's head exploded in front of me. I tasted blood on my lips. My ears rang, muffling the shouts of people in uniform who surrounded me. I tumbled backwards. The V that still held on broke my fall. Arms wrapped around my stomach, cutting off my breath until one of the soldiers yanked me up and dealt with the V.

There was silence now in the store except for my ringing ears. Ano was on his knees, hands behind his neck, a gun pointed at his head. The Vs were dead now. Some of them looked almost exploded into pieces.

Kern and Laurel stood behind the soldiers and no one pointed a gun at them.

CHAPTER 18

THE ARMY TRUCK WAS FILTHY AND DARK. We sat on benches facing each other. They had bound all of our wrists and ankles, except for Laurel and Kern's. Maibe was laid out on the bench and she groaned at each jolt of the truck. Ricker sat on the floor of the truck and leaned back, using his weight to keep Maibe from falling off. A guard holding a rifle sat on the end of one bench.

I saw all of this from the periphery of my vision because I stared at my hands and the rope that bound them. I'd be able to untie it all easily enough, but we were part of a convoy and I did not think we could escape them on foot.

The canvas smelled damp and moldering. I sneezed into my hands and dug my fingers into my eye sockets to keep tears from falling.

All of us captured again. As if we had never been released. We were back at square one, worse than before, because the guards were better than the ones before. Too slick and mean and professional. Too watchful. Too careful.

"It's not what you think," Kern said softly.

I did not respond. He wasn't talking to me anyway. He was explaining himself to Corrina or Dylan or someone else who actually cared about that sort of thing. As if getting us captured could be explained away.

"They're looking for a cure, but we need more help."

"Indentured servitude," Ano said. "Slavery."

"Gabbi," Kern said.

I looked up and saw his face in the dim light. Like stone, no remorse, if anything, a sense of pride and a layer of anger.

"You would have done the same," he said. He looked stricken with shame then, just for a moment, but the emotion disappeared and disdain replaced it. "You don't understand—"

A strangled cry lodged in my throat and I launched myself off the bench. I straddled him, even with my ankles locked together, and used my fists to pummel his shoulders, head, arms. I saw his fists too late. He brought them up and slammed them into the underside of my chin. My head snapped back and stars exploded across my eyes. I was pulled off Kern and onto the truck's floorboards.

When my head cleared, a rifle barrel filled my vision. "Get back onto the bench."

I tried to talk around the blood in my mouth and choked. I spit out a glob by the guard's feet. I couldn't get up on my own and I wasn't going to ask for help.

The guard motioned to Kern and Laurel. "Get her back on the bench."

The two men lifted me back onto the bench. Kern rubbed

his temple and returned to his seat. The others remained silent. I almost blamed Corrina, she was the one who had pushed us to trust the two strange men, but really, I blamed myself for not stopping the stupidity before now.

We rode the rest of the way in silence. I figured Kern and Laurel must have been working with Sergeant Bennings at the fairgrounds. It must have been them who had killed all those Vs on the trail near the underpass. I wondered how long they had actually been Feebs for.

Once, Kern looked ready to say something else, but a warning elbow from his father silenced him. Bumps threw me against Dylan at times, but there was no hint of attraction present. He was like a lump of coal.

Out the back of the truck, neighborhoods passed by, some rich and spread out, others close together and run down, most burned away. When we crossed over I-80, the convoy slowed near the middle of the overpass. The freeway was thick with cars. People had tried to flee—not many had made it out of the city by the looks of it. Taking the freeway would have been the wrong move. But then again, the bike trail hadn't turned out so great either.

Smoke still hazed the sky, otherwise we would have seen the snowcapped Sierra mountains, some hundred miles away. A few miles later, all of it disappeared as we went through a tunnel. Out the other side was the rail yard. We'd ridden the train here often enough that I recognized the medians and markers. A large Methodist church built in the late 1800s was usually the first thing you could see from the train station. Its painted white bricks and stained glass windows were still intact, but the surrounding buildings had burned to sticks.

Here the streets were clear. In fact, the entire drive had been mostly free of obstacles, as if someone had cleared it.

The entrance to this camp bustled with activity. Guards were posted at regular intervals in lookout towers. We rumbled through. Cooking smells drifted into the truck and made my stomach cramp from hunger. A train whistle, long, high-pitched, and familiar sounded.

People, uninfected, walked around. The truck rumbled through the grounds, paused while the driver talked with someone, then continued on, not stopping again until it hit some sort of office building, but there was something not quite office-like about its windows or shape.

The ramp unlatched. The guard motioned us out with his rifle then jumped off.

I stood, wobbly on my feet, my jaw aching, my head throbbing.

A glance at Kern showed he wasn't much better off. He might be bigger than me, but I knew how to throw a punch. His left eye was swollen shut and blood had dripped down and dried on his chin.

I squeezed my eyes shut, then opened them wide. I rolled my shoulders trying to get the kinks out, then stepped behind Spencer to walk down the ramp.

"When you enter the jail, we will need to decontaminate your clothing and all of your possessions. You will get everything back after decontamination."

I could not yet see who spoke, but something about the voice made my stomach cramp. I stepped forward. Corrina crowded behind me. She drew in a sharp breath. "No."

Sergeant Bennings was at the end of the ramp.

CHAPTER 19

SERGEANT BENNINGS STOOD with his legs hip-width apart and his hands behind his back. A clear plastic shield covered his face and his hands were gloved. His eyes skated past me and settled on Dylan. I let out a silent breath of relief. I feared he would recognize me as the one who had killed his soldier on the stage.

"Hello, Dylan," Sergeant Bennings said, nodding in his direction. "You may not believe it, but I'm glad to see you alive. Infected or not."

"I can't say the same," Dylan responded.

Ricker stepped off the ramp with Maibe leaning against him. When she saw Sergeant Bennings she stopped and became rigid.

"I know him." She touched Ricker's shoulder. "That's Alden." Her face was blank yet focused on Sergeant Bennings.

It gave me the chills watching her act out the memory-rush right there in front of me. We'd been inside the fairgrounds with our stack of blankets, figuring out a way into the warehouse.

Sergeant Bennings froze. "How do you know about my son?"

"We went to school together."

He thought she was answering his question but I knew it was part of the memory-rush.

"He's alive and untainted. He won't be allowed to have anything to do with you."

Maibe opened her mouth. Ricker looked at me with wild eyes. I stomped on her foot.

"Ow!" Her face cleared. She blinked and looked at me. "Why did you do that?"

"Shut up," I said.

"You'll find things run a little different here," Sergeant Bennings said. He was talking to all of us but stared at Maibe like she was an insect. "More strict in some ways, more relaxed in others. If it gives you any comfort, I'm not the one in charge. They didn't like how I ran the fairgrounds."

"How it fell apart under your command?" Dylan said.

Sergeant Bennings finally looked away from Maibe. He wiped his mouth with the back of his hand. He reached for the stick at his waist.

"Sir, what about my wife?" Laurel left the line and moved to within feet of Sergeant Bennings. Guards leapt forward. The click of tasers went off. Laurel screamed and bounced onto the ground. The rest of us jumped away, but then suddenly we were all surrounded with clicking shock sticks.

Kern dropped to the ground. Dust puffed up. "Wake up, Laurel. Wake up. Come on!"

"He'll be fine," Sergeant Bennings said. He wiped some imaginary dust from his right shoulder. "The council has clearly become too lax here. Please remember that infected are not allowed to stand within six feet of any uninfected person, or said infected person risks shock and possible execution. Now—" He motioned for the guards to step back.

"We did as ordered. There's no need for this," Kern said.

"Yes, you're right," Sergeant Bennings said. "You will be rewarded. Now—"

He surveyed the rest of us. His eyes rested on me for a moment and then slid on. Maibe vomited spindly translucent trails of saliva onto the ground.

"—please follow me."

"She needs medicine."

Sergeant Bennings stopped and looked at Ricker and then at Maibe. "She'll get it."

Ricker helped Maibe forward. Laurel moaned and then braced himself on the dirt while Kern lifted him to his feet. We shuffled into the building—a large sign over a bullet-proof encased reception area revealed the building had been used as a county jail. The plaque said "state-of-the-art, built in 2004."

They escorted us to an open area. Natural light streamed onto the railings and concrete surfaces and into the surrounding layers of cells. I was prodded into a cell with Corrina, the others walked past and it sounded like they were separated into cells of their own.

A fire alarm bell rang. I sat on a cot next to Corrina and watched Feebs stream across the opening of our cell. "What's going on?"

"I have no idea," Corrina said.

I stood up. No one was watching us. We could leave.

The cell bars clanged shut. The bell turned off. A door opened. A cart, heaped with trays, rolled by. People in hospital scrubs with face masks and gloves pushed the tray. Delicious food smells almost overwhelmed my senses. My stomach cramped at the thought of food.

Corrina and I looked at each other. I surveyed our new little home. Two beds, a toilet, and a sink.

"What do you think is happening?"

I laid out on one of the beds. "Nothing good, of course." Though I hoped we'd get some dinner first before the next awful thing started.

"They said they were working on a cure."

"And look at how that turned out for Leaf."

Corrina sat down on the bunk and then lowered her head to her knees.

"I think that most things have fallen apart or burned down or will have both happen to them very soon," I said. "I think that when a thing breaks, it's harder to piece it back together than to just toss it aside and start again. I think that even if they are looking for a cure, it's for themselves. Not for us."

Corrina looked up at me, her brown eyes staring into mine.

"You know it's true," I said softly, remembering our truce. She had that haunted look about her, that look that said she knew what it was like not to belong so badly that it turned you into something worse than an alien, it turned you into trash people could throw away and never think about again.

I closed my eyes and pressed my lips together. Leaf's numb face appeared. He was smiling, but only half his face moved. The ghost-memory wasn't a happy one, they usually weren't for me. I opened my eyes in the hopes that he would disappear, but instead I saw him sitting next to Corrina on the cot. His legs were crossed, and his arms, his good arm, lay draped over one knee while the other one hung limp against his side.

"If this has affected most of the country, hell, most of the world, maybe there's a scientist in a bunker working on a solution, but that's not going to help us here and now." I jabbed myself in the chest to emphasize my point. "Any help that comes our way comes from us." Even as I said the words, I wasn't sure how much I meant them.

But in the silence that settled between us, among us really, because Leaf still sat there nodding his head as if in agreement, I realized I did mean it.

"I would welcome you to Camp Pacific, but such words would be farcical, and I no longer have a sense of humor." A female voice drew our attention to the cell door. She had the tell-tale marks of a Feeb, but she was also unfettered and unguarded.

"Who are you?" Corrina asked.

"A traitor." She smiled. "That's what new ones like you call me, but I usually change their minds."

I got up from the cot and approached the bars. Leaf's ghost stood up with me and reached out a hand as if to place it in warning on my shoulder. I flinched from the almost-touch. He drew his hand away, a hurt look on his face. I don't know why I flinched. He'd never done anything to hurt me.

I turned back to the lady. She had long gray hair that dangled past her shoulders. Clear blue eyes twinkled with intelligence and sternness, but the smile on her lips was friendly and she held her hands out, palms up, almost in supplication. Her eyes caught on my arm with all the scars, but she didn't ask about them.

I felt the loss of Leaf all over again and how his name was missing from my arm and how that needed to be fixed.

"In two minutes or so, they will have finished dropping of the food, then they will release your locks and dinner will be served. We all eat together in the greenhouse."

"The...what?" I said.

She cocked her head over her shoulder. "The center of the jail."

"They power the locks with a generator, but otherwise there isn't any electricity on this side of camp. They save the power for their side." The woman moved away from the bars toward the next cell.

"Wait!" Corrina said.

"Yes?"

"What's your name?"

"Tabitha. You can call me Tibby, if you like."

"You're a Feeb," I said. "Why aren't you in here with us?"

She smiled and moved on.

"Hey!" I ran up to the bars and shook them. They were supposed to rattle like in the movies, but they were too sturdy for that. I searched the cell. There was a spoon underneath the mattress. I took that to the bars but before I could touch them, the latch released and the cell door opened.

Corrina pushed passed me and onto the walkway. I came out slowly. Ricker burst out of a cell with Jimmy. Ano came out with Spencer and Dylan.

"Where's Maibe?" Ricker said. His face was pale and veins throbbed along his neck. "They took her from me."

Other Feebs came out of the cells, talking and laughing and shaking hands and hugging as if this whole thing were a normal part of the day. Laurel helped a woman with a cane limp out. He had his arms around her shoulders, protecting her from falling. He kissed her on the lips. Fury rose alongside understanding. All our lives traded for his wife's one life. There would be payback.

Kern was talking to Tabitha against the railing. I stalked up to them. "Where's Maibe? What have you done with her?"

Tabitha looked at me with steady eyes. Kern rubbed his hand across the stubble on his neck. "She wasn't with you?"

"No, she wasn't with me. That's why I'm asking, dumbass."

Ricker came up next to me. Then Corrina and Dylan.

Tabitha looked at each of us in turn. I felt the pressure building to an explosion.

"Maibe!" I shouted. "Maibe, where are you? Are you in here?" A breathless feeling filled my chest. I took my eyes off her for one second. But it hadn't been one second. It had been hours. I hadn't thought about her since they had loaded us into the truck. I cursed myself. I had promised to look out for her and now—

"She needed an IV and antibiotics," Tabitha said.

"Where is she?" Ricker said. His voice cracked.

"Take them to her, son."

Son? Had anything they said been true? I opened my mouth but Ano grabbed my wrist and tapped: C-O-O-L. He shook his head at me and I could read the rest of his message easily enough: cool it until we knew more.

Kern stared at our hands and then looked away. "Follow me."

Maibe was laid out on a cot. Inside the cell with her was a long metal pole with a bag of liquid attached. The tubing snaked down and into her arm. Her stupid pink sweatshirt was rolled up to her elbows and looking more gray than pink now. Her mess of dark hair peeked out from her hood. Relief made my knees weak. I grabbed the railing and held on because goddamn I was not going to faint in front of Kern.

Her wounded arm was bandaged. Her breath was slow and steady and she was awake.

"Hi," Maibe said. She smiled and her skin stretched, pale and webbed.

"Hi," I said.

Ricker pushed in beside me. "Maibe, are you okay?" He sat down next to the cot and placed his hand alongside hers without quite touching it.

"It's okay, Ricker. I'm already feeling better." Maibe looked back at me. "She said they let us out for the night because everything's locked up and they don't care what we do."

"Who said?"

"Tibby."

"Well, it'll just make it easier to mob them in the morning and escape." But anxiety snaked through my stomach. Alone with all these strangers, all these men, and nothing to lock them out. I pushed the thought aside for now because if I thought about it too hard I would have a panic attack.

"She said they won't send in any food and they'll turn the water off if we don't return to our cells. Even one of us goes missing and they will punish all of us for days."

I scowled at her. "Are you trying to tell me something?" I knew exactly what she was trying to tell me. Don't mess it up for the rest of us.

Maibe sighed and looked at Ricker.

"She's right," Kern said behind me. "But there's a whole introduction we go through and there's more to it than just the cells."

I whirled around. "I don't play well with others," I said in a snarl. I didn't, that was true enough, but I knew I could have said it differently. Still, they needed to learn fast that no one was going to tell me what to do without earning some scars for their effort.

Kern smiled. "Then you'll fit right in."

Dinner consisted of spaghetti noodles, red sauce, some meatballs that looked a lot like ground up SPAM, and all the water we could drink. Everything was served cold, but it was the best meal I remembered eating in a long time.

Three rows of tables, four tables deep, filled Tabitha's 'greenhouse.' Almost all of the tables were full.

We sat as a group. Kern was at a different table, but he kept looking my way. Every time he caught my gaze I stared daggers at him. I pictured running across the tables to choke him into unconsciousness, but instead I savagely attacked the spaghetti noodles. Spencer ate as if in his own bubble. Ricker and Jimmy were ravenous and chatty, Ano listened but didn't participate much. Dylan and Corrina and Maibe sat across from me and acted like they were some weird nuclear family. I sat on the edge of both the table and an emotional cliff. People were laughing and talking and acting as if this were some community night event and everyone could just go back home to their quiet lives like the world had never fallen apart and we weren't actually being kept prisoner.

I rose from my seat. My fingers twitched against my plate and I pictured slamming it to the floor and walking away and making sure all the people in the room learned it was better not to mess with me. I planned out how the night would go, how I would force myself to stay awake. We could all take a cell together and take turns being on watch and—

"Sometimes, when it gets really bad," Tabitha said, standing over me. "When I think I'm about to lose control, I remember the most beautiful flower I've ever seen, a deep purple morning glory spread open to the sun, climbing the stalk of a yellow sunflower."

"That's the dumbest thing I've ever heard," I said.

Tabitha slid next to me on the bench. I froze.

"Please sit," she said.

I did not move.

She inclined her head my way. "This is going to take a little while to explain."

The rest of the group had stopped talking. Ano rested a hand on my shoulder. "It's okay," he said. I settled back down but kept my muscles coiled like a cat about to spring.

Tabitha scanned our faces. We waited to find out how bad things were going to get.

"We are working toward a cure here. That is the most important thing to know upfront."

"You mean THEY are working toward a cure," Corrina said.

Tabitha nodded. "Yes, and they need our help."

"Why did they imprison us if they want our help?" Dylan said.

"Because you would not have come otherwise," Tabitha said.

"You bet not," Corrina said.

"It's dangerous out there, and I understand your group came through the fairgrounds first, and you should know—that's not how they do things here."

"Then why is Sergeant Bennings here?" I said. "He was in charge and he seems pretty involved with things here too."

"It's unfortunate that he was the one to meet you off the truck. But it's different here," Tabitha said firmly.

I was about to speak again, but Tabitha held up her hands. "Wait, please. Let me better explain."

I closed my mouth and waited. Let her hang herself by her own words.

"We are all here against our will. There is no use in denying it."

I felt surprise at her words. Wasn't she supposed to convince us otherwise? Wasn't it her job to make us play along?

"But in some ways, the uninfected are also here against their will. The same fence that protects them from the sick outside also of course imprisons us inside. Not in the same way, no, but the world has changed, and if we do not want to become the enemy of our neighbors, we will also have to change." She paused for a moment and scanned our faces again.

"Most everyone here has uninfected family on the other side of camp." Her gray hair shined from recently being washed. The wrinkles around her eyes deepened as she grimaced. "It is our lot to prove to them that we deserve to work alongside them—not as their prisoners. We will not allow our neighbors to dehumanize us."

"They already have!" I said. "We are nothing, we are less than human, something to experiment on or get rid of if we cause too much trouble."

"If you believe that then you already are what they think you are," Tabitha said, focusing her stare on me as if trying to peer into my soul.

"It's not what I believe that matters, it's what they believe," I said.

"No," Corrina said. "It's what we believe that matters."

"Yes, that's what we believe here," Tabitha said. "We are their prisoners. Our neighbors, our family in some cases, have taken us prisoners, but we only become the beasts they claim we have become if we also believe the lies."

"They're the monsters," I said.

"They are not," Tabitha said.

"I don't understand," Corrina said. "Where is everyone else? All these uninfected?"

"The camp here is split into two," Tabitha said. "You cannot go on the uninfected side without permission. They cannot come here without protection. We work separately to keep the entire camp going."

I turned away and looked into space, but Kern was there, across the room, staring intently, directly, at me. He moved as if to get up, but Laurel whispered in his ear and he settled back into his seat.

"But," Dylan said, "what does that mean for us here and now? Are you saying we should just accept this? That it doesn't matter how they treat us, that—"

"Of course it matters," Tabitha interrupted.

I looked away from Kern's table and surveyed the rim of cells darkening around us in the evening light. No electricity. When the sun faded completely, everything would become pitch black. "Do they lock the cells at night?" At least the bars would offer some protection.

Tabitha shook her head. "We are only locked into the cells when the uninfected need to enter."

We would not see anyone coming our way during the night. There would be no warning. "We're all sleeping in the same cell."

Tabitha inclined her head. "If you wish. There is a schedule and there are procedures and jobs that everyone shares in. We are not criminals and we will not act like ones no matter how much easier that would make it on our neighbors." She went on to explain the work chores everyone would get assigned tomorrow, how there were still hot showers, but the toilets didn't work because the manuals had been replaced with auto-flushers hard-wired to the electricity. She explained about the pit toilets and the rules we were expected to follow.

"All right," Corrina said. "So we play the game—"

"It's more than a game," Tabitha said.

"We all know that," Corrina responded.

"Of course you do," Tabitha said. "I apologize."

"So we do what we want, and then what? Wait for a chance to escape?"

"If someone escapes," Tabitha said. "They will punish everyone here, but yes, that is your right. You could take such an opportunity and leave us to our fates."

I turned back and slid my legs under the table bench. "How do they punish us?"

"Reduced rations, more work, taking away some of the small luxuries we have like soap, clean water for bathing."

"This all sounds so nice, doesn't it?" Spencer said, his first words spoken the entire conversation.

"And are they running experiments?" Corrina asked.

Tabitha nodded. "There is no other better way to test for a cure." She stood up. "I will not ask you to promise anything. This is a devil's deal, I know it, you know it. Everyone here knows it. But most of us are determined. We would rather die than turn into the monsters many of the uninfected already believe us to be. And we have hope that a cure will be found. Please consider my words, but of course, this decision is a personal one that only you can make for yourself. We are putting our humanity in your hands."

At this she stood up and left the table. We were silent, stunned, thoughtful. I wasn't going to follow the rules. The first chance we got to escape, I would make us take it. But even so, I found I respected her a little bit for being so sure about what to do in an impossible, horrible situation. They hadn't broken her yet.

Corrina stood up from the table and said a hurried, "I'll be back, I want to ask her…"

But she didn't finish, only brushed her hand along Dylan's upper back as she followed Tabitha across the greenhouse, over to Kern's table.

"I THINK WE SHOULD ALL STAY in Maibe's cell tonight and take shifts standing guard. Two people up at a time," I said.

"This sounds good to me," Ano said.

Ricker nodded.

Jimmy looked troubled. "You think something's going to happen?"

I shrugged. "Maybe."

Maibe looked up at the sound of her name. "I'm going to the bathroom."

"Not by yourself," Dylan said.

Maibe looked about to protest, then said, "I need someone to go with me."

Ricker looked at the other two. "We'll go." He elbowed Jimmy and Ano. "I've had to pee for ages."

"Yeah, me too," I said.

"I'll wait for Corrina," Dylan said.

Spencer didn't say anything but made no move to get up from the dinner table.

"Meet back at Maibe's cell," Dylan said. "We'll drag some

more cots in and make it work somehow."

We left Spencer and Dylan at the table and walked through the greenhouse to a hallway that led to the toilets. It was twilight and everything had lost its color, not that there had been much to begin with. Cement ground, a few basketball poles missing their hoops, white paint marking off the court, a tall chain-link fence with barbed wire, several lookout towers with armed guards. They flashed us with their lights and then moved on.

The pit toilets were dug in the middle of the yard, walled off with plywood, and more plywood separating it down the middle. The planks were covered in artistic paint strokes and landscape scenes, including a purple-flowered morning glory vine twined around a sunflower stalk.

"Who did this?" Maibe asked.

"Tabitha," I said, rolling my eyes.

"It looks nice," Jimmy said.

"Why would they bother?" Ricker asked.

I thought about it and weighed Tabitha's earlier words against the pictures in front of me. "Because she might mean what she says," I said finally. "She's not going to let them win."

We used the crude facilities. Really not that bad considering what I was used to. On the women's side were several buckets of water and a sliver of soap. I poured a scoop of sand down the hole after we finished. Ricker and Jimmy could not shut up as we returned to the greenhouse. They joked around with Maibe until I wanted to swat all of their ears, but I kept my hands to myself because I also sort of enjoyed hearing them laugh again.

Only a few people remained at the tables now. A half dozen Feebs were at a sort of bucket washing station, cleaning up the plates and utensils while a few other people scraped leftovers into a compost-type bucket. The light was almost gone, but people did not hurry. It was as if they knew exactly how much time things took and knew they still had enough time to get it all done. People—men, women, children—wandered in and out of the cells, talking in hushed tones, walking by us to use the pit toilets, brushing their teeth, hanging out clothes on the railings.

Corrina sat at a table with Kern. Dylan had joined her, but Spencer was nowhere to be seen.

"Where's Spencer?" I said in a too-loud voice that interrupted people from their tasks.

Dylan motioned us over. "He said he went up to move the cots around."

"Look," Kern said, "There are some of us making plans—"

"YOU," I jabbed my finger in the air at him, "can forget about us having anything to do with YOUR plans."

"I think we should give it a try," Corrina said.

"We're going up to help Spencer," Jimmy said, standing up.

Ricker tugged on Maibe's sweatshirt. "Come on, Maibe. This conversation is about to go nowhere." They clambered up the metal stairs.

I started in on Kern again, listing all the reasons why he couldn't be trusted ever again, why we shouldn't have trusted him in the first place, and how we should have left him and Laurel trapped on that roof. He took it too. He didn't say a word the entire time, but he met my gaze and held it as if knowing that it was part of his punishment.

And suddenly I felt deflated and my voice lost its power and I stopped.

Gunfire erupted outside and people started screaming.

CHAPTER 20

KERN SPRANG FROM THE TABLE as if lit on fire. I chased him and expected someone to stop us when we reached the front doors of the jail but he slammed right through them.

People continued to shout, but the gunfire had stopped. I ran into Kern's back. I pushed him out of the way. "Hey!" he said, but I did not care because a dreadful feeling had settled in my chest.

Out front, the open space was larger than the back, but the separation between sections was clear. Guard towers marked two parts of the fence that kept the Vs out. Another guard tower marked a section of interior fence that kept us Feebs from the uninfected part of the camp.

When they had unloaded us, the truck had blocked the layout but now it was easy to see the train tracks snaking alongside the fence on the uninfected border. On our side there were rows of white hoop houses and piles of dirt and gardening tools.

The fence on this side ran along a street with another fenced parking lot on the other side. Acres and acres of parking lot with weeds growing from the cracks.

Two guards in the tower had white spotlights blazing down onto a figure on the ground on our side of the fence. A dark, black puddle spread out around him.

The guards were screaming for us to get back inside or get shot.

I stepped forward and felt Kern grab my arm.

"Gabbi."

I shook him off. It was Spencer in the light. Spencer in the puddle.

I stumbled to one knee because I couldn't feel my feet anymore. Ricker and Maibe came up next to me. He turned and buried his face in her hair. Jimmy puked and I noticed somehow that a chunk of pasta had landed on my leg. I stared at this little glob because I couldn't stare at anything else. Kern pulled at my elbow and lifted me into his chest. The warmth of his body burned me like the lights seemed to burn off the veins and webbing of Spencer's afflicted skin and smooth it all back out so that everyone could clearly see he was really still so young.

"Careful," Kern said, his hot breath tickling my ear. He pulled me back through the crowd, through the front doors. He told my group to follow him, quickly, don't talk. Go into the cells and don't say a word.

Even though he said it only to us, the entire jail filled up again. People rushed back into their cells and whispered about one of the new Feebs trying to escape and punishment and consequences.

We stuffed the six of us around Maibe's cot. I couldn't look at any of them. I buried my face into the rough cloth of the sheets and tried to stop breathing. What had he done? He knew they were out there. We had all been warned and even I wasn't stupid enough to have tried to escape yet. And then I realized. He hadn't tried to escape. He'd killed himself.

I wanted to rage at him for leaving me alone. What was the point of running away all those years ago for him to just give up now? The anger I felt warred with the suffocating feeling that came over me. I did not want to be in charge. I would mess things up. Spencer was gone.

I wished I had a knife right then to carve his name into my flesh, to at least give him the tribute of knowing he would never be forgotten.

The bars banged shut. The sound of it shocked me. It was dark. There was sniffling, a couple of sobs. No one spoke. No one talked about what had happened.

MINUTES OR HOURS LATER, there was no way to tell, the bars unlocked again and swung out. Tabitha came with a candle in her hand. The light bounced off her face and made her features ghoulish. "I am so sorry." She paused, stared at the candle. "They've given us fifteen minutes to use the bathrooms and return to our cells for the night."

We forced ourselves outside. I leaned against the plywood walls and stared at the guards in their towers and the lights they moved around, checking for Vs, and Feebs like us. I waited out the fifteen minutes. The stream of people tromping back and forth stopped. I waited for trouble to come my way for being late. Let them shoot me down like they did Spencer.

Instead, Corrina came out with a candle. The light made her frizzy curls glow orange. "Gabbi?"

I did not answer.

"We are going to try and sleep now. I…I'm sorry. It would help the rest of us if you came back. They're afraid without you."

She turned back and went inside.

I picked myself off the ground. I brushed my hand across the cold concrete to guide my way down the hallway and into the main part of the jail. The smells of washing soap and food waste hit me. Someone in one of the upper cells sang a lullaby in hushed tones that echoed.

A bright point of light appeared as if out of nowhere, but once my eyes adjusted I saw that it was a candle held by a man at the foot of the stairs I needed to climb. His body must have blocked the candle until he turned. I tensed my muscles, wondering if the night terrors would begin now and how hard I would have to fight to keep my body intact.

In another few seconds my eyes adjusted to this new point of light and I realized it was Kern. This did not make me feel any better.

I kept my fists balled and walked up to his candle. He held it to my face for a moment, casting his own face into long, ominous shadows.

"Gabbi, I'm sorry—"

"Stop," I whispered.

He moved the candle closer to his own face and the light made his eyes glint. "We can't do much tonight. Maybe not for a few days. But as soon as they let us out, we'll give him a proper burial tomorrow—"

"—Is he still…"

"No, he's in a different part of the building. It was the medical room. It still is, really, we have a few medicines and…" He glanced up the stairs and then back at me. "Not that any of that matters right now. Try to get some sleep if you can. There's another one of us at the top of the stairs. They're going to lock us all in tonight."

He moved away from the bottom step and I began to climb. My feet felt like lead blocks and my heart ached, but I was so exhausted, I knew that even the nightmares I was sure to have would not keep me from sleep.

"Goodnight, Gabbi," Kern said from below me.

The guard at the top step was an unfamiliar woman who I remembered laughing a belly laugh at someone's joke at dinner. Now she was somber. "I am sorry for your loss," she said simply.

I counted the cells and held back when I reached ours. I wasn't good with small spaces. Closets and me didn't get along. It was so dark and small in there and my breath hiccuped in my chest. Tears began to stream down my face. Please. I didn't want that memory right now, not after Spencer. Not right now.

"Here, Gabbi, we saved you a place." A hand grabbed mine and pulled me through a tangle of limbs and bodies to a warm spot on the floor. They'd thrown down a cot cushion and some blankets. Ano, Ricker, Jimmy, and Maibe surrounded me and patted my arms and head and legs. The memory-rush faded. It was pitch black and there was no way to see, but I could touch and smell everyone I still loved in the world.

I wish I could say I fell asleep right away, but I stayed awake for a long time listening to everyone breathe, listening to the silence, listening to the beating of my heart as if it held a secret message that could fix all of this if I only learned the code.

I AWOKE FIRST, even though I had fallen asleep last.

There was light now. It streamed from the cell door since there were no windows in the cells. Someone's knee pressed into my neck. I moved it away and also repositioned a heavy leg that Ano had thrown across me. A swatch of Maibe's pink sweatshirt, looking decidedly grimy in the morning light, showed up between Jimmy and Ricker. Corrina and Dylan were tangled together on a single cot. Her hair dangled across both their faces. Even in sleep, he held onto her as if she might evaporate at any moment. We had piled into the cell together like a colony of rats, a pack of dogs, a group of humans who needed to belong to somebody.

An ache started in my throat as I surveyed the room full of people I dared not care about and yet had fallen into that trap no matter how many times I'd raged against it.

A click-clack of metal against metal drew my attention to the cell door. Tabitha stood framed by the bars. She looked over my group of hapless runaways and throwaways. She did not say anything.

"Are you in charge somehow?" I sat up and pushed at Ano to wake up.

"In a way." Tabitha tilted her head. "I'm the spokesperson for us. I relay instructions, problems, decisions. It's easier, and safer for them, to go through one person they trust than to send in uninfected all the time." Something hard sparked in her eye at that moment, some harsh truth that told me her supposed complacency during her speech yesterday wasn't all there was to know about her.

"What happens next?" Ano said.

"There will be no breakfast today. Chores have been

suspended. There will be a bathroom break at lunch."

"Is this because of Spencer?" Corrina asked softly.

"We are all of us responsible for the choices that others make. Whether we wish it to be that way or not. Until they can check over the defenses and we draw away the Vs attracted by the noise—"

"We?" I said. "What do you mean we draw away the Vs?"

"Not you," Tabitha said. Her gray hair lay in long strands around her shoulders like a cape. "It'll be Kern and a few others the council trusts to go outside and do the work. It's not safe for the uninfected to get so close to the Vs."

"Last night at dinner, I'd almost forgotten we were prisoners in here," Corrina said.

"I do not ever forget." There was a heavy note of bitterness in Tabitha's voice.

TABITHA HELD HER ARMS OUT to the sides and in one fluid motion raised them above her head until her hands touched palm to palm.

"Breathe out on a count of five and bring your palms down the center of your body, pausing at the heart, and continuing until you touch the floor with a flat back. "

It was three days after Spencer had died. Yesterday, Kern and his team had returned—dirty, bloody, exhausted, two of them bitten and in the fevers. This was the first morning we weren't on lockdown. This was the first morning of the exercises.

All of us Feebs were out of the cells and had formed three staggered rows on the greenhouse floor. The cement was icy, our breaths came out in trails of mist. The skylights built into the ceiling three stories above us could make you forget the dungeon-like feel of the cells.

Air traveled in and out of my lungs like a river. My heartbeat remained steady. For brief moments, my mind became blank. The wound on my ankle burned with a brightness that warmed my body in spite of the cold.

The stillness in the air matched the stillness from those stretching around me. I didn't know any of them. Yet when Tabitha asked us to go down on hands and feet and arch our backs toward the sun, we did it as if one body. When she moved us back to our feet and we stretched out our arms and positioned our legs as if we were an army ready to throw a volley of spears at our enemy, we did this as if we had always practiced this together. When we moved into a shoulder stand and our dozens of pairs of legs stood straight into the air like trees, I felt part of the room, part of those around me. It was like we were turning ourselves into Faints. Everything outside this stillness began not to matter.

We matched our movements and our breathing like it was a choreographed dance, like it was the march of an army. The silence in the jail was interrupted only by the low beat of blood flowing through our bodies and the air moving in and out of our lungs and Tabitha's soft, firm voice.

We were exercising to beat back the memories.

It didn't keep away the knowledge that Spencer had practically killed himself. It didn't keep away the bone-deep sadness that Leaf had been killed, and before him, we'd lost Mary, and ahead of us, there was more death. All of that settled deep into my DNA. It would never separate from who I was now.

The different exercises held the mind so still, it chipped at the walls I'd erected to protect myself from feeling anything. This was all we had now—each other, this cold cement room, this disease that both protected and imprisoned us. Our lives were bright dots in a dark night that blinked out for so many sad reasons.

Tears leaked down my cheeks in the last position. It spread us out on the cold floor, breathing in and out, slower each time, deeper each time. Sometimes I paused and wondered what it would feel like to stop, just stop it all. My arms and legs melted into the ground and became a part of the soil somewhere deep beneath this tomb. Under there it was dark, protected, lonely, and yet the peace of it called to me. I didn't want to understand what Spencer did. I did understand it.

THE BELL BUZZED and broke conversations like someone had shattered a vase. We returned to our cells. To the tomb within a tomb. I tried to shake off feeling trapped, but it hovered at the edge of my brain like the memories we all still fought back. The exercises helped a little but not completely.

As Tabitha promised, the cells locked for a few minutes. Enough time for them to check everyone was inside somehow. Cameras, binoculars, I had no idea what they used. The water pipes rumbled and Tabitha pushed in the cart of food alongside several guards. As soon as the uninfected left, the cells unlocked. A group of people went straight for the cart. My heart rate sped up as I wondered if it was first come, first serve, and whether there would be any food left by the time we made it down.

Instead, Feebs I sort of recognized from our first dinner unloaded the cart and began separating, chopping, and cooking breakfast for everyone. There was oatmeal, and a sort of spicy sausage, and cans and cans of beans. Hot coffee. It would have felt like a feast if not for Spencer's missing spot at the table. Everyone else talked quietly about what they could have done, had he really done it on purpose, why did he try to escape, if only they could have stopped him. There was nothing we could have done. He had decided.

Near the end of breakfast, Kern joined us. His shoulders were stooped in exhaustion and circles deepened the intensity of his dark eyes. Since our group was so new, he said, we would be assigned jobs within the jail. Outside chores were for those who had proved they could follow the rules.

I spent the day with Maibe, washing and scrubbing dishes under Tabitha's watchful eyes. Jimmy, Ricker, and Ano were sent to clean out the bathrooms. Dylan had once done some construction work so they set him on a few maintenance projects around the greenhouse with Kern. Corrina was sent to help with the laundry. I planned for how we might all sneak away to memorialize Spencer properly. They didn't seem to be afraid of us having knives, there was no shortage of utensils for meals—as we discovered while washing all of them after breakfast, lunch, and dinner that day.

I tucked a steak knife in between my jeans and skin. It would do the job I needed it for when the time came.

Everyone returned from their various outside chores, dirty, exhausted, but talking, and even laughing sometimes. The groups went their separate ways, some into the showers on shifts, others into their cells to change and wait their turn. The dinner ritual repeated itself: Tabitha reminding us to stay inside, the clang of the locking bars, the noises as the food was wheeled in, the release.

After dinner, Tabitha called all the Feebs out to the yard.

Spencer's body had been taken outside and rested next to a pile of dirt and a hole dug a few dozen feet away from the fence. Several other graves were marked. A sheet covered him from head to toe.

Two uninfected guards watched from the other side of the fence while two Feebs lowered him in with ropes. Tabitha said a few words on our side of the fence. I declined when Tabitha asked if I would like to say something on his behalf.

We returned to our cells and I waited until we would barely be able to make out our work before calling over Maibe and the boys. I figured by the time we were done everyone else in the building would know what we'd been up to, but I would deal with that later.

We whispered quietly to each other as the boys each raised a bare arm for my knife. I did Maibe last and then I handed the knife to Ano to do me.

Corrina walked into the cell and stilled when she saw our bloodied arms. I waited for her rebuke, but all she said was, "I'll do it for you."

Her voice shocked the knife out of Ano's hand. It clattered to the cement floor.

"I'll do it if you'll let me," she said.

"What are you doing?" Dylan said, walking in behind Corrina.

"Shh," Corrina said. "I'll explain later."

"We are remembering Leaf and Spencer," Jimmy said.

I picked up the knife and held it out, to Corrina, handle first.

The pain burst into my skin at her first cut and then turned into a burning glow that radiated all the way to my fingertips.

Spencer had a lot of letters in his name.

When Corrina was done she wiped the blade on her jumpsuit and then contemplated my arm. "You're running out of room."

A ball seemed lodged in my throat.

Ano let out a howl, drawn out, full of experience and pain. The rest of us joined in, though Dylan and Corrina did not. But at Dylan's bewildered look, Corrina grabbed his hand and squeezed it.

We let out another group howl, long and agonizing and loud. When our noise stopped bouncing back at us from across the jail, when the howls had died to whispers and then died altogether, when we opened our eyes, not realizing we had closed them, I said, "Now go to sleep, cockroaches. We've got early morning exercises tomorrow."

February

CHAPTER 21

The days here follow mostly the same pattern. Morning exercises with Tabitha. The cells lock, the cells open, we prep food, we clean up food. Repeat.

Not once have they let me or any of us outside. Not once during that first week did they bring us in for questioning or testing. I'd welcome getting tested right now. I'm going crazy keeping myself from bursting through those front doors. If I don't get out soon I might explode.

They take people away sometimes, but everyone comes back and talks about blood being drawn, mental intelligence tests, exercise tests, vitamin injections, more blood drawn.

Nothing like the fairgrounds.

Maybe things are different here. Maybe they really are looking for a cure.

AT THE BEGINNING OF THE FOURTH WEEK in the jail they took Dylan away, but no one noticed at first because the hot water had stopped working. There were shouts and cursing before breakfast from the people who discovered that fact firsthand.

Dylan came back that same day before dinner. The hot water did not. He found Corrina right away and kissed her. He looked relaxed, unharmed. "They only took blood and asked me some questions about how I got infected," he said at dinner, around what was now our regular table. Others joined us from time to time, to make conversation, check in on us, get to know us. I didn't really talk to them, not really, but the rest of the group did.

"Was it Sergeant Bennings?" Corrina asked.

"I didn't see him," Dylan said. "They've got a real lab here, professional equipment. And it's just like Tabitha said." He paused to shovel in another bite. Dinner had come in as raw potatoes and cans of gravy, along with barely enough propane to cook it all. The food was mind-numbingly hot and delicious.

"Everyone is working on something, the uninfected I mean, but on their side of the camp." He paused again for a drink of water and then glanced my way. "And there's a special cleanup crew. People who're allowed to go outside the fence and deal with any Vs causing problems."

Jimmy, Ricker, and Ano swiveled their heads in my direction, all three at the same time, like a comedy act.

"Don't look at me like that," I said. "We knew that already. Remember Kern?" I didn't say Spencer's name out loud but I didn't have to.

"Like what?" Ricker asked. "Like this is the perfect job for you and maybe it'll make you less grumpy if you're able to kill a few Vs every day?"

"What are you talking about?" I wasn't in the best moods these days, but considering the circumstances I thought I had been doing a pretty good job of keeping it together. I would never admit it to Tabitha, but the morning exercises were helping.

"You're a bit scary, Gabbi," Ricker said. "No offense." He held up his hands to ward off the mean look I gave him.

"And what do you think, Ano?" I said.

To his credit, he did not immediately answer, but then he said. "It's a good idea."

"I want to join," Maibe said.

"Absolutely not," Corrina said.

"Don't act like you can tell her what to do," I said, my blood rising.

"Don't ruin this for us!" Jimmy shouted. He had stood up. He was shaking.

I felt stunned. "What are you talking about?"

Corrina put a hand on Jimmy's shoulder. He shook it off. "I'm going to see if there's any more gravy."

"He likes it here," Corrina said.

"We see how you look at the fences," Ricker said. "You're thinking about running away."

"We're being held prisoner!" I said. It should have been the most obvious thing in the world to them. "We aren't supposed to be here. What about Dutch Flat? What about escaping?"

No one answered.

"Dylan said they didn't even hurt him," Ricker said. "They're really looking for a cure this time."

"You can't believe that. You can't. Not after everything. Not after what they did to Leaf."

"Even Leaf said it was an accident," Ricker said.

"Ano? Maibe? You can't possibly think—"

"I will go with the group," Ano said. "Stay here, go there. Die one way or die another."

I couldn't believe what I was hearing. A few weeks of calm, of food, of the safety being a prisoner gave us, and they were ready to give up? It made my head spin, how quickly things had changed. I didn't believe it. I couldn't believe it. They weren't stupid enough to think everything was going to be okay now, were they? "Maibe? What do you think?"

She looked uncomfortable with all the attention directed at her. She probably wasn't used to having her opinion count for much, but it mattered to me what she thought. No matter how many times I might have dismissed her out loud, deep down, I knew she was smarter than me. I knew she was worth listening to.

"I think it's been okay so far," she said, but she must have seen the crushed look on my face. "But that doesn't mean things will stay that way."

"It's not like you're going to get a chance to escape anytime soon," Dylan said. "They're not letting anyone out unless they trust them. We're not exactly high on their trust list."

"It hasn't been so bad yet," Corrina said softly. "That doesn't mean I'm okay with it, it's just…I thought Tibby was giving us a line when she did her whole 'race for the cure' speech. But it seems like they really are trying."

"We're calling her Tibby now?" I said.

"Tabitha, then," Corrina said. She looked at me like she was worried about me. Like there was something really wrong with me and she wished she could fix it. "We thought maybe if you could get on their V team or whatever they call it—"

"We? You've all been talking about me? The problem that is me?"

Their silence was answer enough. My appetite disappeared. They thought I was going to ruin it for them. "They treat us like criminals and you're okay with that? You're really okay with that?"

"They need us," Ano said. "They need us to help find the cure. They need us to fight the Vs for them. It's too dangerous for them otherwise."

"It's different here," Dylan said. "When I was working with Sergeant Bennings, they treated anyone infected like they were rabid animals, like—"

"—we've turned into zombies that deserve to die," Maibe said it like it was fact.

Jimmy returned with a token amount of gravy. He didn't look at me.

Corrina pressed her lips together, ready to protest the word zombie like she'd done a million times in the past, but then tilted her head. "We do sort of look the part," she said with a toothy grimace.

The tension broke. I surveyed our table. I'd gotten so used to how all of us looked. Wrinkled. Sickly transparent skin that, even on the darkest of us, veins and bruises snaked up and around and across. Bloodshot eyes, achy joints. Crippled memories.

"I vant to eat vour vraaaaaiiinns," Ricker said suddenly. He lifted up his hands like two cat claws and swiped at Jimmy's head.

"Zombies don't talk like that, idiot," Jimmy said. "That's a vampire. And vampires don't eat brains."

"I vant to eat vour vraaaaaiiinns," Ricker said louder, moaning it out and grabbing Jimmy's head with both hands.

"Get off!" Jimmy said.

Maibe started giggling. Ricker turned to her in appreciation and did his little comic relief act for a third time while Jimmy fought him off.

"Not funny!" The look of horror on Jimmy's face sent Ano into laughter.

"You know I hate vampires…zombies…whatever you're supposed to be!" Jimmy said.

That sent the rest of us laughing, even me, until Jimmy swiped Ricker's bowl and licked it clean.

"Hey!" Ricker said, dropping his arms and his zombie/vampire expression.

"Yum," Jimmy said. "If this is what brains taste like, I could be down for this."

"That was the last of it!" Ricker said.

"Sorry, not sorry," Jimmy said.

"You will be." Ricker pushed Jimmy onto the floor, but Jimmy grabbed Ricker's shirt and took him down too, and then they wrestled. Ano laughed again and pushed Ricker in the back to unbalance him just as he was about to pin Jimmy.

I left them that way, laughing and fooling around and forgetting for a moment this new world we all lived in.

Tabitha walked by. I followed her outside to the pit toilets. I thought about Jimmy's outburst. I thought about what Maibe said. I thought about how they looked—full of food, well-rested, and ready to stop running. "I want to join the team that goes outside. The ones that go after the Vs."

She stopped in mid-stride and replaced her foot on the ground. She turned to me with the same care. She led us in the exercises every morning after all. Even though she was older, there was a power in the way she carried herself. She hid her strength, but you could see it when she moved in the mornings. She scared me a little bit.

I forced myself not to squirm under her gaze, but it was a close thing. She had those eyes that seemed to pierce into you, to probe for weakness or for faintness of heart or for some sort of darkness. A smile curled at her lips. She brushed away a loose strand of hair. "Why should they trust you?"

That was the question she asked, those were the words she spoke, but I knew what she was really asking was why SHE should trust me.

"You probably shouldn't," I said. "I'm a runaway. I don't follow the rules. I mess simple things up. I get really angry and lose my temper a lot."

She raised her eyebrows.

"But I don't mind taking chances. When I care about something, I can be pretty loyal." Even as I spoke the words to convince her, I knew how dumb they must sound, but I couldn't force out any promises about dying for her cause or fighting to the death or standing up for what was right no matter what. They would be lies and she would know it.

"Why would I want a runaway on the team?"

And even as she said 'the team' I knew somehow she meant HER team and my curiosity soared into the atmosphere. "I probably know better than a lot of other people on the team about how to move around without being seen, how to hide, how to run, how to fight."

She inclined her head in tacit agreement. "Yes, well, this might be true. For one reason or another, those of us infected and brought here have very little military background, if any. Father's father, that sort of thing."

"I don't have any code of honor," though even as I said the words, I realized I clearly did, it just wasn't what many other people counted as honorable. "I'd be willing to take jobs no one else wanted as long as I knew why, as long as it made sense to me. I know what it's like to live on barely any food and to sleep anywhere I can and to still take care of business."

"How many Vs have you killed?"

"A dozen—at least," I said. "With my own hands or a cross-bow or bat. I don't mind getting my hands dirty."

She nodded.

"I would kill uninfect—"

"—Hush," Tabitha said.

I stopped and pressed my lips together. I looked up at the guard towers. Surely they were too far away to hear any part of our conversation. But then I remembered the locked cells. How did they know everyone was inside if they didn't have a way to monitor us? Tabitha's face was like stone and my shoulders sagged. I had almost convinced her and then I misstepped and I would be stuck inside washing dishes and following the rules for the rest of my life.

A couple with their kid in tow passed us on the way to the bathrooms. They greeted us with warm hellos and she nodded pleasantly in their direction. Once they had disappeared behind the bathroom's plywood walls, she stepped closer to me and I flinched.

"Kern is team leader," she said in a low voice.

"Okay."

"You will have to work with him. Follow his rules."

A sour taste filled my mouth, like I'd just bit into a slice of lemon. It was hard not to look at him during dinners. It seemed like I kept catching his eye no matter where I was or what I was doing and I hated that I kept looking. I hated how an electric shock went through me every time he looked back. He was a traitor, he was a liar. He was a lot like me.

"This is nonnegotiable," Tabitha said.

"Done," I said and tried to say it like I meant it.

"If he says your actions put other team members in danger, if you jeopardize your missions, I'll throw you off the team."

"How is it that you are the one who gets to decide such things?"

She looked at me as if I were stupid.

Instead of getting angry I felt embarrassed. "Forget it," I muttered. I paused, took a deep breath, and then locked eyes with Tabitha and said, "I will work with the team. I will follow directions."

If Spencer or Leaf could hear me now, they would have been rolling on the floor, holding their bellies, laughing so hard. It was good Ano wasn't around to hear me. Tabitha didn't know how ridiculous the promises I just made were—for me. She might guess, but she didn't know. Maybe it wouldn't be that hard once we were outside the tomb that the jail had become.

Tabitha nodded and said, "I'll see what I can do."

I could do it. I could follow Kern's directions.

I could probably do it.

Shit.

CHAPTER 22

IN FEBRUARY HERE IN NORTHERN CALIFORNIA, the weather lets you taste the sunshine of summer without its heat. It also never let a runaway forget the cost—February still dropped below freezing sometimes. We felt that in the cells. No heat except for our bodies tucked under a few wool blankets. But even though it was warm the way we slept—all in a pile of bodies—I always got up before the rest. I couldn't stand to be in the cell closet for longer than I had to.

Today, I had decided to bring back the hot water.

I had seen the others collect various food waste containers to be dumped later. Some of them were transparent milk jugs, five-gallon buckets, even some tubing.

I needed something dark to collect heat, and then a second person to help me set up. That's where Kern came in. I was going to prove to Tabitha that I deserved to be on the V team.

Kern sat at the table with a group of his teammates.

Sometimes they went out in the mornings and didn't come back for several days. When they returned from the outside, people would shake their hands and nod their heads in respect.

I wanted that respect. I wanted that specialness. I wanted to go outside.

I swallowed my pride and took my plate of food and walked past Maibe and Ano and the rest of our group—who all tried not to look like they were watching but weren't very good at hiding it—and I sat at Kern's table.

The conversations stopped for a moment. They glanced at me, at each other.

Kern paused, a piece of cheese halfway to his mouth.

I tried to smile but grimaced instead.

He set down the piece of cheese. "What can I do for you?" He enunciated each word.

"I need your help."

He raised an eyebrow.

"It's to help out everyone here."

"And why would you want to do that?" he said in this maddeningly asinine tone. "You've made it pretty clear you're disgusted—"

"I never said—"

"I'm pretty sure you did."

"Let me finish!" I said in too loud of a voice, half rising off the bench.

Conversations stopped again. Someone snickered at the end of the table.

"Neil Madsen," Kern said and the guy shut up, "this is Gabbi. Gabbi, Neil." Neil's face was thin, gaunt at the cheeks as if he continually sucked them in. His nose was bulbous and red and his long neck stuck out of his shirt like a sickly giraffe.

Neil nodded at me, not in a good-natured way, more as a flinch from the elbow he got from the woman sitting next to him.

"Leave it, Lilia," Kern said.

Lilia looked older than Neil, maybe middle-aged, but it was hard to tell because of the Feeb skin. Her thick, golden brown, curly hair hung on her head like a helmet and she didn't even try to smile.

"Over there is Enos and Julian." They were like caricature opposites of each other. Enos was thick and burly and muscled. Julian was so thin and he hunched his shoulders making his whole body look warped like a bow.

Enos rose up to shake my hand but stopped midway, his arm in the air. His eyes dilated. "You look so much like my—"

Julian punched Enos hard in the shoulder. "Snap out of it."

Enos's eyes refocused. "I got a fresh dose of the Lyssa virus while we were outside yesterday." He showed me the ugly gash on the back of his neck. "Still shaking it off I guess. Sorry."

"Don't worry about it," I mumbled as I tried to keep the yearning out of my voice. They'd gone outside, away from this tomb.

"Go ahead, then," Kern said.

I settled back and took a calming breath. I knew more than just this table watched. I knew Tabitha must be watching too.

"It seems to me that no matter how much we don't like each other—"

"I never said I didn't like you." He smiled an impish grin.

I gritted my teeth even as I noticed that his smile set off his brown eyes and lightened the exhausted lines of his forehead.

"You're not going to make this easy," I said.

He crossed his arms across his chest. "I'm going to make this the opposite of easy."

"So you know I want to be on the team. Did Tabitha tell you?"

"In fact, she did not. But why else would you be talking to me right now? I don't see you as the kind of person happy washing dishes every day. I'm surprised you lasted this long."

"I do have people here I care about. You've seen how good I am at protecting what I care about. I recall you were on the receiving end of my help not so long ago."

Kern nodded. "Fair enough. So, how can I help you be on the receiving end of my help?" His face held a leer in it. Nothing too obvious, nothing I could exactly put my finger on, but I felt it all the same. I almost lost it. I clenched my fists. He was doing this on purpose just to see if he could get a rise out of me. I would not give him the satisfaction.

"I'm not going to talk about it here," I said, realizing this was partly an act Kern was doing for the table. I headed to the bathrooms. A wolfish whistle and laughter followed me and Kern outside.

I pushed through the double doors and the cold hit me deep in the chest. The guards faced me. It was hard to believe they were protecting us when they did that. Footsteps shuffled next to me.

"All along the fence here." I waved my hand to the right of us. "And here too," I said, waving to the left. "And on the ground, and if we have any black cloth, like landscaper cloth, or black plastic, or—"

"What are you talking about?"

"Hot water," I said. "Or at least lukewarm water—for bathing or cleaning."

"Are you kidding me? We've already looked at the system. It's broken. It can't be fixed with what we have here. The propane they give us is barely enough to boil water for coffee in the morning."

"I'm not talking about fixing the system. I'm talking about going around it. Ignoring it all together. Pretending it was never there in the first place. Plus, it won't be hot water and it won't be every day, just on the sunny ones at first but later—"

"People are going to shit themselves if they get their hands on some hot water."

"Then they can clean themselves off with the water too."

Kern laughed. "I told her you were worth bringing in."

"What did you say?"

He winced.

"I thought it was your job to bring in any Feebs you found."

"Yeah, well, we make a lot of 'mistakes'. Most of the time. Feebs get away."

"But not my group. Not me."

He shrugged his shoulders. "Not you."

I stalked to the furthest point of the fence, to our makeshift graveyard for Spencer. His wooden marker would crack and splinter in the heat this summer. Eventually it would disintegrate and all that would be left was the hump of dirt that marked where his body lay. Even that would eventually settle and then he would be forgotten.

I rubbed the scabs on my arm.

Not forgotten.

I walked up to Kern—within inches. Our breaths intermingled, not smelling all that bad, considering. His brown eyes widened at my closeness. I could feel the heat from his body coming off in waves. His breathing shortened. Hell, my breathing did too. There was no denying the spark between us.

"So, will you help me with the hot water?"

"Of course." He swayed in my direction, as if to kiss me, but then caught himself.

I stepped back and socked him hard in the stomach. The air whooshed out of his body and he doubled over.

"What the hell is going on," he said between gasps as the blood rushed to his face.

"That's pretty much my question exactly," I said simply and then walked back inside to sounds of laughter from the guard towers. I returned to dinner, this time in my normal spot.

Kern returned a few minutes later. His face still red, he walked in as if nothing had happened. Neil jostled him in the ribs while making some sort of joke. The others laughed, but then Kern said something short that silenced them. He glanced my way and I held his stare to reinforce the fact that he was an idiot for thinking that helping me with a little hot water was going to get him out of hot water with me.

But then he smiled and I saw it was going to be a much bigger battle to make him pay. But he didn't know I had hardly any lines I wouldn't cross when it came to payback, no matter how much I had wanted to kiss him back.

"TELL ME WHAT YOU WANT to do about the hot water," Kern said.

I hid my surprise and tossed the damp dish rag onto the wash bucket. Maibe and I had washing duty again. "It's not that hard."

"Hot water?" Maibe exclaimed.

"Warm water," I said quickly. "Don't get your hopes up.

Lukewarm water."

Kern motioned me on. "Let's get on with it then. I don't have all day."

I explained about the materials I'd seen around the jail and what we still needed to track down. Then I explained the setup.

"That's it?" Kern said.

"It's not magic. It's just using infrared waves the sun is already producing for free. Someone else would have thought of it eventually."

"How do you know any of this?" Kern said. "I thought you were a runaway or a dropout or something."

"She's super smart," Maibe said. "She spent hours and hours in the library and—"

"Shut up, Maibe," I said.

She closed her mouth like a fish.

"You can't just go around telling people things. The less they know the better."

"Well, that's a sorry way to live," Kern said. "Nobody ever gets to know you? The real you?"

"Plenty of people get to know the real me." If the definition of plenty was Ano, Ricker, Jimmy, and now Maibe—and Corrina on my good days.

"I guess I'm not on that list."

I gave him my most patronizing smile. "Better luck next time."

"I don't give up easily."

"I've noticed," I said. "I didn't take you as very smart to begin with, so…" I shrugged.

Maibe's eyes widened. Kern smiled that damn smile of his and said, "We'll see."

By the time we finished, it was lunch, and we had scattered

dozens of transparent jugs of water across the yard. Kern was pretty much allowed to leave the jail when he pleased—after lunch he came back with rolls of landscaping cloth. We used this as a heat sink to help warm the water.

"Here, grab this corner," Kern told Maibe. She held the cloth flat as Kern unwrapped it from its paper barrel. She kept looking at him, as if about to ask something and then deciding not to.

"Just spit it out, kid," Kern said.

"Are they really looking for a cure here?" Maibe said.

Kern paused, then continued unrolling another section of cloth. "Yes."

I don't know why, but when he said it this time, part of me believed it. A spark of hope rose in me.

"But it's not going to work," he said.

"How do you know?" I said, not willing to give up the hope so quickly.

"What do you mean?" Maibe said.

"Think about it. So they find a way to make us not be sick like this anymore. So then we're like them again? We go outside and get bit and turn into a V?"

"The cure would make us immune," Maibe said.

"We'd get a vaccine or something," I said, "and we'd never be able to catch it again."

Kern shook his head. "The scientists have been working for over a year on it. There are too many variations. Even if they come close to finding something that will work, it won't be permanent."

I didn't know what to do. There were so many things wrong with what he just said. I couldn't process the cure stuff so I stuck on the other part. "Did you say a year?"

"But I only got infected in November," Maibe said.

"It happened to me in August," I said. "I thought we were some of the earliest cases. They said we were some of the first."

He looked up and then away. "This camp was set up a year ago. That's when I was infected," he said as if confessing some great sin. "They were fearing the worst in case they couldn't stop the spread. They were right."

"Whoa," Maibe said. "I didn't even think…how come…"

"This is as done as it's going to get," Kern said. He left Maibe and me to stare at each other in disbelief.

"He said a year." Had all of this been planned somehow? Did they know it was going to happen like this?

Maibe shook her head. Something bright flashed across Maibe's face, as if someone had flicked a mirror. She blinked and the flash disappeared.

I looked up at the guard towers, but none were turned our way.

"That was weird," I said.

"Yeah, well, Kern likes to make things weird," Maibe said quickly. She began dancing from foot to foot as if playing hopscotch.

"That's not what I meant—"

"I need to use the bathroom."

"You just went half an hour ago."

Maibe shrugged. "All this water makes me need to go again."

I looked around at our crazy array of buckets, bags, and black cloth. Maybe the sun had glinted just right off the water in one of the jugs.

Maibe disappeared into the pit's plywood walls.

I scanned what I could see of the camp. Two guard towers,

the edge of the fence that separated us from the uninfected side. The gap of space where the graves were. A flash of light again.

I went into the bathrooms. There was no one in any of the stalls, but a plank of plywood lay at a weird angle under one of the sinks. I kicked it and it moved.

"Maibe, what the hell are you doing?" I crouched on my hands and knees and pushed aside the plywood. There was just a big enough hole for me to crawl into. When I came through the other side, I was in this gap between the stalls. It backed up to a section of fence the guards couldn't see unless they came down off the towers and patrolled on foot. Maibe was there against the fence. Talking to Alden.

"Maibe, what the hell?"

She whirled around as if caught in the act of something she knew she wasn't supposed to be doing. She recovered and motioned me over.

"This is Alden." She nodded in his direction. He had Sergeant Bennings eyes. Blue, clear, cold. But he was all of thirteen or so. His blonde hair peeked through the green beanie he wore.

"This is going to get you killed if Sergeant Bennings finds out."

"He won't find out," Alden said. I looked at him more closely. He stayed far enough from the fence that Maibe couldn't possibly touch him, but he acted like he wished he could get closer.

"Then Ricker's going to kill you when he finds out."

"Who's Ricker?" Alden said.

"No one," Maibe said.

"Yeah," I said.

"Just like Kern is no one," Maibe shot back.

That shut me up.

"I don't have much time," Alden said. "I just wanted to give you this." He pushed a thin package through the fencing. It was a chocolate bar. He'd gotten her chocolate.

Maibe took it and thanked him.

He smiled and said, "Dr. Ferrad has a whole drawer full in her lab. She won't miss it."

"Dr. Ferrad is here? But she's the one who experimented on Leaf! How could you—"

"I know," Maibe said, cutting me off. "I've been asking Alden to watch her for us. He's been telling me what he knows about the uninfected side of the camp and I've been telling him about this side."

"You've been telling him about us?" I looked at her in disbelief. This whole time I thought she was this scared little girl who could be tough when she needed to but otherwise just wanted to be safe. Here she was proving me totally wrong. A little bit of pride rose in me.

"I trust him," she said.

CHAPTER 23

WHEN PEOPLE DISCOVERED the warm water that afternoon, there were shouts of joy and laughter. Kern gave me all the credit.

Tabitha looked at me in the sort of way you look at a dog you're considering at the animal shelter. "Come with me," she said. I followed her out the front of the jail. Tabitha waved to the guards and they returned the wave and let us through. Just like that, I was past the doors and outside.

We stopped in front of a ramshackle shed with spiderwebs that hung from the outside rafters.

The door opened and Kern blocked the opening.

"Good, you're already here," Tabitha said, walking by him.

I moved to follow, but he blocked my path. I waited, daring him to speak first. I would not. I would wait all day in silence and burn a hole through his jacket. He braced his arms on either side of the doorway as if it were the most natural thing in the world to take a break right in my way.

I looked up at him and gave him that look I saved for those really special people who liked to give you trouble while you were spanging.

"She's on the team today," Tabitha said.

Kern stepped aside and bowed. "Well, then, come right in."

I entered the room and saw candles lighting up the table. Shadows danced on the walls and across the half dozen people in the room. The same half dozen people at Kern's table the night before.

"The council wants us to raid another grocery store, but the next closest one is six miles away," said Kern.

Tabitha glanced up from the pile of papers on the table. "Our secondary target is here," Tabitha tapped the map.

"That's ten miles away," Kern said.

"Yes, but there's a grocery store on that same block," Tabitha said.

Kern nodded and folded up the papers. He held out one map to Neil and Lilia.

"Get her outfitted," Kern said to Neil.

Neil motioned me over to a metal trunk. It creaked open and I saw vests, gloves, knives, goggles, all arranged neatly in piles.

"This one should fit. You'll get a knife, but no guns. You're on lookout today with Lilia."

At the sound of her name, Lilia turned and examined me like a lab specimen.

"We'll see how you do and then see about getting you some other gear," Neil said.

"I don't need any other gear. It'll just slow me down."

He eyed me carefully and then shrugged his shoulders. "You were out there a long time then, before coming here?"

"A long time," I said.

"Well, we need all the help we can get."

Kern called for us to load up. We left the shed and stepped into the bright morning sun. There was a red minivan in the grass. Its side door was open and so was its trunk. The seats had been torn out and replaced with benches. Dust and dents covered the van from bumper to bumper. There was even a vent in the top. It wasn't our old van, but it felt a little bit like coming home.

"Gets great gas mileage," Lilia said and laughed.

"SO WHAT PART OF YOUR STORY was even true?" I sat alongside Kern in the back of the van. Lilia drove and Neil sat in the passenger seat. Two more of Kern's team sat in front of us. Enos, the older man with thick ropes for muscles, and Julian, thinner, younger, and nervous.

"What do you mean?" Kern said.

"I mean, your mom was obviously alive at the greenhouse. You weren't outside because you'd escaped, but because Tabitha or someone else had sent you out. Did you even have a sister?"

Outside, the houses that hadn't burned into ashes still looked decimated. There was no one to clean up the car wrecks, the dead bodies, the broken glass, the trash that flew everywhere in the wind. One side of the street might be totally gone, the other side mostly intact—the street itself creating a fire barrier. It was slow going around the obstacles. Sometimes those obstacles were Vs, dead from dehydration or some other catastrophe. But not all of them were dead. We were already forming a tail.

"I had a sister, but Vs got her, like I said. That much was true."

"Why did you act like you had escaped?"

"We'd tried telling others about the camp at first, but it had always gone badly. They didn't believe us, thought it was a trap. People died." He paused, looked out the window. "So we changed our tactics."

"It WAS a trap."

He didn't answer.

"Why are you telling me all of this now?"

He looked at me with a hooded expression. "There's a lot more going on here than you know."

"I could've guessed that."

He shook his head. "You don't even know. My mom was a big player before she got infected. She's pissed at how they've been treating her."

"She seems so in control," I said.

"Yeah," Kern said. "Sure seems like it."

Lilia stopped the van. "We have arrived."

Before I could ask anymore questions, Kern slid open the door and jumped out. "Neil, you're with me."

The contrast from dark to light blinded me.

"Everyone else does as Lilia says. Food first, medicine second, everything else third," Kern said. "But for God's sake, pick up some decent spices this time."

We were in an empty parking lot of a little corner grocer, the ethnic kind. Indian, it said. Saliva kicked up in my mouth because even though I hadn't eaten much of that type of food, I had tasted fresh naan once. Buttery, fluffy, gooey on the tongue.

"Enos has watch outside. Gabbi, you're with me and Julian," Lilia said.

"I thought Kern wanted me outside," I said, forcing my mind

away from the bread memories.

"I'm not having you watch my back. You're inside with us where I can see you," she said.

"That's fine with me." I smiled, showing her my teeth.

She grunted.

"How big is the tail?" Enos said.

"Too big," Lilia said. "Get moving."

We hurried to the market. One window had already been bashed in. The glass shards crunched underfoot. The interior of the shop smelled wonderful in spite of the underlying layer of rot. Some food had gone bad—a back section of prepared foods that had turned into a black mess. We loaded cans and jars and spice packets into boxes we carried out to the van under Enos's sentry. Lilia pointed out a few labels to me saying they were Tabitha's favorite so make sure to grab them.

I crouched next to Julian on the floor and handed him jars of tikka masala.

"Don't know why she said it's Tabitha's favorite," Julian whispered, a hint of a smile in the dim light. "It's pretty much my favorite, and Kern's favorite. We won't be leaving any of these behind."

"I haven't tried it," I said.

"You'll be in for a treat then for dinner tonight."

I handed him another jar. "Hey, guess what?"

"Hmm?"

"I don't have to wash a single stupid dish today."

A smile appeared on Julian's lips. "Yeah, I had that job when I first came to camp too."

"How did you end up here?"

"Don't remember. Got sick—fell into the fevers, you know,

and then woke up in camp."

"So what are Kern and Neil doing?"

Julian's hand froze midair, then he grabbed the jar, fit it into the last slot and closed the cardboard flaps. "Stuff for Tabitha." He jumped up and walked the box out of the market, then returned with an empty one. "Here," he said. He pointed to the next aisle over. "Go pack those chickpea flour boxes."

Suddenly, there was a pop-pop-pop outside.

"They're here," Enos said, running inside.

We packed up and scrambled into the van. Kern and Neil hadn't yet returned, but that didn't seem to worry Lilia. She drove the van in a donut and pealed out of the parking lot, sideswiping one of the Vs who came at the passenger side at a dead run.

She slammed on the brakes. I flew forward and hit my cheek against the driver's seat. Enos crashed into me, bending my back into an awkward angle. Lilia was yelling.

Enos grunted and pushed himself off. I unwound and turned upright. Black spots dotted my vision. I shook my head, trying to clear them. It didn't work. I realized the black dots weren't in my mind, but were the faces of all the Vs that had surrounded the van.

"Where did they all come from?" Enos said. "There shouldn't be this many. We cleared this area two weeks ago."

Lilia's hands shook on the steering wheel. She turned around, her face white and splotchy and webbed. "We're going to get trapped. We have to get out before—"

"We're already trapped," Enos said. "Lilia, snap out of it. Breathe it out."

Lilia's reached for the door handle. I shouted for her take her hand away. Enos and I scrambled for the door at the same time, getting in each other's way. She was having a memory-rush. She would open the door thinking the Vs were still far away but they were right outside, eager to tear her apart. Enos and I fought to untangle ourselves.

Julian hooked her around the neck and pulled her out of the driver's seat. I slammed the lock down so that even if she tried the handle it wouldn't work.

Lilia gasped for air in Julian's arms. "I'm okay. I'm okay."

Julian released her. My chest heaved. Enos was catatonic staring into the hazel eyes of a V just on the other side of the window. He reached out to touch her chin. I slapped him hard on the cheek. His head flew to the side and the dazed look cleared from his eyes. We were all present now. We hadn't died yet. We were still surrounded by Vs.

Lilia rubbed her neck. "We could shoot our way out."

"We should wait for Kern and Neil to come back," Julian said.

Enos shook his head. "Shooting will draw more of them. Kern and Neil don't have enough ammo."

"Then what do you suggest," Lilia said, a snarl in her voice.

Enos didn't respond.

I looked up at the vent. If it worked once, why couldn't it work again? "We go through the vent."

Everyone looked up.

"I won't fit," Enos said.

"We don't all need to go," I said. "Just one of us."

"And then what, genius?" Lilia said. "Do a dance on top of the roof as they swarm?"

"And then I make enough noise to draw them away."

"We should wait for Kern and Neil," Julian said. "They'll

show up and distract them."

One of the Vs punched the back windshield. Dozens of cracks streaked through the glass. Enos pushed himself down onto the floor.

"We can't wait," I said, feeling sick to my stomach and also exhilarated. This was what I was supposed to do—go outside, fight for my life, take chances, feel alive again.

Lilia looked from Enos to Julian and than to me. She threw up her hands. "It's your life."

They boosted me through the vent. I scrambled onto the metal top, parts of it sinking under my weight and then popping back out. I tried to tell the different between now and before. Maibe's pink sweatshirt seemed to flit around, first near the van, then further down the street. I pinched myself. She wasn't here, it was a ghost-memory, it wasn't real.

I took a running leap off the roof and reached for the bat strapped to my back. I grabbed at air. There was no bat, I'd left it in the van. I tumbled into a somersault. The ground scraped up my bare arms. The moans and shrieks paused, shifted. The mass of them had turned. They had surrounded the van three or four deep. Some looked freshly infected—angry red wounds that wept yellowish fluid. Others looked near death, their skin drawn tight around their faces, but loose everywhere else. They came at me as a mob. I jumped to my feet and reached for the bat again and cursed at myself and Lilia and everyone else in the van for pushing me through that vent without a weapon.

The three of them peered at me through the front windshield. As soon as the Vs were clear Lilia gunned the van. The tires screeched and rocks flew from underneath as she drove away. Two Vs separated from the mob and shambled after the disappearing van.

They'd left me.

Part of me was actually surprised. I had hoped—

No time for that now. I ran from the Vs, across the parking lot. I veered back to the store we'd ransacked for supplies. The Vs veered with me, so sharp and precise. There should be a back door. I could lose some of them through the aisles, come out the back, maybe climb the roof or find another vehicle that worked—

I was grabbed around the ankles and I went down hard. My chin split open and the hot gush of pain flooded my brain for long seconds. I twisted around and beat at the V around the head. His fingers clawed into my legs and reopened my wound. His nails were long and yellowed. His teeth brown and disgusting. He bit into me and I howled and kicked away, still on my back.

Two other Vs caught up and circled me, blocking out the light. I screamed again and fought with my teeth and feet and hands. I got past them but a third caught me and slammed me to the ground again. I was so tired. So hot. I turned my head to the side. There outside the store was my father, sitting on a bench. Red-faced, jeans ripped at the knees. He was tapping his fingers on his thigh.

Tap-tap-tap. Tap-tap. Tap-tap-tap. Tap-tap.

Again and again.

He smiled like this was what he'd expected because he always knew I wasn't strong enough to make it in the real world.

Fury gave me strength. I would not let him see me give up. He would not get that satisfaction.

I kicked out until I heard a crack and the V's grip loosened. I scrambled up. I stopped.

The Vs were dead in piles around me. Blood seeped from bullet holes. My father's ghost-memory vanished from the bench. Neil and Kern were there. Behind them the van waited, engine running, door open, cardboard boxes spilling medical supplies onto the ground.

CHAPTER 24

"WHAT HAPPENED?"

Everything was dark and the voices spoke as if from a distance, as if muffled by something.

"We said you'd be coming back. We told her to wait."

"She didn't listen."

"If she wanted to risk her life, what was that to us?"

"We got out of there because of her."

Tires screeched. I tumbled around. My mind spun. I tried to open my eyes. They felt so heavy.

I WOKE UP FROM THE FEVERS inside one of the cells. It reminded me too much of a closet. I turned over and threw up from the side of the cot. Tabitha shifted on the chair next to me and wiped a damp cloth on my forehead. I raised my hands, but ropes stopped them. My feet were tied up too. Not so tight as to cut off circulation, just tight enough to keep me from hurting anyone during my fevers.

"Congratulations," Tabitha said. "People are raving about the food you brought back."

"Is everyone okay?"

She hesitated. "Enos didn't make it."

"Oh." I wished I could feel bad for him, but I hadn't really known him.

She dipped the rag back into a bowl of water. "Everyone's talking about how you went all Amazon warrior out there."

"It's Maibe's fault," I said, half-smiling.

"How is it Maibe's fault?"

"I was just following in her footsteps." I explained about the broken-down van.

"Interesting. Maybe I'll talk to her next—"

"No," I said, sitting up. The ropes twisted at my wrists. "She's too young."

Tabitha picked up the rag again and squeezed out the water. The drops pinged back into the bowl. "That's all right, then. Not Maibe." She looked over. "What about you?"

Ano sat at the end of the bed. He patted my foot under the sheet. He'd come to stay with me during the fevers. We never left each other alone.

He shook his head. I relaxed.

Tabitha set down the rag. She smiled but it felt fake. "I wanted to make sure you were going to be okay. Rest up now. We've cleaned the wound. You even got some ointment on it. Lucky you. Take your time." She stood up and left the cell.

At the entrance, Kern rushed up and stopped her. He glanced at me and the ropes that bound my ankles and wrists. I wanted to apologize for Enos even though I couldn't remember what happened.

Ano moved into the chair Tabitha had left. "I'm glad you came back alive."

"The Vs are mobbing one of the gates," Kern said calmly. "Two people have already died."

"Which gate?" Tabitha asked.

"On the uninfected side."

"All right." Pause. "Is she ready?"

"She'll have to be," Kern said.

"Do it."

Kern left and shouted out an alarm. Even from my cell I felt the panic from his words spread through the jail like lightning. Ano tapped the code for question mark on my ankle. I gave him a look that said: how the hell should I know?

"Who was killed? Was it my boy?" a woman shouted up.

"What about my mother? Is she still alive?"

Others began shouting out names and questions. Almost everyone had family on the uninfected side of the fence.

"Untie me," I said. "I can help."

Before Ano could move, Tabitha took a knife from her belt and slashed through the first rope.

IT WAS AFTERNOON. The sun was pale and a bank of clouds was dropping a light mist onto us. There were no guards to monitor our movements, no locks to keep us contained—as if our side of the fence had been abandoned altogether in the face of this greater threat, which was probably the truth of it.

The mist chilled my face into numbness. The thick metal

doors of the jail closed behind me. I was in the middle of the group, near Ricker and Ano and Maibe. I couldn't see much over the heads of those ahead of us. First a parking lot cracked and eaten up by weeds, fencing and barbed wire further off in the distance, several buildings.

We ran for the gate that separated the sides. Some of the Feebs sprinted, I guessed, to find their loved ones.

Instead of staying with the group, Kern went the opposite direction.

"Where's he going?" I asked Tabitha.

She looked at me with a shrewd gaze and said, "He is following directions. Can you?"

I shut my mouth against an angry retort and ran to catch up with the group.

I heard the gunfire long before I saw the battle. My adrenaline shot up and my focus narrowed. The gunfire became louder. All along the twenty-foot-tall fences people were shooting at the Vs. Parts of the fence seemed dangerously twisted and ready to break open from the mass of flesh building up against it.

Groans and grunts and screams drifted through the air. Ricker looked at Maibe with a raised eyebrow and said, "What do they think we can do here?"

A Feeb motioned us to an open shed. Suddenly Feebs were handed weapons. Bats, sticks, shovels. When it was my turn, I peered into the gloom of that dark shed and saw Alden decked in head gear and gloves, handing out weapons.

There, in the corner, a familiar shape leaned against the wall. A crossbow.

I brushed past him and even though he was suited up he jumped away from my touch as if I had burned him. I hefted the crossbow's familiar weight onto my shoulder. Then I ran for the part of the fence that looked most in danger. Dozens of Vs pressed in, bowing it as if it were made of plastic. These Vs looked like zombies. Slashed clothing, deep wounds, hair full of mud and leaves. The Vs swarmed the fence. For every V that fell away, another replaced it.

I took up a position on the line, and too late realized I was next to Sergeant Bennings. I swallowed the riotous anger that filled my throat and threatened to take me over like a V. My first arrow sunk deep into the forehead of a woman in her forties with a torn shirt that exposed a dirty bra underneath. She crumpled sideways to the ground.

I notched another arrow but before I released it, I noticed that Sergeant Bennings stared at me through his mask.

I let the arrow fly and it buried into the neck of a screaming V.

Sergeant Bennings used a sword to skewer a V through the links. The stench of entrails gagged me.

I used up all my arrows and then grabbed the bloody shovel of a Feeb who had been torn to pieces after getting too close to the fence. All I could do was use the stick side to push them back. A futile gesture except it gave Sergeant Bennings and the others with real weapons extra time.

What felt like hours later, but was probably minutes, the Vs finally stopped replacing themselves. And then it was over.

I was covered in blood and gore. A few flies buzzed around in spite of the cold. I found Ano, Ricker, and Jimmy further down the fenceline, also covered in gore. "Have you seen Maibe?" I asked.

Ano and Jimmy shook their heads. Ricker slumped down.

"What happened?" I said sharply.

"Got infected again," Ricker said.

"The V grabbed his stick and pulled him too close to the fence," Jimmy said. "We jumped in and beat it off, but it had already taken a chunk out of his arm."

"Get him back before the fevers kick in," I said. "You know how this works."

They led Ricker off to the jail to endure another round of fevers. I was lucky I'd been bandaged up so well otherwise the blood on me would have gotten inside and renewed my fevers too.

Further on, a crowd of Feebs kneeled and gathered at one end of the field. Most, Feeb or not, seemed to be wandering around in a daze, but this group was different, intent on some sort of task.

I hurried over and saw Dylan flat on the ground, his leg a grizzly line of bites. Corrina tended to it. His flesh was even paler than normal. Sweat ran off his forehead. He whispered and his eyes fluttered open and closed. Memory-fevers always hit hard and fast.

Two Feebs jogged over and spread out a sheet. They moved Dylan onto it and carried him back to the jail.

An uninfected woman yelled out. She sat on the ground and cradled a bloody hand in her lap. Her face mask was streaked with blood on the ground next to her.

One of the Feebs said, "It's the only way, Helena. You know how this goes."

She blubbered something about not wanting to die, not wanting to turn, not understanding why this was happening to her.

"It's not so bad," the other Feeb said. "We'll get you through it."

She sobbed softly. Even I could see the alarming flush of her cheeks and the twitch of her injured arm. Finally she mopped her tear-streaked face with her good hand and lifted her head to stare at the two Feebs. "Do it, then."

One of the Feebs took out a cleaning kit and painstakingly disinfected Helena's wound, then did the same to the other Feeb's uninjured thumb. Then he took out a knife and made an incision on the thumb, collected the blood into a syringe and injected it into Helena's arm, just above her wound.

When he was done and had packed up the kit, he moved onto the next uninfected, now infected, who would join us on the Feeb side of the fence.

Helena's blood donor sat next to her on the dirt, holding her around the shoulders.

"It's not so bad, especially when the memories are good ones. And there's ways to control the bad ones, ways to help manage the nightmares. At least now the family won't be so split apart."

"Dear brother," Helena said. "We will still fight like cats and dogs, there just won't be a fence to separate us now."

He hugged her a little tighter. "There are good people on the Feeb side."

"There are good people on this side too," Helena said.

"I know," he said quietly. "Come on, let's get you to a cell before the fevers hit."

He steadied her on her feet, but after only a dozen steps she collapsed and he carried her through the gate that separated the two sides.

Five other uninfected were laid out on the ground in various states of injury and all were receiving some form of the 'kit.' I moved on and finally found Maibe at the shed, talking to Alden as quietly as was possible when someone stood several feet away from you. Blood streaked her clothing and her face. Her hands were crusted with mud and more blood. "Where were you?" I said.

"Fighting," she said almost quizzically in reply.

A cold shadow fell over me. Sergeant Bennings. The sword was at his waist. He was covered in blood from head to toe, but his gear was intact. Two men also in medical gear stood behind him with rifles and a pole with a loop at the end.

"Set aside the crossbow and come with us," Sergeant Bennings said.

My hands tightened around the crossbow, not that it mattered anymore. It was out of arrows. "What are you going to do?" I set down the weapon.

One of the soldiers wearing heavy rubber gloves yanked my arms in front of me. A plastic zip tie cuffed my hands.

Maibe moved, a protest on her lips, but froze when the sergeant's pistol leveled at her.

"Dad," Alden said, stepping between the two of them.

"Step away from my son. Do it slowly. Do it now."

Maibe trembled like a leaf about to fly off a tree. She took a step away, and then another. Alden's mouth froze in a wide 'O.'

Sergeant Bennings grabbed Alden. "Are you scratched or bitten or hurt?" There was real concern in his eyes.

"I'm fine."

"You are not supposed to be here. You were supposed to stay safe in your room—"

"I'm not going to do that while everyone else is fighting. I'm no coward," Alden said, even though his medical gear was pristine. He might have handed out weapons but he didn't do any fighting.

"I know you're not. I know it. But since your mother…You're all I have left."

"I have to help. I can't just sit by and let everyone else do the work for me!"

Sergeant Bennings brushed a hand through his no-longer-military-length haircut. "You're right, but not her." He jerked a thumb at me. "This one killed one of my guards."

Those last few words brought back the man on stage under the lights, the water as it streamed off me, the way his chest had bloomed with blood, the moment I'd realized Leaf was dead. I swayed on my feet and darkness began to close in.

"I wasn't helping her. I was helping Mai—"

"Throw her in solitary. Lock down the jail."

They tried to drop the rope around my neck. I went crazy like a dog, like a V, to throw it off. I wondered if this was what Mary had felt.

I ran.

CHAPTER 25

I RAN THROUGH THE GROUPS still receiving the Feeb kit and
dodged into a nearby building. It wouldn't be long before they
caught up. I skirted around a secretary's welcome desk and
entered the back. Where there should have been offices, there
were rows and rows of cages. My skin was numb from the cold.
My fingers tingled. Were the cages really there?

I stepped forward. It was dark, but these cages were all metal,
these were not camouflaged with drywall. It wasn't a ghost-memory. These cages were real and they looked—occupied.

A screech like from a hawk pierced the air. I veered toward
it as if drawn by a siren. I didn't know where I was going but
I had to keep going.

Another screech. Everything was in shadow. One of the
shadows raced for me and threw itself against the bars. His
face materialized into a man. Someone who was no longer
anything but his rage, his fear, his hatred.

I stepped back, my skin prickling, my stomach cramping. This was a room full of caged Vs.

Shouts behind me. I raced down the aisles and tried to lose myself in them, but my movements stirred the Vs into a frenzy. It became a riot of noise. Shrieks, screams, bodies thrown against the bars, hungry arms reaching out to me. I swore my heart stopped beating, but then I realized the noise was good. The noise would cover any sounds I made.

"You have to leave now or not at all. Now is the time."

"I'm not ready. There's too much to prepare still. You gave me no warning!"

I crossed an aisle and stumbled into lantern light. Two people held lanterns over their heads. They hovered over a wheelchair. Both saw me at the same moment. Tabitha and Dr. Ferrad.

"What are you doing here?" Tabitha said, the light hollowing out her cheeks. "You can't be here."

"They're after me," I said. "They're going to lock me up. Help me."

"Turn off the lights," Dr Ferrad said. "They'll act like a beacon."

We were plunged into darkness. This did not quiet down the Vs.

"They're going to find us," Tabitha said, her voice floating in the darkness. "We have to hurry. Do you want out or not?"

A long pause. "I'm so close to a cure."

"Yes or no?"

"You know it's a yes. You know it. You're loving this."

Steps pounded a nearby aisle. Flashlights flared like lasers. "They're coming," I said.

"Gabbi, stay where you are. Dr. Ferrad, I've promised you—"

"Yes but what you're asking for in return—"

"There's no time for this," Tabitha said, frustration rising in her voice. "I already got what you needed."

I decided if they weren't going to do anything I could still run. I worked my way around where I thought the wheelchair was.

A shuffle. A screech.

"Hold her!"

"I need her!"

Something wrenched at my hair. I reached up, felt hands formed into claws. I stumbled backward and fell onto the ground. My head burned and blood dripped warm down my cheek. Tabitha turned on a lantern and flooded our section with light. A V stood over me, my chunk of hair and scalp in her hands. She flung it aside and reached for me.

I felt my world crash apart. Mary's black, straight hair was in mattes around her head. Her shirt was torn, her jeans practically non-existent. She had bruises everywhere and the IV snaked into her arm. She looked at me and didn't see me.

Panic threatened to choke my throat. Was it her or another V and I only wanted it to be her? My friend, the one who looked after me and made me laugh when I felt my lowest. The one who dreamed about living out in the country surrounded by friends. The one I had promised never to let down. The one I had abandoned when she had told me to run.

I wanted to cry out. I wanted to kill them. I wanted to gather her up in my arms. I wanted to die.

The blue light of the lantern washed out her skin. Her hands came around my neck and squeezed. She cocked her head as if listening to a small animal scream.

So I tried screaming. "Mary, it's Gabbi!"

I swore I heard my name from her lips. Her hands loosened.

I sprang out from under her, pushed her off. She snarled, her face turned into a hateful grimace that made me shudder.

Dr. Ferrad lifted a needle into the air and shot Mary up with something that made her crumple.

"Leave her."

"I'm not leaving without her! That was the deal," Dr. Ferrad said.

Tabitha raised the lantern higher and their faces turned into skulls with holes for eyes and mouth. Tabitha stared at Dr. Ferrad. There was a mean set to her chin and a dangerous gleam to her eyes. I shivered. I had never seen Tabitha like this before.

Shouts from far away. "Over here. Go around. Cut her off."

"I'll bring her," Tabitha said. "Kern is waiting. Go now or never."

Dr. Ferrad opened her mouth to argue. The blue light disappeared into the black cave of her mouth. She turned and ran away into the dark.

Tabitha dragged me up by the arm. Mary was crumpled at our feet. I struggled but she dragged me down the aisle.

Boots stomped up, flashlights blinded me.

"Trust me," Tabitha said in my ear. She pushed me so hard I fell forward onto my knees. "Here! Here she is!"

March

CHAPTER 26

THE LONG SLOW DRAWL of a train whistle interrupted my meager breakfast. I wondered at the noise that would surely draw Vs to it. I sat cross-legged on the cold floor and knew I would need to stretch to limber up again and be ready for whatever came next.

The first time they opened the door, they asked me what I knew about Dr. Ferrad disappearing. I said I didn't know anything. I asked about Mary, about the V. The guard said he didn't know anything, mimicking me, and laughing.

They had delivered two breakfasts since then along with some water for me to wash off the gore dried into a hard crust on my clothes and skin.

I didn't understand what had happened between Dr. Ferrad and Tabitha. What I did know was that Mary was alive and somehow they were all working together to get out of this prison. That was enough for me to take a chance that maybe Tabitha had a plan after all, that maybe she hadn't just sacrificed me and Mary so Dr. Ferrad could escape.

Four breakfasts later, they told me they weren't going to kill me. They were going to send me somewhere else, to be useful, they said.

Two guards came in full face masks and gear that covered them from head to toe to finger. They brought me out to the train platform—some plywood planks alongside the tracks. The uninfected wore face masks and covered their skin. There were other Feebs. Some I recognized from the jail, but others not at all.

And then I saw Corrina and Dylan. They stood ahead of me. Tabitha must have sent them. Somehow, they were here to help me escape. Then I saw how their hands were tied in front of them. Their clothing was dirty and torn. They were prisoners like me. My hopes deflated.

The air stunk of exhaust. The train was seven cars long with a yellow engine at either end. The engines had attachments almost like snowplows, like we'd put on Old Bully. Metal grates covered the windows of the cars and a sort of metal bumper ringed them as if to hold back a paparazzi crowd.

The next two cars were freight. There was one car left—it was also a passenger car. They marched all the Feebs inside this last one. A hazel-eyed guard zip tied the hands of any unbound Feebs as we entered. When it was my turn I held out clenched fists, palms facing down, and held my breath.

Leaf and I had researched once how to break free of different restraints after a bad run with bad people. When the guard wasn't looking, I'd be able to squeeze out my hands and get free.

There was debris everywhere on the floor. Papers, broken glass, bits of metal. The car stank of unshowered bodies and a thick musty smell. In the back, some of the chairs and tables had been replaced with a cage.

"Gabbi?" Corrina said, shocked to see me. They let me sit next to her and Dylan.

"What happened?" I said.

"What happened to you? We thought…we didn't know what to think. They wouldn't tell us anything." Corrina looked behind me, craning her neck. "Where's Maibe?"

"What do mean where's Maibe?"

"I thought…she disappeared when you did. I thought you must be together."

"Maibe's gone?" I slumped against the seat and tried not to listen to the voice deep inside that told me it was my fault.

"Sergeant Bennings' son is gone too," Corrina said. "Though we only know that by rumor. No one's talking about it."

I finally noticed something was wrong with Dylan. He moved in a rocking motion and sweat poured down his face.

"They'd locked down the jail since the V attack. Since you and Maibe disappeared. They slashed the containers you made to warm the water." She shook from anger, exhaustion. "We were going to escape this morning, or try to anyway, but Dylan got reinfected and we had to go back. We're lucky they're sending us to another camp instead of shooting us…."

She was talking about Spencer. I shook my head. "Forget it."

"We have to find a way to escape," Corrina said, but even as she said it her eyes slid to Dylan. There was no wheelbarrow this time.

"And the boys?" I said.

Corrina didn't speak for a long moment. "I don't know. They were back at camp still."

I flexed my hands against the plastic. Tabitha's words rang in my head, trust me, she'd said. I didn't know what her and Dr. Ferrad were planning, but they were both Feebs—that counted for something, right?

A soldier's boots stomped on board. I locked eyes with Sergeant Bennings. He wore his military cap and his cold eyes scanned the passengers, then settled on me again before flicking over his shoulder. "Bring it into the cage."

Two people in white medical suits, clear face masks, and gloved hands carried Mary in by a stretcher. She was strapped down at the head, arms, chest, and legs. She was out cold. Sergeant Bennings took several steps back as they lifted her inside the car and then into the cage. The entire train car tensed as if someone had brought a bomb on board.

Without thinking I stood up. "Mary." A blow to my stomach curled me over in pain. Black spots danced across my vision.

"Stop that!" Corrina yelled.

"Sit down," Sergeant Bennings said.

"Breathe, Gabbi, just breathe."

"I'm trying!" I said between gasps.

When my air came back I looked up. None of the other Feebs looked at me.

"I'm so sorry, Gabbi," Corrina said.

Tears pooled in my eyes. Blood roared in my ears. It was so simple: stay alive, don't get hurt, don't get caught. It was impossible. Maibe missing, the three of us caught, who-knows-what happening to the boys. And Mary. I had failed them all.

The cage shut with a clang. The white suits positioned themselves outside of it. Sergeant Bennings moved to the opposite end of the car next to the hazel-eyed guard. He picked up a phone and spoke into it as the train began to move west—into the valley. The floor underneath me shook and trembled.

There was an impact against the train. A thump, as if a body had slammed against the outside. A Feeb, an older woman, her clothing a tattered mess of layers and a long scratch running angry red down her cheek cried out. "They're coming," she said.

The guard peered out the window. His cap was jammed low over his forehead and I wondered why he had no problem being so close to the Feeb. He laid a gloved hand on her shoulder. She grabbed the hand with her own and he squeezed it.

"The bumper will take care of it until we reach the ledge."

"The ledge?" she said.

The train thumped its rhythm on the tracks alongside the counterpoint beat of Vs throwing themselves at us.

"Think of it more like a pit. Whatever crazies are nearby will run along with us and fall into a trap at the ledge. There's one at every stop. That's why they use the whistle."

"Oh," she said, on the verge of tears.

"Aunt Jewel, it's going to be okay," he said.

"Step away from her, soldier," Sergeant Bennings said, his voice deadly. He'd hung up the phone and his hand rested on a gun holstered to his belt.

The soldier left Aunt Jewel's side and returned to the end of the car, not meeting Sergeant Bennings' eyes. As if on cue, the train whistle sounded. There were more impacts against the train, but the car didn't flinch, even if the rest of us did. Then the impacts stopped.

I guessed we had passed the pit and imagined all those Vs trapped like sardines in a can, like how they had been inside the high school gym.

Hours later the train whistled again, and the unnerving thumps returned. Minutes after that, the train stopped. My legs had gone numb and my mind had gone blank. Tabitha had not rescued me. I cursed myself for believing that she would.

Feebs got on and off. The same hazel-eyed guard marked it against a clipboard. Two uninfected huddled at the other end for a few minutes, discussing something with the white suits in hushed tones.

Mary moaned and tossed around on her stretcher. The white suits opened up the cage and injected her. She settled down again. Saliva dribbled from the corner of her mouth. I felt sick to my stomach.

Fences glinted in the distance. So much noise. Voices, shoes, the train engine, shouts of recognition.

"What camp is this?" Corrina asked.

"Camp Potomac, I think," said Aunt Jewel. "They're supposed to be taking me to my youngest nephew. Said they found him hiding in the attic of a house they were clearing. My sister is… my sister turned V, but he's safe and they're bringing me to him and his brother."

I began to work my wrists against the plastic. I got my thumbs out, and then got the rest of my hands out.

Corrina hissed at me.

"What are you doing?" Sergeant Bennings voice. His eyebrows drew together and his skin wrinkled into deep grooves. The plastic of his mask glinted. He hadn't shaved in days.

"Hold out your hands," he said.

I held them out like I had before.

"No," he said. "One wrist on top of the other. Hands flat."

My stomach sank. I did as he told me. His gloved hands

tightened the plastic around my wrists. He used a second one to tie my wrists to the metal rail on the seat in front of me.

"Do you know where they are? Alden and Maibe?" Sergeant Bennings said. His gloved hand pinched mine.

"Even if I did I wouldn't tell you."

Corrina drew in a sharp breath. She didn't have to say anything for me to get that she thought I was acting like an idiot.

Sergeant Bennings drew out a knife. Corrina yelled. He slashed down, cutting the plastic he'd just used. He dragged me into the aisle by my hair. My scalp exploded into a thousand needles of pain as the wound Mary had made opened up again. People were screaming. Corrina stood up. He released my hair long enough to punch her in the gut. She fell over, gasping for breath.

He used his knees to hold me down, my back to the ground. I didn't understand why he hadn't shot me yet. One hand held my zip tied arms over my head and pinned to the floor. The other held a knife to my throat. The hazel-eyed guard hovered in the background.

"Tell me where Alden is." Sergeant Bennings said each word carefully as if he thought I wouldn't understand him.

"I. Don't. Know." I spit on his mask.

He used his knife hand to wipe off the saliva and then wiped it onto my shirt. The knife was back at my throat. "You know something." He pressed harder.

I couldn't swallow for fear the knife would bite into my skin.

I laughed even though I knew it would send him over the edge.

The gleam in his eye went all crazy bright.

There was a commotion near the front of the car. It distracted him enough that I tore my hands from his grip and punched him hard in the throat. He made a choking noise and the knife clattered to the floor. Corrina's bound fists flew through the air. They thumped Sergeant Bennings hard on the side of the head and he went down. I jumped up just as the hazel-eyed guard and the white suits jumped off the train car. Feebs crowded the windows.

I began tearing at the plastic with my teeth. Corrina grabbed Sergeant Bennings knife and slashed through the zip tie. I searched Sergeant Bennings pockets for the key to Mary's cage. Nothing.

"Find me two thin pieces of metal," I told Corrina.

She scrambled onto the floor, searching through the trash for what I needed. She brought back five pieces. I took two of the long ones and bent one in several places. I'd learned how to pick my first lock years ago. I would rake the lock on Mary's cage until it opened. Between Corrina and me, we would carry Mary and Dylan out of here.

I stopped. There was no way the two of us could carry out two people, especially two people who acted half dead and crazy.

Aunt Jewel shot up from her seat at the window. Her eyes were glazed and she began slapping at her shirt and pants and arms. "Oh, my God. Oh, my God," she screamed. The car of Feebs turned away from the spectacle outside the windows. She was in the grip of a memory-rush, anyone could see that. Before we could stop her, she ran out of the car, flapping her arms as if she were on fire.

In her mind, she probably was.

Then gunfire sounded in a quick burst.

The train window was smeared with skin oil and fingernail

scratches and it blurred the shapes outside. People in masks and dark clothing held weapons—AR-15s, hunting rifles, handguns. They aimed the weapons at a group of uninfected soldiers. One long rifle pointed at two people kneeling on the ground.

Aunt Jewel. The other, the hazel-eyed guard, kneeling between her and the gun. The gunmen, clothed all in black and wearing a cloth mask, hit the butt of the rifle against the side of the hazel-eyed guard's head. He crumpled to the ground. His aunt threw herself on top of him, crying.

People cried and whispered around me. Something about killing us all. Corrina was dragging at Dylan's arms, trying to get him off the chair, but he was still in a memory-fever. Mary was in her coma, strapped to a stretcher, sedated, almost peaceful. I bit my lip and a metallic taste filled my mouth.

I helped Corrina drag Dylan to the entrance, but a person in all black clothes blocked our way. I looked up into the masked face of one of the gunmen and felt a jolt. There was something almost familiar about the eyes.

"All infected off!" he yelled.

They forced us off the car, single file. Two of them dragged Mary out of the cage on her stretcher and she disappeared before I even realized they had moved her. We huddled in front of a freight car until they shouted orders for us to form a line. They cut the ties from our wrists and forced us to transfer supplies from the train to two pick up trucks.

We had filled the truck halfway when a siren sounded and the masked gunmen yelled for us to stop. Mr. AR-15 jumped on top of the truck roof and shot his weapon into the air, then whooped and shouted, "All infected, and those working with the infected, will pay for bringing this curse upon us!" The other gunmen jumped onto the trucks, firing off their own shots and yells.

I crouched, bracing myself for the moment when they would turn the guns onto us. As if my wish had made it happen, the AR-15 lowered and pointed at me.

"You are coming with us." He jumped off the truck and slammed his boots onto the boarding planks. My muscles seized with fear. I would explode into his face and gouge out his brown eyes and break the teeth in his smirking mouth.

"Gabbi, get up," Kern said quietly out of the lips of the guy with the AR-15. And I thought I might as well die there as anywhere else if Kern was going to start haunting me.

"Gabbi," he said in a whisper only I could hear.

I waited for Kern's ghost-memory to superimpose over the masked man's face. And it was there, in the brown eyes, the lines of his mouth, but his face stayed masked, and that wasn't how a ghost-memory was supposed to work.

Suddenly I was lifted from the ground and thrown onto the back of one of the trucks. Mary was on the stretcher next to me, surrounded by boxes. Dr. Ferrad had wanted Mary. They'd come back for her, and for me. They were here to save us after all. Cardboard corners dug into my side and thigh and arm and cheek. It was going to be okay. They were going to get all of us out. Corrina and Dylan and the nephew and his Aunt Jewel.

Gunfire erupted. Sustained bursts that made me want to clamp my hands over my ears. The engine rumbled and the truck's movement threw me flat on my stomach. Acid burned in the back of my throat.

Kern yelled above me. The truck lurched, then straightened out and gained speed. I pushed myself up and looked back and swallowed a scream.

The Vs had pushed over the fence and broken through. They ran for the train, for the trucks, for the people on the ground. For Corrina and Dylan. The Feebs and uninfected fought back with hands and feet and teeth. The truck raced away. Corrina stood up, her hair wild, her face blank, her hands weaponless, Dylan useless at her feet.

"Wait," I screamed. "You can't do this! You can't just leave them. You can't just—"

The truck picked up speed. A V jumped and held onto the edge of the bed. No one could hear me over the shots Kern's team fired at the Vs, but they hadn't seen this one yet. The shots were so loud they called Vs from blocks away. More Vs overwhelmed the tracks, the train, the cars. Corrina and Dylan disappeared underneath that darkness. They were dying. They would die. Kern and his people couldn't shoot fast enough.

The world closed in around me until all I saw was a narrow, dark tunnel of Vs running me down, hands reaching out, wounds, physical and mental, on display for all to see, ready to crush me under the weight of their hate and violence and despair.

The V held onto the side of the truck and pulled himself up. I held onto Mary's stretcher. She'd wanted a garden and a place for her friends to live all together. Her face was twisted now into a grimace. Her eyes fluttered open and closed. Leaves and twigs were tangled in her hair. The camp was gone, Corrina and Dylan were gone. The Vs were not. They still ran for us, from behind, along the sides, in front of us.

The V locked eyes with me like a predator does with its prey. He looked like a rather nice old man in cargo pants and a sweater that once might have been a coral color but now was caked in mud. I didn't know why I couldn't move. Corrina and Dylan were gone. Kern had let them die. I hadn't saved them. I hadn't saved Mary either. I wanted to die.

I held out a hand and the V grabbed it and pulled himself up. Kern slammed into his shoulder and pushed me out of the way, on top of Mary and a box corner that dug into my thigh. Mary screamed out, a horrific screech, and her hands reached for anything to grab and pull and tear apart but there was only empty air.

Kern flipped me over. I saw blue sky and the V tumbling off the side of the truck. Kern had unmasked his face. His hair was wild and his black vest ripped near the collar, showing bare skin underneath. In his eyes was a ferocious, bewildered light.

"What wrong with you?"

In reply, I bit his leg.

He howled. "What the hell, Gabbi?"

I didn't let go until he knocked me unconscious.

CHAPTER 27

I COULD NOT REMEMBER the last time I'd brushed my teeth. This bothered me. I opened my eyes to see if Spencer had snagged toothpaste like he'd promised. I sat up and brushed off the comforter. This motion made me dizzy. No, it wasn't the sitting up that made me dizzy. I was still moving. I was still on the bed of the truck. Cardboard boxes surrounded me, obscuring everything except for the blue sky and a pant leg at the edge of my vision.

Kern sat on the wheel well, rifle resting on his thigh. A strip of cloth was wrapped around the leg I'd bitten. He looked at me but didn't say anything. The driver took us fast enough down the street to outpace the Vs that followed and slow enough to avoid the wrecked telephone poles, crashed cars, dead bodies.

I remembered the train and Kern. Corrina and Dylan gone. Maibe lost. Jimmy, Ricker, and Ano still imprisoned in the camp.

Everyone on the trucks were dressed in black. Jeans, shirts, vests, shoes, all black. As if there'd been a clearance sale at the local Goth store. Some wore professional gear: a bulletproof vest, a utility belt, military-style boots with the pants tucked in. They had their masks off now and I recognized them. Neil and Lilia and others. They were Tabitha's team.

"I'm sorry I hit you. You wouldn't let go." Kern maneuvered around the boxes and stood next to me, one hand holding the truck railing to keep himself steady. Yet another Kern stood over the woman and her nephew, and another Kern took off his mask and stood over me while I let the V grab me.

"Are you okay?" Kern asked.

I raised my fist to punch him. He grabbed it halfway in the air and held it. We rocked in the same direction when the truck took a sharp turn around a crushed mailbox. Every few seconds a shot rang out when a V got too close.

"You killed them. Corrina and Dylan and the others. You killed them," I said, but there was no energy in my voice. I felt dead inside. I didn't know if I was accusing him or me.

"I'm sorry, Gabbi." He did look sorry. His eyes were sunken and his jaw was tense, as if he were gritting his teeth to keep from crying. "We were going to save them but the Vs were too many. It was get out or die." He let go of my hand. "Hit me if you want. I deserve that and more."

I dropped my arm back to my side. The ache in his eyes told me he meant what he said. I told myself there were others who still needed saving, but I wanted to cry anyway. Corrina had been a good person. Dylan too. I wished I'd told them that. "You said you were going to kill all of us. Make us pay."

"We were acting, Gabbi. Pretending to be them."

"Pretending to be who?" I said, confused.

"The Feeb-haters. Laurel and I have run into them a few times. A nasty group of uninfected. Survivalists, I think. Some of them were in the camps at first and left. They want to exterminate every type of infected person and anyone who works with them."

"But why did you pretend—"

He looked at me like I was stupid. "The uninfected can't know it was us. They'd turn on Tabitha and the rest of us."

I pressed my fingers into the inside of both eye sockets, to relieve my headache, but also to clear away the Kerns that still overlapped in my brain. I wanted to sweep everything off a cluttered table to make room for the puzzle parts to fit together: trains, impostors, Tabitha's power, Kern's followers, Dr. Ferrad's mission.

"Here."

I felt a small box pressed into my arm. Kern held out some juice. A cranberry something that tasted tart and energizing. The liquid sugar spread from my stomach to the rest of my body and my brain cleared a bit.

"You have to understand. We had to do it, Gabbi. Dr. Ferrad is close to a cure, but they wouldn't let her work on it. We had to get her out."

"What do you mean? That's what they wanted. This whole thing is supposed to be for a cure."

"I don't know. But Tabitha—"

"Your mom."

Kern paused. "Yeah. My mom says it's true and she wouldn't believe Dr. Ferrad if it wasn't true. They hate each other."

I still couldn't put the puzzle pieces together. "What are you talking about?"

"My mom was a director type person where Dr. Ferrad worked. I don't know. They have a history. My mom wouldn't just believe her—"

"Stop. You know what? It doesn't matter. I have to get back to Camp Pacific. I have to get back to Ano and Ricker and Jimmy."

"If you go back Sergeant Bennings will kill you."

"No. He's dead now. He was in the train car. With Corrina and Dylan."

Kern paused. "It doesn't matter if it's him or someone else. They sent you away. If you go back, they'll kill you."

"If I don't go back, he'll punish my friends."

I finished the juice. Kern watched me without a word.

Finally, I said, "What?"

"Why did you let that V grab you?"

My hold on all of this felt so tenuous, like a string ready to break. He looked at me as if he really cared. As if it had hurt him that I'd tried to hurt myself. "A memory-rush, I guess. I saw this, well, I saw a man who'd hurt me once years ago and I had to get away." I lied because I couldn't bear to admit out loud that for one brief second I'd decided to give up.

After a long moment he relaxed his shoulders.

There was a shout from inside the cab. I tensed. Kern didn't look worried. "We're here."

We passed through a narrow opening in the street. On either side was a barricade of cars and debris. When the two trucks passed through, metal gates closed behind us. The Vs hit the gate soon after. The metal creaked and bulged.

"That won't hold for long."

"Long enough," Kern said.

The trucks slowed and stopped. A small RV and three trucks

drove up and formed a circle. Kern jumped down and helped two other Feebs lift Mary's stretcher off the boxes.

"Hey! Where are you taking her?"

"Come and see," Kern said without pausing.

I jumped off the truck and followed them into the RV. Inside were Dr. Ferrad and Tabitha, arguing.

They stopped when they saw Mary.

"Put her over here," Dr. Ferrad said. Mary moaned when they set her on the bed. Dr. Ferrad checked her pulse, opened up a metal case, then pulled out a needle. She checked the fluid level and reached for Mary's arm.

I grabbed Dr. Ferrad's wrist. "What are you doing?"

Dr. Ferrad froze, and for a moment I knew she didn't see me. Her eyes cleared and she shook her head. "It's to sedate her. I don't want her to hurt herself against the straps."

Kern pulled me away. "Gabbi."

I shook him off. "What's going on?"

Tabitha looked at Kern. He nodded. "I told her."

"Then you already know this is all for a cure," Tabitha said.

The RV's engine rattled to life. Tabitha glanced out the window. "Vs are in." She said it like she was pointing out someone had knocked at the front door.

Kern jumped down the RV steps. "Come on, Gabbi."

"I'm staying with Mary."

Kern looked to Tabitha as if she could force me to change my mind. Instead she said, "Where are the rest of them?"

Kern didn't look at her. "Vs overran us before we could get anyone else out."

Tabitha sucked in a breath. "It doesn't matter."

"It matters!" he said.

"Get moving, son. We still have a lot to do."

He looked as if ready to argue, but then left. Tabitha turned to follow.

"Where are my people?" Dr. Ferrad said. "My assistants?"

Tabitha paused at the door. "There is one truck of your people going with you now. The rest of us will meet up with you at the designated spot. Don't be late."

"You don't have to do this."

Tabitha stared at Dr. Ferrad. "Yes, we do."

The door shut and I scooted to Mary's side. The engine rumbled and I lurched backward. She looked so small like this. Dr. Ferrad reminded me of the college woman who had tried to study us for her PhD. Mary had made me laugh so hard telling a joke about it the day she'd gotten infected.

"You said she was different?"

Dr. Ferrad sighed and looked up from a map she'd spread across a table. "I gave her a megadose of the bacteria, but it was outside the window. It shouldn't have worked. It didn't work, not completely, but she's aware more than other Vs are. I need to find out why."

"That will help you find a cure?"

"I remember you and your friends. Mary helped save you from the Lyssa virus."

I flinched.

"Where are the rest of your friends now?"

My face must have crumpled because she took a step forward and held out her hand. "I'm sorry. I didn't mean—"

"I don't know where they are. Some of them are dead. The rest of them are missing."

Dr. Ferrad looked out the window. It was just the RV and

the truck. The other vehicles had separated, drawing the Vs away from us.

"Do you know what I traded Mary and my freedom for?" She stared at me, her eyes an abyss. "Tabitha wants power. The cure will give her power."

"What—?"

"I aerosolized the double infection. She's going to use it to infect everyone at Camp Pacific."

CHAPTER 28

"I MADE A DELIVERY DEVICE that allows you to catch it in the air, but only if you breathe in the spray. You can't pass it like a cold or flu. Theoretically."

"What do you mean theoretically? Is it in the air or not?"

"I haven't done all the necessary tests! It's not like I can work under standard experimentation guidelines." She looked over to the driver. "Anton. Turn left here."

"The meetup point is further on," he said.

"I know," Dr. Ferrad said. "Just turn."

His hands stayed on the steering wheel for a moment, then made the turn.

We swayed as he maneuvered around a burned-out car that had exploded glass in every direction.

Dr. Ferrad drummed her fingers on the seat. I suddenly felt a desperate thirst. "Do you have some water?"

Dr. Ferrad refocused on me and flicked her head at the

cabinets. "Check in one of those."

I searched until I found a fresh bottle and downed half the liquid in one breath. The water felt clean. It washed the cobwebs out of my mind. "You're not going to meet up with Tabitha and the others."

"Would you?" She said. She faced me, her brown eyes perfectly matching the brown in her hair. The Feeb wrinkles and webbing somehow made her look solemn. She still waited for my answer. She honestly wanted to know.

"I don't know," I answered lamely.

She turned away, as if disappointed. "Well, once Tabitha gets the cure, a real cure, a permanent cure—"

"If you find one," I interrupted.

She stared at me, burning holes in my head. "I will find it. And when I do, Tabitha doesn't get to be the one to control it. Do you think she'd give it out to whoever needs it?"

"I—"

"She won't. I know her better than you. She won't."

Mary moaned on the bed again. She tossed her hair around, but her eyes remained closed. Dr. Ferrad went to her side and checked her pulse. "They have a remarkable ability to metabolize chemicals. It's quite spectacular."

"Is she going to be okay?"

Dr. Ferrad shook her head. "I don't know. The Lyssa virus is it's own special kind of monster." She stood up, lost in thought. "And the bacterial infection—I don't understand the vector. Why are there so many? It's not airborne, it's not through ticks like regular Lyme disease…" She shook her head, remembering where she was. "You can come with us, you know."

"What?" I stood. "What do you mean?" Where are you going?"

"I can't tell you where we're going, but I'll need people to help protect my experiments. I'll need people like you to help while I find the cure. I'm sure Mary would want you with her."

"But my friends—"

"They've already got the double infection. Tabitha won't hurt them." But she looked away when she said that, as if she didn't completely believe what she was saying.

I went to Mary's side. She was here. She was here and alive and sick. I could help her somehow. I could stay and she'd remember me and I'd help her get better. I could not worry so much about running for my life. I'd be safe and contained— like in the prison. My mouth soured. Ano and Jimmy's faces appeared. They looked gaunt, exhausted, worried. We were around the bathtub while we held vigil for Ricker's fevers.

They were still at camp. They didn't have Dr. Ferrad's protection. They needed me more than Mary did. Especially now, especially when I had messed up by trusting Tabitha and Kern and thinking even for a second that getting caught at the prison wasn't a bad thing. I had known better, but I had begun to believe the lies Tabitha told me. I had wanted to believe so badly.

I stepped away from Mary even as my heart broke just looking at her. She would have killed me if she found out I'd even thought about leaving the others. "I can't stay."

Dr. Ferrad examined me from head to toe. I shivered under that gaze. She had been there, going through her own fevers the same time as us—after we'd lost Mary. We'd escaped before she'd recovered. I thought Tabitha had a piercing look but it didn't hold a candle to Dr. Ferrad.

"You're making the wrong decision."

Anger flared inside of me. "What do you know about any of

that? You don't know me."

"You stay out there, you're going to die. Come with me and you get a chance to be a part of something big. You get a real chance of surviving long enough to get the cure."

"If you actually find it—"

She opened her mouth but I cut her off.

"I'm not staying."

"The crazies are tailing us," Anton said quietly. He glanced at me through the rearview mirror. "If you step out there, they'll be all over you."

"Your cars are making the most noise. I'll run fast and quiet. They're more likely to follow you than me." I told myself Dr. Ferrad would take care of Mary because she was wrapped up in Dr. Ferrad's research for the cure. I needed to take care of the others.

"Why take the risk?" Dr. Ferrad said. She moved to block the RV's side door. "If you don't go with us now, you might never see your friend again. You'll probably die out there. I need you. The cure needs you."

Something wasn't right about this. "What exactly do you need me for?"

"I told you. Protection. Caring for your friend." This time she managed not to look away while she lied to me.

My hands tingled as I thought about what to do. "Get out of my way." Lame. Especially since Anton kept driving and Dr. Ferrad didn't move. Actually, she did move. She pulled out a gun from her waist. "I can't let you leave. The cure is too important."

My mind spun and I saw red. She dared to keep me away from my friends. She dared to hold me prisoner. She dared to tell me what to do. Before I could think about it too hard, I barreled into her stomach. She yelped and the gun skittered across floor of the RV, disappearing underneath the front passenger seat. Anton shouted. I grabbed Dr. Ferrad's hair and pulled until she yelled out in pain.

We were flying through the air. Anton must have slammed on the brakes. I hit the back of the driver's seat with a hard thump. Dr. Ferrad landed on me before falling flat to the ground. I fell on top of her.

I scrambled up and raced, dizzy and swerving, for the side door. I jammed my finger on the handle. Anton was sitting back up. He had found the gun and he was pointing it at me.

I jerked open the door anyway and flinched in anticipation of the shot. A man blocked my path, his left cheek torn into shreds. He reached out with ugly, bloody fingers and clawed at my neck. I cried out as he broke skin. A loud bang deafened my ears. His head puffed out a cloud of a pink mist that seemed to hang in the air for several awful seconds. He dropped away. I ran through that mist, slapped a hand to my bleeding neck, dodged another V, and another one who clawed on my shirt, almost catching it.

Two more shots rang out. The RV roared back to life and sped down the road away from the Vs. Dr. Ferrad stood in the doorway and gave me a look that made me shiver. As if she would make sure I would regret this.

I tumbled onto the hood of the truck. The five Feebs stuffed inside the cab just stared at me, eyes wide, guns drawn, looking confused. Then they looked past me and I didn't bother turning around. It had to be more Vs.

I pushed myself off the hood. "Follow Dr. Ferrad!" I slapped the window as I screamed it. My hand left blood behind. I ran around a half-burned house that spilled its interior onto the yard like animal guts. Clothes and furniture and insulation that hung in strips and floated in the air like cobwebs. I heard the truck's engine fade as it disappeared after Dr. Ferrad.

I didn't understand what had just happened. I didn't want to understand. Why had Dr. Ferrad pulled a gun on me? Was Mary safe with her? The sinking feeling in my chest said that I had made the wrong decision. And now Mary had no one to protect her and they were gone.

I noticed the garage window was still intact. I used my sleeved elbow to break it. I climbed inside. The garage was empty. I pressed in between two benches and waited and prayed for the Vs to pass me by and for my pulse to slow down and for the fever to hit from the wound on my neck. I wanted that water again. I wanted so desperately to pour it over my neck and scrape the wound clean. I began to drown in the heat of the fevers, they rose like waves when the tide comes up, higher and higher each time. There was no time for this. Ano and Jimmy and Ricker needed me. Tabitha and Kern were ahead of me, they had too much of a head start. I couldn't stay here and there was no one to go through the fevers with me—

"JUST STAY BACK. I'll help her."

"Are you sure?"

"There's blood. You can't risk it. Give me the water."

"What's going on with her?"

"She's in the fevers."

I felt a cool splash on my neck. A rough scraping renewed the pain that had turned into a dull throb. I opened my eyes.

A grotesque face swam before me. Weird, oversized eyes that shined. Blonde fur that hung over the face like hair. A huge snout covered with dirt, no mouth. I blinked. The shapes swam into better focus. Safety goggles and a painter's mask, but I didn't recognize the face. It was too well covered up.

Another face zoomed in. I flinched backwards, but the wall stopped me.

"Oh good, you're awake."

Her voice. Her voice—

Her hair framed her face like Mary's had. Long, dark, matted. Her pink sweatshirt was torn at the shoulder and looked brown now, crusted over in dirt and blood.

"Maibe?"

She smiled.

I decided that even if it was a ghost-memory, I'd enjoy it while it lasted.

She pressed a rag to my neck.

"Ow!" I slapped my hands over it.

"It'll get infected," Maibe said.

"It's a little late for that," I said.

"Haha," Maibe said. "You're such a comedian. Blood poisoning is so funny."

I waited for her to disappear, but she pushed my hands away and doused the rag in water again. She attacked my neck. I gritted my teeth and let her work. I decided she wasn't a ghost-memory after all. Mostly, because I had never seen Alden dressed up in this ridiculous getup before. Ghost-memories conjured up what had already been experienced. As far as I knew, they didn't make up new stuff.

"How are you here?" I croaked.

"We've been following you since the train station," Alden said.

"What? By yourselves?"

"I'm getting much better at this surviving thing," Maibe said. She patted the bat strapped to her back and smiled.

"About time," I said trying to crack a smile but it only managed to crack the skin on my lips.

Alden stepped forward. He wore jeans several sizes too big and rolled up at the cuffs. The t-shirt was this collared polo with a logo embroidered on the front. A ridiculous, heavy duty painter's mask and suction goggles obscured part of his face, making him look like the monster I'd first thought I'd opened my eyes to. "Did you see my father?"

I turned my head away. "He was there in the train car when the Vs came."

Alden slumped his shoulders. Maibe reached out to put a comforting hand on him, but stopped when he flinched at her touch. She was infected.

"Dylan and Corrina were in the train car too," I said, wanting to get the bad news out all at once. "And Tabitha is going to infect every one at camp and turn them into Feebs."

Maibe locked up, stunned. "They were supposed to be at camp. I left them at the camp."

"Corrina said they got in trouble after you and me disappeared." I didn't say because they were trying to find her, but the look on her face said she'd already figured that out. "They were being moved to a different camp when Kern and his people took the train." I couldn't bear to continue. If they hadn't taken the train, the Vs wouldn't have overwhelmed the area. Sergeant Bennings and Corrina and Dylan would still be alive.

Alden retreated to a corner of the garage. Tears slipped down

Maibe's cheeks. I felt it too. The pain carved a hollowness to my chest that I hated. I couldn't stand it another second. I forced myself onto my feet. I was woozy, dizzy, my neck felt hot to the touch, my scalp still burned. "Tabitha's gone crazy."

"We have to stop her," Alden said. He waited for me to agree. I didn't really care what happened to everyone else, except that it made me sick to my stomach to let her get away with it.

I realized I wanted to help. I wanted to finally stop something terrible from happening instead of picking up the pieces afterwards.

"We have to get back to Ano and Ricker and Jimmy," I said.

Maibe stood a little taller. She wiped the tears from her cheeks.

I glanced at Alden. "We have to stop Tabitha."

WE FOUND BICYCLES. I felt the pressure of getting back to the boys like a pair of strong hands squeezing my throat closed.

Sometimes we biked down the blocks and Faint shadows passed by curtained windows, or crossed streets in a slow, rambling gait, or puttered in the front yard, acting as if it were spring in the garden instead of the end of winter. Some of them shut down in mid-motion. Others looked strangely doll-like. Others even looked normal. The Vs didn't attack them, as if somehow the Vs new the Faints carried something that would harm the Lyssa virus.

I brushed off the jitters from all the Faints wandering around like zombies of old, slow and brainless and trapped by the need for motions they could no longer control. I focused instead on making the exercise clear away the cobwebs in my brain.

We stopped at a hardware store and stocked up on weapons and a bolt cutter. When we left, we picked up some Vs on our tail. At first glance they'd looked like Faints and we'd gotten too close. Before the fairgrounds, we had been able to move around without getting noticed. Now, the world had become infested with the infection. Every move drew them to us.

We pedaled as fast as we could. The houses were like burned-out clown masks. Beams and studs tumbled about like matches with burned ends. We lost them around a corner and then another corner. They caught up at an intersection blocked by a dozen crashed cars we had to hike the bikes over.

I couldn't keep my hands dry. Every few seconds they slipped off the handlebars and I wiped them on my pants. My legs were getting tired now. Maibe was falling behind a little. Alden kept our tail. He wouldn't let her go last, but that meant the mob was closing the gap.

When we got to Camp Pacific's fence, I worked on it with the bolt cutter. The mob was only a couple of blocks away. There were more of them than had been at the high school. They flowed like water over the smashed cars, broken light poles, and burned-out skeletons of houses in their path. I had never seen a group that big. Even when we made it to the other side of the fence, it wouldn't hold them back for long.

"You need to get up on a roof," Maibe said to Alden.

My hands slipped off the bolt cutter. I wiped them again on my pants and went back to work. I was only a third of the way done with what we needed.

"No. I'm not a coward," Alden said.

There were no guards in the towers. You could feel it in the air. This sense of heaviness, this sense of wrongness.

"Tabitha will infect you," Maibe said. "They'll rip off that mask—"

"You don't know they're inside yet. They might not have made it."

I forced myself to move faster. The groans behind us became louder, more vicious.

The sound of a garbage can falling over snapped my focus to the left. There, coming from the opposite direction of the mob was a V pushing along a trash can. She dug through what fell out and was ripping it to pieces. A raccoon.

Her pencil skirt was ripped and her hose was dangling in strips from her bare legs. Her hair had fallen out of a bun. Suddenly she whipped her head around, searching, angry, laser sharp.

She dropped the bloodied pieces of raccoon like so much refuse. Her hands hung at her side, one finger sticking out at an odd angle. Broken, but she didn't notice. She sprinted for me. We didn't have time for this. I scrambled backward, losing my grip on the bolt cutter, and tripped onto my tailbone.

She had green eyes and a missing front tooth. I jumped up and swung out, punching her in the jaw. She reached out her hands and something dark blocked the sun and she fell to the side with a crack.

"Did you miss me?" Maibe said, a bat resting against her shoulder.

A shadow detached itself from a building and an old woman ran to us, her hands out like claws, her eyes bloodshot and vacant, her gait stiff and slow. She should be watching TV and drinking tea, not out here with a bloody foot and a torn dress that revealed a bruised shoulder.

She ran for Alden, but Maibe stepped in front of him and used the bat again. The woman fell flat on her bottom, her dress hiking up to thighs covered in more bruises and scratches.

The old woman growled and tried to get up. Maibe walked backward, facing her. She glanced at me for a second, then turned back and screamed, "Alden!"

He stood there, white as a sheet, frozen to the ground as the V crawled on her hands and knees to him. She grasped at his shoes and caught her hands in the laces somehow so that when she tried to stand she fell onto her face.

I ran and threw her off and then slapped Alden hard enough to skew the mask sideways. "Do you really want to become a Feeb after all we just did to keep that from happening? Are you serious with this shit right now?" I straightened his mask and made sure his goggles were on tight.

"I...I..." He waved a gloved hand in front of his eyes.

I pushed him to Maibe, but she was looking at something over my shoulder.

The Vs were half a block away now. Maibe picked up the bolt cutter. I took it from her and attacked the fence.

CHAPTER 29

WE HURRIED THROUGH THE GAP and ran for the uninfected side of the camp—Alden with his ridiculous mask and goggles, Maibe with a bat, me with the bolt cutter.

The light was fading. I'd lost the morning in the fevers and we'd lost more time getting back to Camp Pacific. My body vibrated with dread. There was no going back, not through that V mob. But what we would find inside—it might be worse.

As if the world wanted to emphasize just how awful a place it was now, a train whistle sounded close by. I thought that might mean there would be a battle soon between Tabitha's people and the uninfected coming back with reinforcements. The whistle rang strong like a horn and made the Vs go into a frenzy. Some of them screamed, others were climbing up the chain-link. The fence swayed and wobbled. A few had found our gap and were already inside.

The light was fading. The chill sunk into my bones even

though we were running.

"Gabbi!" Maibe yelled at me.

I pivoted and saw she was leading Alden into a building. I didn't know what her plan was, but since I had none, I changed direction.

The building's shadow swallowed them up. I followed into an old community hall. The kind of place that held dances and exhibits. It was empty. Our shoes made crazy-loud slaps that echoed off the walls. My heartbeat felt out of control, and our breathing—we sounded like Vs.

The train whistle rattled the glass windows. Maibe and Alden raced through a door on the other end. It bounced hard on the outside wall and came back. I held out my arms and slammed through it to the outside.

There was a row of trailers. Empty. I turned back, but the Vs had already cut off that retreat. A light flickered hundreds of yards away. In the jail. Fear clogged my throat. It was too far. We would never make it and even if we did, the Vs would lay siege to it.

"This way," Maibe said. She had stopped next to one of the trailers and was motioning me over. I wanted to strangle her.

"You got us trapped!"

Maibe's face went pale. "This is how we got out. We can get back into the jail this way."

Vs burst from the building. Small, large, fast, slow. Their shadows were everywhere. Outlines of heads and arms and flashes of teeth. We were surrounded. Maibe dragged me behind the trailer. They grabbed at my clothes and hair. I wrenched myself away. I followed Maibe as if she were the only thing alive in the world at that moment.

We shimmied under the fence that sectioned off the toilets from the jail. Suddenly we were in that little gap and through the hole in the plywood near the toilet pit. It smelled over-whelmingly like diarrhea. I covered my nose with my sleeve.

Alden was there. Fear made the whites of his eyes huge, even behind the goggles. Maibe was bent over, hands on her knees, breathing hard.

We didn't rest for more than a few seconds before we were racing into the jail. I was the last one in and I made sure to lock the doors behind us. I grabbed a metal bar and jammed it between the handles. It would hold for a little while, but even still, through the little windows I could see dark figures pressing up against the fence.

We entered the greenhouse, where we had eaten meals and done our exercises every morning. The moans grew louder. They were going to drive me insane. I clapped my hands over my ears. I was losing it. I had to get it together.

Each cell contained a messy pile of sheets. Not just sheets, I realized, but someone in the sheets, going through the fevers. Time seemed to stop as I saw the glass of water set next to each cot—on the ground, because there was no table in the cells. Some of them had IVs hung from the top of the bars and drip-ping into a vein. Others had a Feeb in their cell, keeping watch, sponging off foreheads, helping the sick sit up and sip water.

The uninfected men and women I had only seen from a distance were transforming before my very eyes. Their skin becoming thin and dry, their veins more pronounced. Some of them screamed in agony, others sobbed, and others babbled in replayed conversations. It was like the whole world had gone mad. We were in the center of it and the first ring was these new Feebs and the next ring was the Vs outside anxious to tear into pieces.

We'd come too late and now there were too many pieces to pick up.

These people couldn't be moved and there were hundreds, maybe thousands of Vs trying to get in here. Vs that we had led here.

Lanterns set up on the tables created little glowing circles of light that revealed Feebs scurrying around, carrying supplies up and down the stairs and into the cells. One of the lanterns revealed a familiar face.

Ricker.

He saw us too and dropped the blankets from his arms. He shouted over his shoulder and Jimmy and Ano appeared. Ricker came up, eyes glowing in the light. He moved as if to hug Maibe but then got shy and just smiled the biggest smile. Then his eyes flickered to Alden and narrowed slightly.

I met Ano's solemn gaze and my heart sunk a little. "She did it. She infected them all, didn't she?"

Ano nodded.

Jimmy hugged me around the waist and I patted him on the back. I felt it too—we were back together. It was better together, even if we WERE all about to die. "It's bad," Jimmy said.

"No kidding," Ricker said.

"We have to leave as soon as possible," Ano said.

I shook my head. "There's Vs everywhere outside. They followed us. We're probably surrounded."

"Gabbi?" Kern said, incredulous, yearning, and angry all at once. "What are you doing here?" He came up behind Ano. The lantern light made shadows dance across his face.

"You knew Tabitha was going to do this, didn't you? She infected them all!" I shouted. "She's as bad as any of them!"

"She's my mother." But he looked ashamed as he said it.

It took everything in me not to lash out and strike him. He'd brought the Vs that had killed Corrina and Dylan. But that thought only lasted for a moment. I'd brought these Vs with us—the ones even now pressing in from all sides, closing off any chance of escape, darkening every window.

But I wanted to hurt him, because he'd made me want to believe him, he'd made me start trusting him and all of that was destroyed. "Just so you know, Mary's long gone with Dr. Ferrad. She's not going to let you get anywhere near a cure."

"Mary?" Ano said. His eyes gleamed. "What about Mary?"

"What is this about Dr. Ferrad?" Tabitha appeared next to Kern. Her voice was cold. Neil and Lilia were with her and looked nervously between Kern and Tabitha.

I tasted salt on my lip. Tabitha was staring at me, waiting for an answer. She would be waiting a long time.

I flipped her off.

"Come on," I said to the only friends I had left in the world, "We're getting out of here."

Tabitha's eyes narrowed. She looked ready to strangle me.

"You have bigger problems than me right now." I waved around. "Can't you hear that?"

The moans from inside the jail quieted for a moment as if to make way for the moans outside the jail. Tabitha paled. Everyone felt it—the tomb the jail had just become.

"Get everyone in the cells and lock the bars," Tabitha said.

Kern, Neil and Lilia flew into action.

"What about us?" Jimmy said.

Tabitha didn't even pause. "You can die out here with the Vs."

I locked eyes with Ano and could almost read his thoughts. We would force our way into one of the cells, no matter what it took.

Flood lights flipped on, bathing the room in an otherworldly silver glow. I froze, as if it were the first time I'd been caught in the act of stealing something—not knowing that acting so guilty was what had given me away. Gunfire sounded outside.

The doors to the front of the jail flew open. People in uniforms, gas masks, and guns streamed inside. They fired shots behind them. Vs followed, grasping, crawling. Dark shadows that formed even darker pools of blood on the ground.

Kern crumpled at the base of the stairs. A soldier had hit him over the head with the butt of his rifle.

I ran to Kern. A lump caught in my throat. I checked his pulse, I checked to make sure he was still breathing. He was alive. His eyes were rolling around as if he couldn't focus.

I dragged him into a nearby cell. The shell-shocked face of a Feeb greeted me. His hand was on the arm of the Feeb in the fevers. "What's happening?"

"Stay inside!" I dumped Kern on the ground, but then was pulled out of the cell. I landed hard on my back, the air knocked out of me. I stared up at the three-story ceiling. It framed the face of a man with a bloody nose that had spread a horrible stain down the front of him.

All around me people were fighting the Vs. Some of the cells had closed, protecting those inside. Other cells had not closed in time. Soldiers fired over the screams. Many of the Feebs fought hand to hand.

This V's hands were around my neck. His breath stank of

rotten meat. I fought him with everything I had. I couldn't afford to get bit. I couldn't afford to die now, not when we were all together again. I dug my fingers into his eyes and closed my own so that I didn't have to see the ooze after I felt the pop.

He howled but his hands remained, pressing harder, tighter. Black dots appeared in my vision.

Suddenly his hands disappeared and then the rest of him fell over. One side of his head was missing now. A soldier stood above me, covered in gore. The glare of lights obscured his face and then he turned and held out a hand to lift me up.

Sergeant Bennings.

He was alive. He'd just saved me.

"Dad?" Alden seemed to part the stream of battles around him.

Sergeant Bennings paused. Then he unlatched a cannister and threw it deep into the greenhouse. It began releasing yellow gas.

I thought it must be tear gas, but then the Vs started dropping, and then the Feebs. He strode over to Alden and replaced the painter's mask with another gas mask on his belt. And then he waited.

I ran to Jimmy and grabbed his shirt. "Put it over your mouth." I did likewise and hoped it would help. I didn't want to wake up with Sergeant Bennings in control again. I didn't know who would be worse at this point, him or Tabitha. It didn't matter. I didn't want anyone else in control of me ever again.

Maibe motioned frantically. Ricker and Ano were on either side of her. They were close to the front door. It was like someone had dipped them all in a bucket of blood. Jimmy and I crept over to them along the wall.

Sergeant Bennings turned, surveying the room from its center, shouting orders to his soldiers. His hand was clamped so hard onto Alden's shoulder. The screams, the gunfire, the shouting, it was all slowing down. Sergeant Bennings was winning.

Jimmy and I hurried, stepping over dead bodies, passing by cells of people who had managed to close the bars in time and cells that didn't turn out so lucky.

"You," Sergeant Bennings said through the mask. It warped his voice into a garble that barely made sense. I looked, ready to face his gun head on, but he pointed the gun at Maibe.

"No!" Alden tried to hit the gun out of his hand.

I jumped and pushed her out of the way. Sergeant Bennings fired. My shoulder became a white hot ball of pain.

CHAPTER 30

"WE SHOULD KEEP GOING," Ano whispered and I wondered why he was whispering except that of course Officer Hanley might hear us and kick out our campfire for a second time that night and we didn't have enough supplies to start a third one, especially since Ano was sick.

"She's still bleeding," Maibe said, also in a whisper, but that wasn't right because Maibe had never met Mary because Mary had pretty much already died but that wasn't right either.

"This place gives me the creeps," Ricker said.

"Yeah, but what choice do we have?" Jimmy said.

"But we can't stay for long," Maibe said. "I need somebody's shirt or something. I don't know."

"Here, I'll do it," Ano said. Pain lanced through my shoulder as something wrapped and tightened around it. Stars burst on the insides of my lids.

"Try not to kill me, Ano, okay?" I said in a raspy whisper

that sounded strange even to my own ears.

"She's awake," Jimmy said.

"And she can hear you," I said. "Help me sit up and somebody better tell me quick where we are and how we got here."

I struggled to open my eyes as someone pushed me up and put what felt like a pillow behind my back. Four faces stared at me, their skin cracked and bruised and papery and dirt-streaked. Their clothes dirty and torn and smelling like something awful. So awful it made me want to gag. Their faces were a rainbow of worries.

I was laid out on a sort of table pushed up against the wall so I could lean back. We were in a mechanic's office, judging by all the tools on the pegboard. It was a small workshop, but tidy nonetheless.

"We made it about four miles before you fell off your bike," Ano said, ever a good lieutenant.

"I don't remember falling." Though I vaguely remembered getting out of the jail and through the path of dead Vs that Sergeant Bennings' people had made.

"You've been unconscious," Maibe said.

"How long?"

"Not that long," Jimmy said. "Ten minutes?"

Ricker left, leaving a gap, but then returned holding a bottle of water. He uncapped it and I drank it greedily, then I pushed it away. "The rest of you should finish that."

"We need to clean your wound. The bullet went through, but it should be cleaned," Ano said.

I was about to protest but then he said, "There's more. A whole case of water in the closet back there."

I sighed and leaned back. "What's the situation outside?"

"Bikes are hidden, but it's not really cleared out here," Ano said. "There's a lot of Vs. They're slow. They look starved, weak, but…" He shrugged. "And, of course, Faints." He tilted his head to a corner of the room. The other three looked in the same direction.

I winced. Of course.

I craned my neck and followed their gaze. An old man with stooped shoulders fiddled with something on a workbench in the corner of the room. He wore a type of apron. Stains darkened his pants and I realized the gagging smells came from him because in his fog of infection he no longer remembered when, or maybe how, to use the bathroom.

His arms were bare except for a tattoo of eagles and the American flag that had long ago stretched and sagged as his skin had aged. Eventually he would be too weak to work and he would lie down and die and there was nothing we could do about it except be grateful it hadn't happened to us. I was surprised he had kept himself alive this long.

I sank flat onto the table. "We stay the night here. I'll be ready to move tomorrow." I said this with more conviction than I felt. "And somebody needs to give him some water. And if there's any food, that would help a hell of a lot too."

I drifted into darkness.

In the morning, I woke up from the pain in my shoulder. I had tried to move, to shift onto my bad side and had paid dearly for that movement. My tongue tasted stale and my mouth was dry like cardboard. I slowly moved different muscles, starting from my toes up to my legs, then all the way to my neck, being careful of the wounds there and on my scalp that still burned. I'd failed pretty miserably at not getting hurt, but at least I was still alive. I bit on my lip when it came time to move my shoulders, but I forced a stretch anyway and decided now was better than never.

I swung my feet off the table and waited for my head to stop its wobbling. When I steadied, I stood and grabbed up the water bottle and guzzled almost all of it, and then splashed the last of it on my face.

Maibe and the boys slept in a heap together on the floor for warmth, safety, comfort. I looked on them in wonder. They were all still alive. We were no longer caught. I continued preparing for the rest of the day, for a full day of bike handlebars. I looked around for the old man. Faint or no, he could still harm us if the right memory caught him.

There he was, in his corner, but no longer working at the bench. He sat on a stool, his hands resting on his knees, his eyes focused on me as if he actually saw me.

Insect bites had raised angry red welts around his bare ankles. "Who are you?" His voice was low and it crackled from disuse.

"I'm just passing through," I said softly.

"Young lady, that was not my question."

"Gabbi. My name is Gabbi and I mean you no harm."

"I can see that just fine, what with you bleeding on my gear over there. I bet you couldn't hurt a fly right now with that shoulder."

I smiled. "Maybe," I said. "But don't try me."

He laughed a low, soft guffaw. "Sounded just like my wife right then. Did you see her? She went shopping but shoulda been back by now."

"No, I haven't, but I'll keep an eye out for her."

"Thank you, I'd appreciate that." He turned and rummaged

around in a drawer on the workbench. He pulled out something rectangular and shiny. He looked about to toss it then thought better of it and walked it over to me. He held it out, his hands grimy from the kind of grease that came from working on cars, but were otherwise clean, though the sewer smell grew stronger with his nearness.

In his hand he held a granola bar.

"Here, looks like you need this more than me," he said.

"No," I said quickly, looking at the way his skin hung off his bones, how thin his wrist was, how gaunt his cheeks were this close up. "You eat it."

"I'm not hungry. Haven't been for days," he said. The look in his eye spoke of some deep awareness—as if while he was trapped by the Faint infection he also sort of knew he was trapped.

I didn't know how that could be possible. "I can't," I said, a strangled note in my voice. The horror of his self-awareness flooded into me and I didn't know how to respond except that I couldn't take the last bit of food this man had.

He opened the package, the plastic wrap crinkling loud in the silence of the room. Daylight filtered in through the window and I saw, at least on this side, that the way was clear of Vs.

He pulled off a small piece of granola, smaller than a dime, then crumbled it into dust between his fingers and let the crumbs drop to the floor. My stomach cramped. My nose picked up faint hints of sugar, chocolate, nuts.

"If you don't eat this, I'm sorry to say it's all going to go to waste," he said, frowning at me.

I held out my hand and it shook a bit from hunger. He placed the granola bar in it.

"Thank you."

He smiled a big smile. A few teeth were missing and other teeth were crooked but all that had happened and healed long ago. "That's better."

I pinched off a section of the piece he had touched and let that tumble to the ground. No need to invite more germs if I could help it. I gobbled up the rest of the bar and when I finished he appeared with a bottle of water. I thanked him again and drank my fill.

By this time the others had woken up and were stretching and drinking water and otherwise trying not to look as if they were watching me and the Faint.

The sugar spiked my endorphins and even though I wasn't looking forward to the bike ride today, I knew it was time to get started.

"Thank you, but we need to get going now. We have a long bike ride ahead of us and it's going to be slow—for obvious reasons," I said, motioning to my shoulder.

"Well, I was thinking about that all last night. It's really a mechanical problem you're facing…" His words disappeared into a series of mumbles and he went still. I got the sense that we'd lost him.

Ricker looked like a parrot stretching his head out as he massaged his neck. "He was mumbling and working on something all night."

I decided that it would be best if we snuck out while he was still lost. Then it would be as if we'd never been there. We gathered our stuff and grabbed a few extra bottles of water, but left plenty for the mechanic in case he came out long enough to drink any of it.

I was the last one to leave the shop. I felt a hand on my good shoulder. "You'll want to take this along with you."

I turned. The old mechanic let his hand drop and stood back to showcase what he had brought out.

An electric recumbent.

At least I think that's what it was. It had two wheels and pedals and handlebars, but its seat was low and upright and you would need to extend your legs forward, not down, in order to pedal. There were extra contraptions mounted on the back wheel and on either side of the seat for supplies and batteries.

I swallowed around a lump that had risen in my throat at this unexpected kindness. The whole world was full of monsters now but this Faint might have just saved me. The seat position, the electric pedaling, I could go a lot more miles on this than on a regular bike.

"Here now, this is for you as I've got no need for it." He wheeled the heavy thing through the door. Ricker exclaimed but Maibe cut him short, reminding him of the Vs close by.

The old man held the bike steady until I lowered myself onto it.

"All right, you all get gone. I've got plenty of work ahead of me today and can't waste time in conversation." With that, he went inside and closed the door to his shop with a soft click.

Wonder filled their faces. A hint of jealousy too.

"What can I say?" I said, smiling around the pain in my shoulder and neck and head. "I've always been quite the people charmer."

Ano laughed, silent laughs so deep that tears sprung to his eyes and streamed down his cheeks. Jimmy giggled. Ricker socked both of them in the shoulders.

"So where are we going?" Maibe asked.

The boys quieted down and waited for me to answer because somehow they had decided that I was the decider. But they would bring me up short if they had problems with my decision, and I would listen to them.

"I don't know of any better plan except to just, I don't know, follow the plan we'd originally set out to follow before it all got taken sideways."

Ricker scratched his head, "Uh, what was the—"

"Dutch Flat," Jimmy said, unable to hide the eagerness in his voice.

"It's up in the hills, out of the way," I said. "I still remember the route Dylan said we should take. We could make it in a couple of days depending on whether we get killed along the way, or captured again—you know, our normal day-to-day problems."

Maibe contemplated some dark thoughts I could not read, but the boys had already accepted the decision as having been made. Still, that wasn't my style. "Unless anyone's got a better idea?" I asked.

Ano began pedaling and the other two followed.

Maibe held back for a moment.

"Do you have a better idea? Maibe?" I snapped my fingers in her face and instantly regretted it. Even though it was my good arm it still managed to trigger a flash of pain in my shoulder. I gritted my teeth until the pain subsided to a dull throb.

Maibe's eyes refocused and she brushed at her head as if swiping at a cobweb. "Dutch Flat. Sounds good to me."

CHAPTER 31

THE ELECTRIC RECUMBENT made the journey easier, but that didn't mean it was easy. We had more than sixty miles ahead of us, but on the other hand, each mile took us further away from the population centers. We decided to split the remaining miles into two days. If I'd been well, I could have done more each day, but I wasn't.

In the morning, after leaving the mechanic behind, the skies became overcast and drizzled a light rain. We took shelter under an overpass, like old times. When the rain cleared a few hours later, we trudged on. The sun shined clear but pale, enough to send the birds into an uproar. It sounded like a zoo, dozens of different calls filled up the silence and covered the little bit of noise our bikes made, though it also made it difficult to hear anything coming our way.

I thought maybe it was early March, but there wasn't any way to know for sure, not anymore. Still, there was that heaviness in the air, a humidity and a promise of more warmth to come, and the poke here and there of green amongst the ashes of burned-out fields and neighborhoods and strip malls. The weeds would grow first, and then other things would follow.

I thought about the Feeb-haters and how strange the mechanic Faint had been and what all of that meant. I thought about Dr. Ferrad and Tabitha and Sergeant Bennings, and Kern sometimes too. None of it made any sense to me. The way they had all tried to control things and hurt people. We'd fallen under the spell of the empty safety they'd offered, but all of that was over now. I wouldn't let us fall for it again.

We made terrible time through the last few towns, stopping and scouting for supplies, working around Faints, outrunning Vs. There weren't many but there were enough. Still, we made thirty-six miles that day according to the recumbent's odometer.

I was the slowest, even with the recumbent, but Ano made sure to stay behind me and called for a stop every now and then to have Ricker rebandage my shoulder.

That night we bedded down in a barn that was empty except for a horse long dead from starvation, little more than skin and bones now. A few chickens scampered around the yard as if everything was normal. Jimmy hunted for their coop and came back with a shirt-load of eggs, more than we could possibly eat in a week, but we sorted through them just the same and started a fire and found a flat piece of metal we decided to use as a skillet.

Some of the eggs had gone bad and we tossed those outside into the dirt, but most were just fine and we feasted on omelets filled with some green bits of weeds that Corrina had once shown us were okay to eat.

This lapsed Maibe into a brooding silence, but there was nothing to be done for it. Corrina and Dylan were gone and Kern and Tabitha were probably captured. Sergeant Bennings and the camps were still alive and well and pretending like Feebs didn't deserve what the uninfected deserved.

I sighed at my morbid thoughts and stared at the hypnotizing flames of the fire. My belly was full and that satisfaction spread to the rest of my body, even dulling the pain in my shoulder.

Maibe came back to the fire after switching watch with Ricker and crouched next to me.

"What are we going to do at Dutch Flat?"

"Anything we want," I said because I didn't really know.

"We'll find shelter first, and then food and supplies," Ano said.

"And then?" Maibe said.

"And then stay out of trouble for a while," I said, but my answer satisfied neither of us.

The next day was clear and bright and promised spring around the corner. Yesterday's rain had cleared away the smoke from the fires of the past few months and the sky was that crystal blue color that hurt the eyes sometimes because it was so bright.

We had fewer miles today and my shoulder was feeling okay as far as that went, but we all knew the miles would be mostly uphill.

We set out early in the morning, the dew not yet evaporated from the grass. The smells out here were cleaner and whenever we encountered something that didn't smell right we went around it—there was no reason to look at gruesome things. When we rode by a gas station Maibe and Ano went inside for a map and snacks, though we had packed a great number of eggs in the satchels of my bike. When they came back out their shirts covered the lower half of their faces. Even though their arms were full of supplies, their expressions said it wasn't worth whatever they had seen inside.

I unfolded the map across my lap and traced our route. "Less than twenty miles to go," I said in a whisper because we had been operating pretty much on silence the whole time and it seemed wrong to break it.

Silence, except for the birds because they had been going all morning like yesterday, but it wasn't an unhappy silence. More a respect for the new state of things, a way to let it sink in that the birds and other animals would take over more and more ground and fill the space humans left behind.

As we climbed into the lower foothills, the few strip malls disappeared and all that was left were rolling fields and farm houses and oak trees and creeks and granite rocks and animals left out to pasture. The elevation change cooled the temperatures, but my pedaling easily kept me warm. I tried to save the battery by only using the electric assist on the steepest parts.

We coasted down a hill to a creek bed with a small bridge crossing and a road sign that said "Dutch Flat 3 miles."

As if by telepathic message we halted at the sign and took in our surroundings. It was greener here than in the valley. Trees—pine, oak, elm, maple, birch—dotted the landscape, thick blackberry bushes, grasses, other plants I didn't know the name for. It was a lush place and seemed well protected.

"Umm, I think we might have a problem," Ricker said. He pointed down the road that crossed the creek, climbed back up, and then turned around a hill or mountain—I didn't know exactly when the foothills became mountains but I knew we were pretty close. Behind the hill a column of smoke rose lazily into the blue sky.

"Does that mean the town burned down?" Jimmy said.

"Looks more like something from a campfire or chimney," Ano said.

"So there's people already there," Maibe said.

"Could be Faints," I said.

"But they'd have burned the whole town down by now if it were Faints," Ano said.

"Maybe," I said. "Probably." And Vs didn't have enough sense left to start a fire except by accident.

"I bet it's either from Feebs or uninfected," I said.

"We have all the luck," Ricker said.

"We could go back," Jimmy said. "Take our pick of a farm or town or whatever. We don't have to keep going."

He made sense, but I balked at the thought. The way Dylan had described it, a little Gold Rush town in a valley, protected by hills and a creek, and maybe a dozen houses with gardens and well water and electricity already off the grid—it sounded like heaven. It sounded like exactly the kind of place Mary had wanted. And it seemed like a little bit of a betrayal of Corrina and Dylan if we came all this way to turn around at the last three miles.

"Let's take a look," I said. "We don't have to go into town if it seems dangerous. Ano, raise up a hand if there's anything funny and we'll stop and go back."

Ano looked like he didn't think it was a good idea but he took the lead and we slowed almost to a walking pace. He held up his hand several times and we stopped and waited and listened, but each time he shook his head and we continued. It bothered me that he was in front. It should have been me up there.

The trees grew taller and more stately, coming together over the narrow road in a sort of canopy that let in dappled sunlight. Our pace did nothing to keep my muscles warm and I began to shiver in the shadows of the road.

Maybe this wasn't such a good idea.

We pedaled over another creek crossing and then up the meandering road. When Ano reached the top of the rise, he stopped but didn't hold up a hand. I biked until I was alongside him at the top and then put a foot down. The others did the same and we spread out across the rise, covering the street with our bikes, and we looked down the gentle slope onto Dutch Flat.

The sun shone directly in our eyes, which meant we'd traveled east of the town and curved back around on the road to it. It was as Dylan had described it. Three or four intersecting blocks, an old clapboard hotel, some houses on one side, and on the other side, a small grocer, an antique shop, a post office that advertised a thrift shop inside, and a faded blue sign marking a small laundromat and coffee shop.

The streets were easy to picture as the dirt roads they used to be. This must have been the main strip of town.

Smoke curled into the air. It was obvious now that it came from a chimney from the tallest building, the three-story hotel.

We were several hundred yards away. Other than the smoke, the town looked peaceful, quiet, tucked away, eager for company.

A person stepped off the wooden walkway on the post office side, arms filled with what looked a lot like laundry. She crossed over to the hotel. She had long hair that fell halfway to her back, untamed and wild.

"You've got to be kidding me," I said.

"What?" Ricker said.

Maibe looked at me.

"Are you seeing this. Did you see her? It's not some ghost-memory I'm having?"

"I saw it,"Maibe whispered.

A smile crept onto my lips. We coasted down the slope and stopped in front of the hotel. Two people stood on the porch now, both carrying rifles.

"Maibe?" Corrina said. "Gabbi?"

Dylan lowered his rifle and smiled in such a way that my heart dropped into my stomach and I remembered that for the longest time I couldn't understand how Corrina had ended up with him. His eyes drank us all in and I thought he rested on me for a second longer than the others and hope flew like a balloon let loose into the sky.

"Gabbi's hurt," Dylan said and my balloon popped. But that was just as well.

Corrina handed Dylan her rifle and hurried down the steps. She took Maibe into a fierce hug, then stepped back and wiped tears away. Dylan clapped each of the boys on the shoulders and told them to get inside because there was food and water and even some soda cans left over from the little grocer across the street.

Corrina came over to me and while I didn't get a hug, she was nice enough to probe my shoulder wound until I exclaimed in pain, which was better than hugs and tears, because it would have been just a little too much coming from her and I might have had to vomit in my mouth a little bit.

"Sorry," she said at my exclamation. "Come inside, I've got some stuff we can put on this."

We all went inside, Corrina and Ano propping me up as I stumbled on the steps and realized how the only thing that had been keeping me going these last few miles was sheer will.

They sat me down in a chair. Corrina left and came back with a box filled with bandages, cleaning supplies, and other basic first aid stuff.

"Any painkillers in there?" I asked since the jostling that had gotten me into the hotel had renewed the throbbing.

"No," she said. "We're not that lucky, but I have something else that might work. You came just in time for tea," she said, smiling. She left again and the others settled themselves down near me. Dylan leaned the rifles next to the door and limped back to sit down with us. Maibe began peppering him with questions and he explained how they had escaped the V mob— by luck, but not without injury. He pointed to the bandages that wrapped his leg.

Corrina came back with a pot of tea and crushed some weird-looking leaves into it. "Yarrow, willow bark, chamomile to soothe. I've got some comfrey to pack in with the bandages, but I need to clean the wound first."

Bandages covered her arms too, bites and scratches that would leave an array of scars behind sort of like the ones I'd carved into my arm.

I sipped the tea she handed me while Dylan explained how they'd thought Maibe and me had been killed and how they'd escaped Dutch Flat. When he was done I explained what Tabitha had done to Camp Pacific and what I had learned from Kern about the Feeb-haters, and then I kept talking and told them about Dr. Ferrad and Mary, and Sergeant Bennings' still being out there, and the weird Faint in the mechanic shop, and all the Feebs still imprisoned in the camps.

Once I was done, I sat back, exhausted, relieved. The knowledge had been a burden I didn't know I was carrying and now everyone in this room would help me share it.

Jimmy's face was pale. Maibe had a resolute set to her features, while Ano and Ricker whispered to each other. Corrina looked at me with wide-eyed thoughtfulness. Dylan stared at the wood floor stained with thousands of footsteps as if by sheer force of will he could change the state of things.

I waited for someone to say it.

The words built up in my chest until I couldn't contain them anymore. "We can't keep running away," I said. "We have to do something. We have to help."

May

CHAPTER 32

Everyone had probably thought I'd have gone with it—join the resistance, the revolution, the insurgency, the underground. Do whatever Tabitha told me because it was for our own good in the end. Kill the Vs, turn all the uninfected into Feebs.

It would have made a great story. The classic kind of story— underdog turns around and wins it. David defeats Goliath.

If you can't join them, fight them.

If you can't beat them, be them—or something.

It's like no one understands that when you start taking power that it makes you just as bad as the ones you want to take it from.

It's not like we're going to win or anything. That's so far beyond the point of all this, if you think that's even the goal here, well, then, you just wasted a whole bunch of your time reading what happened to me for pretty much nothing.

It's not about winning, it's about fighting back and making sure that we don't become like what we're fighting. That's really hard to do, almost impossible. Just pick up any history book from any library, you'll see.

Well, any library that made it through the fires. But that's so obvious it should go without saying.

The point is—

"GABBI, I THINK IT'S TIME," Maibe said.

I set down my pen and closed the notebook. It was dark in the van. We'd covered the windows with blackout curtains and the only light was a little battery-powered pen light I'd picked up during our last supply run. It wouldn't last much longer.

"How come you always write in there?" Maibe asked. "It's always before we do something big—you have to write it down."

I turned off the light and stretched my legs and then rolled my arms to warm up the muscles. My shoulder and neck were a mass of scars now mostly healed, except for a general weakness that hadn't gone away even with weeks of careful training on a weight set Dylan had found.

"I don't want them to be the only ones telling the story. They tell it wrong. They make themselves out to be the heroes when they're just as bad as the other side."

"Which side?"

"Both sides, dumbass. Both sides." But I grinned to take the sting out of my words.

Maibe smiled, letting me know she got the joke at her expense. She handed over the binoculars.

I peeked out between the curtain and the window frame. One uninfected with a gun watched over several Feebs who worked at digging something out of the dirt. They were in the middle of a field rimmed with trees that obscured our van from their sight.

Alden had gotten us a message about two cousins who were about to be shipped off.

"So what's the plan?" Maibe said. She'd changed out her pink sweatshirt long ago for something a bit more stealthy—a dark sweater and leggings, though the weather would soon turn too hot for much more than shorts and a t-shirt. We'd all have to go clothes hunting soon if we didn't want to melt during the summer.

"Gabbi?"

"Yeah," I said, and coughed. "About the plan…" I trailed off because even though we'd staked the place for several hours already, I hadn't thought of anything yet. Corrina, Dylan, and Jimmy were back at Dutch Flat taking care of the last group of Feebs we'd brought them. I cursed myself for letting Ano and Ricker go out on their own this time to search for Mary and Dr. Ferrad. I should have made them stay and finish this job with us first.

"They're leaving," Maibe said.

"All right, all right," I said. "We'll rush them and in the confusion—"

Maibe's look silenced me. Yeah, it was a pretty stupid idea.

"Okay. Something will come to me in a minute. Trust me." I grinned, showing her all my teeth.

She rolled her eyes. "Yeah. Okay, so I think we should…" and she explained her plan and I listened and I nodded my head because it was a solid plan and I could trust her with my life and know she'd do her best to take care of it.

WHAT WILL THEY DO FOR A REAL CURE?

Find out what happens to Maibe and her friends
in the final book in the Feast of Weeds series,
Eradication (Book 4).

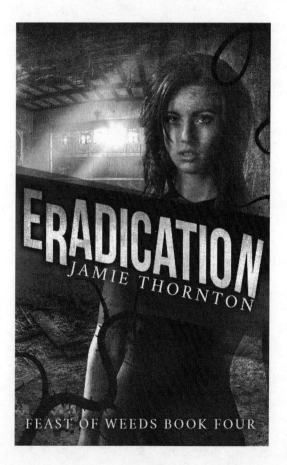

IGNEOUS
BOOKS

ABOUT THE AUTHOR

Jamie Thornton lives in Northern California with her husband, two dogs, a garden, lots of chickens, a viola, and a bicycle. She writes stories that take place halfway around the world, in an apocalyptic future, in a parallel universe—her books don't always stick to one genre, but they always take the reader on a dark adventure.

Join the Adventure through her email list to receive freebies, discounts, and information on more of her dark adventures.

Sign up at:

WWW.ZOMBIESAREHUMAN.COM

IGNEOUS
BOOKS

LooseChangeling

A CHANGELING WARS NOVEL

A.G. STEWART

Trade paperback and ebook

Nicole always thought she was regular–issue human…until she turns her husband's mistress into a mouse. The next day, Kailen, Fae–for–hire, shows up on her doorstep and drops this bomb: she's a Changeling, a Fae raised among mortals. Oh, and did he mention that her existence is illegal?

Now she's on the run from Fae factions who want to kill her, while dealing with others who believe she can save the world. And there's the pesky matter of her soon–to–be ex, without whom she can't seem to do any magic at all…

Trade paperback and ebook

Murderers. Madmen. An ancient red–handed spirit named Molly. Patwin County is an unsettled place, full of shadows and secrets.

When Laura Livingstone's mother vanishes, Laura and her husband must find her before evil engulfs the county. As they search the streets of San Augustin, they uncover a terrible secret and fall into a supernatural horror beyond their imagination.